To Jean

Enjoy.

RUSSIAN DOLL

Fondest regards

Ives Magol.

Russian Doll

Lucy Lloyd

Comely Bank Publishing

First published in 2017 as 'Shotlandiya'

This edition published 2018 by Comely Bank Publishing

ISBN: 978-1-912365-01-2

Copyright © 2017, 2018 Lucy Lloyd

The right of Lucy Lloyd to be identified as
author of this work has been identified by her in accordance
with the Copyright, Patents and Designs Act 1988.

Original cover design by Raspberry Creative Type
Text printed in Adobe Garamond Pro by 4edge

A CIP catalogue record for this book is available from
the British Library.

For Team Lloyd

Raised in Glasgow, Lucy Lloyd studied biochemistry
before becoming a BBC radio producer.

Today she lives in Edinburgh with her husband and two daughters.

Russian Doll is her first novel.

CHAPTER 1

'That's only trouble,' Sam said.

I jerked the hot coffee over my hands in surprise. I thought he was still dealing with Ian Rankin in the studio. We weren't allowed the guest coffee, but the big man was distracted by the TV screen on the wall.

'What's that?' I tried to hide the mug by my side and walked round to look. It was an aerial shot swirling around a pointy rock in the ocean with ant-sized people sitting on it.

'The Russians having a picnic on Rockall.'

I squinted at the jiggling picture on the screen. 'Are they having a picnic?'

'No!' Sam snorted. He sat down behind the desk and picked up his sketchbook and charcoal, scanning what he'd already done as he spoke. 'It's trouble I say. You don't mess with Russians. No sense of humour. That for a guest, that coffee, is it?'

I nodded, mumbled something about being waited for, and scuttled off back to my desk.

It turned out Sam was right. They weren't having a picnic. They were claiming colonisation of a barren rock sticking out of the Atlantic 230 miles west of North Uist which Britain had imaginatively called Rockall. It was nothing to us, really, but we had the economic rights to the seabed; that is, Scotland did when we inherited it during the break up. We'd been independent for 18 months, and at the Scottish Broadcasting Corporation, or SBC, the official broadcast line was that the Russians had completely taken advantage of our not-so-blissful honeymoon period to stake a claim to our drilling rights; yet the chat in the corridors was that Angus McCulloch, our Foreign Minister, was completely out of his depth, both literally and figuratively, when he waded in to sort this out.

Russia then, of course, was riding high on its wave of transatlantic resurgence fuelled by the popular right. There was no automatic condemnation from the US. Our application to NATO was in fraught negotiation. Our petitions to the EU were being considered. We were ripe for the taking. How easy it seems now. How exposed we were. How tempting a piece of venison we must have seemed.

A few days later I was stepping out of the main radio recording studio when I had to jump back to avoid being crushed in a stampede. Angus McCulloch himself, leading the herd of advisers to the lifts and exit, scanning his phone and batting away the questions Graeme from News was trying to lob at him.

'Off the record then – just an inkling of the forecasts!'

Angus stopped, his bald pate shining in the low spot lights; his deep Glasgow accent commanding the room. 'I have completed your interview, Mr. Davidson; now do me the honour of behaving in a civil and professional manner by letting me exit the building without being hounded like a fox. I refuse to be ripped apart for your sporting delectation.' The advisers glared and muttered, then trotted after their master.

I went into the tea room opposite. Graeme followed, glowering.

'If he were a woman I'd say he was all fur and nae knickers.'

'I'd rather you didn't, Graeme.' Isobel, Education Correspondent, followed on his heels and joined me in waiting for the kettle, 'it might make me think less of you.'

Graeme needed to let off steam. 'He's a shyster, always a

shyster, and now he's dealing with people who are better at that game than him and he's totally out of his depth.'

'Are the Russians still on Rockall?' I asked, my head having been buried in a mammoth two day set of tricky recordings.

'On Rockall?' blustered Graeme, 'they're on the bloody mainland being handed Scotland on a plate! They've got a warship in the Firth of Forth. Submarines have been spotted off Caithness! It's the new treaty, the new 'Northern Alliance'. Angus swears it's good news, but in reality it's because he's met people who are tougher and dirtier than him and he's cacked himself but is too proud to ask for help.' Graeme stabbed a finger down at the carpet, down south, 'You know Westminster offered to help? They had their men here, standing at the entrance of Holyrood, ready to negotiate. They know the real threat. They've got patrol boats level with the Tweed, but Sandy thinks he can do his old Govan hard boy act to a bunch of Russian crooks and thinks they're going to crumble.'

'It might not come to that,' soothed Isobel, 'surely the First Minister is going to step in, surely NATO will...?'

'Ah, she's got her marriage issues, which of course we don't know about, and is fighting to push through the hospital reforms, and NATO's not going to bother if a country that won't pay its dues says it's all under control.'

Graeme liked to keep the fading BBC hack traditions alive. He shouted at subordinates, drank his coffee strong, and spent half his time fumbling for his fags.

'We're totally fucked, I'm sure. Anyway, I'm off for a smoke,' he said, patting down his chest pocket in reassurance.

'Well I'm glad you've got your priorities straight,' said Isobel, ushering her tea out and giving me a wink.

I left the building and emerged into the rain. It had been one of those days in November when there's no apparent sunrise. The rain hammered off Dean Bridge and sprayed out from under buses. On that narrow pavement, with the five-foot wall between us and the deep drop to the surging Water of Leith below, we were at the mercy of the rain firing squad. The orange glow from street lamps and white glare of car lights bounced and swirled as my corneas drowned.

I slammed the security door shut behind me. The storm splattered against the sandstone walls. I dripped onto the floor. Made it. Soaked.

A bag was lying at the foot of the stairs. A khaki bag. Above me the rain pounded off the cupola, but now another sound joined it: footsteps. I leaned over to look up the curving stairs.

He appeared: late-twenties, tall. Dirty blonde hair cropped short over a pointy face; ears sticking out beneath sharp stubs of hair. He slowed when he saw me, but no part of his face flickered in acknowledgement. I stepped back, aware I was staring. Staring at his luggage tags. He grasped the bag and returned to the stairs as if I wasn't there at all.

I flicked my keys out and quickly unlocked the door, then closed it behind myself. Surely it was unmistakable? The Russians were coming, and one had moved in above me.

I was up early the next morning. We'd been summoned to Glasgow. The SBC's headquarters were still there, neatly boxed up in glass on the edge of the Clyde. Edinburgh was a smaller office populated by us speech radio producers, some journalists and a handful of engineers. Glasgow was the trendy powerhouse, with the development executives, all the TV departments, music shows and drama. All of radio in Scotland had been summoned to a meeting, so there was only one place we could be.

The train was busy as usual, but quiet. It let me think. Last night I'd listened out for sounds in the building. The front door slammed a few times. The steps were in use above me. Once, I'd scuttled to the spy hole in my front door and had seen a back disappearing outside, my self-imposed solitude in my flat giving me a sense of vulnerability I hadn't experienced since my own breakup.

I stepped out at Queen Street and went to cross directly into the underground before stopping. There was something of a hubbub occurring. I moved down towards the bustling pavement and decided instead to walk to Central Station and take the overground to the SBC. Traffic was snarled up around George Square and the City Chambers. Something was attracting attention. I stepped further and could see Sir Walter Scott as usual on his tall platform gazing over the city, but his sight now also took in two large army tanks squatting in the middle. Soldiers sprawled over the vehicles, pretending to be bored and ignoring the camera phones pointing at them. They weren't Scottish soldiers.

'Hello?' A small group of Russian soldiers stood close to me now, but I hadn't seen them and I started. The speaker gave me a smile. His colleague leered. I turned without comment and made my way on autopilot across the city centre as my mind whirred.

They'd arrived so suddenly or maybe they hadn't. Since the breakup Russia had been doing what Russia liked doing, which was messing around in our waters and being rapped on the knuckles for it, so nobody had really paid attention. When they took up camp on Rockall I'd watched our puny boat alongside the Russian megaship, nagging them to get off. I'd watched the delegation of Russian diplomats descend on Holyrood with their accompanying 'guard' or soldiers, who multiplied by the week. After Graeme's outburst, I'd caught up, and read of planes arriving with young men, not even wearing uniform, but who set down in hotels and hostels, speaking in Russian to each other but stilted English to the staff. It was like twilight festival season in Edinburgh with powerful handshakes and mocking smiles. I'd watched the news footage of files being carried by harried ministers with stern faces and shadowed eyes. Then that bizarre news conference which Graeme had followed up on, like it was all great news, with Angus japing about 'our new friends' and agreements over a few drams. They had a lot more oil than us, a lot more power. Power: that Scotland as a small newly-independent country wanted to sidle up to while continuing to show the finger to England.

Now those tanks sat in George Square by the cenotaph marking a nation who sacrificed generations of men in two world wars, who had long ago fought off the English with a minority army. But this wasn't an occupation, so Angus said. He didn't tell us what it was. Maybe he really didn't know then. I suppose we all kept calm and carried on.

The SBC seemed more subdued than usual, or maybe it was just in my head. I swiped my card, got through the gates, and then started to climb up the great wide central staircase. It stretched out ahead of me, broken down into small sections with mezzanine layers holding tables and chairs between levels. On the first floor a group was standing. The SBC Head Sandy McQuilken was in front of them. Stout and ruddy-cheeked he pressed his tie down against his chest. Then he did it again, nodding as a sleek man spoke with an assured manner to him. Then he did it again, unaware of this nervous tick. The men behind stared with arrogant eyes. Russians, that's what they looked like.

I did my usual scout round for an available hot desk, saying hello every few rows to someone I knew. I found one and switched on the computer, throwing my coat over the chair to mark my territory then I made my way up to the canteen to order a coffee. The morning radio teams were passing out – gossiping, swapping 6am war stories and working off the daily adrenaline rush. TV researchers and directors were charging up on caffeine for the long day ahead. Meetings were being held, newspapers were being read. I bought my coffee and made my way back to my desk. These meetings were always late on starting so I would have plenty of time for some social media checking.

'Anna: meeting: now.' Jennifer was swooshing through the rows of computers and herding everyone towards the meeting room. Unusual. She was usually the last in with her packed schedule of meetings and programme listening for compliance.

I grabbed my coffee and followed my editor. The meeting room was big, but not big enough with all my colleagues from bases around the country squeezed in. The Aberdeen and Inverness lot were there, all tired with tight smiles from their early start, and the rest of my colleagues from Glasgow and Edinburgh were in attendance with their own air of nervousness. It felt like redundancies were on the menu again. I found a seat on the outer row from the central table. Four seats were empty at the head.

Marc Polmont, Head of Radio, walked in. This wasn't a good sign. Jennifer rushed in after him, herding in a few more stray producer lambs, and then she sat to his right. Then in came two of the men I'd seen on the stair mezzanine. Most definitely Russian.

'Hello everyone.' Marc wasn't well liked. Well, that is, particularly by his current audience. When the BBC fractured with the breakup of the Union, the speech department was hard hit. When the Beeb represented all of the U.K., London requested a certain proportionate quota of programmes from north of the border. Edinburgh in particular had a significant workforce churning out a variety of speech programmes which were broadcast on Radio 4, 3, 2 and the World Service. When the BBC was sliced, so were we. There was very little money for Scottish radio to produce such labour-intensive programming so the department was reduced. After some political dealing and serious pleading, the department now made some programmes for the network with a contribution from the licence fee in Scotland going to London in return for both programme making and access to the resources and output from Broadcasting House. It was a delicate political treaty which had a huge impact on the payroll with us.

Marc had stepped in during this period, and he'd never seemed to fight our corner. He had always been a news man. Things that weren't live were old news. The documentary indulgence was a relic of a past age from when producers had secretaries and drank their way through long lunches.

'Eh,' Marc always dithered at these meetings. With a pug face he looked like he should be a bullish man, but in reality he had an evasive manner. I wondered if he always sensed the resentment with us. 'I've brought you all here to talk a little about the current environment and how, as a department, we're going to interpret that.' He cleared his throat. Jennifer was watching him closely. She was a cool and composed customer, but her look today was shrewd.

'You'll all be aware that we as a country are in the middle of a diplomatic argue...' He looked across at our two guests '...disagreement' nodded at them for approval, which he got by way of a sharp, short nod, 'and as a department it's important for us, for you, to interpret that in the correct light. I'll be talking to each of the teams about how this is going to happen, but I'm particularly conscious that with the new series of Talking Point already in production, and with the architectural series and the...' He looked at Jennifer, who looked at me.

'Shetland Song,' she said.

'Right, yes, we have to be conscious to be producing from an accurate viewpoint. And with regard to the Russian question, we need to reassure and be mindful that the audience might view what is happening here as being threatening. Which is isn't.'

'Sorry,' Andrew Coulter had his hand partially raised. 'If I could just clarify? What...what...what do you mean? We aren't making programmes about the political row over a distant piece of rock.'

'Yes, well.' Marc was floundering.

'If I may, Marc...' A man in dark-rimmed glasses and a neatly pressed shirt and tie leant forward from the adjacent seat. He gave a practised smile of someone used to being listened to. Marc leant back. He looked relieved, in both senses of the word. The stranger continued. His voice was a strange mix of Russian harshness and American twang. 'As producers you are of course responsible for delivering programmes that adhere to the SBC and the BBC's editorial guidelines. We are not asking you to change that.' He held his palms out towards us. Trust me, I'm a friend, he gestured. 'What would be concerning, and we want to address this before it arises so you know where to turn if you feel you need assistance, is if you were trying to make a judgment on content, perhaps, or an interview aside, perhaps a piece of scripting where you tie up a piece of history with a little contemporary observation, and you pass comment on the situation: then we are here for you. Unfortunately some news outlets are not completely educated on the reality of the discussions taking place and are, maybe not deliberately I hope, misleading the British public and causing unnecessary scaremongering across the British Isles. What we don't want is for any misjudged commentary to be produced from this department. It would reflect badly on you, and undermine your position as impartial documentary makers.'

Beverley raised her hand. 'Excuse me, sorry, just to be clear. You are talking about the network programmes? I'm not making any network programmes...'

The stranger smiled again to show he understood the confusion. 'Of course, as producers of programmes for Scotland too we are very concerned that impartiality, and accuracy – the cornerstones of SBC programme making – stand firm. Again, if you have any questions about pieces you are making for programmes that touch upon the Rockall question, be it a joke, or a comment, please do ask and we can advise you.'

'I'm sorry,' Andrew again, 'who are you?'

'Ah, I apologise,' the man laughed, 'my name is Grigory Rankovic. We are with the Ministry of Foreign Affairs in

Moscow and I am here to assist you with the media operation. This is my colleague Aleks Petrov. He will assist you too. We are both here to help.'

His colleague didn't look too helpful. His eyes swept the room. His expression was masked. He didn't acknowledge his introduction.

'Okay, great, thanks to everyone for coming.' Marc practically climbed over his Russian friends on the way out.

'Right, everyone,' Jennifer was standing up, 'we can chat through this again tomorrow in Edinburgh and I'll –' she nodded at our northern colleagues, '– speak to some people on the phone.'

The room emptied. I stood up. Andrew was beside me.

'What the fuck was that all about?' I asked him.

He shook his head and looked at my coffee. 'I don't know. But I think we'll be needing something a bit stronger than that.'

CHAPTER 2

So that's how the Russians were suddenly involved. They weren't editors, we were assured, but they were there around the office. Jennifer tried her best to keep their creepy presence from us. It was obvious, though, that they were leaning on her, or leaning on Marc who was leaning on her. Suddenly Marc wanted to hear output he'd never been interested in before. As I mentioned, Marc was a news man. We as a department were viewed as a group of over-academic, blue-stockinged snobs. When news wanted to broadcast on the arts, they'd package up an eight-minute piece in an afternoon. When we wanted to follow a story about the arts, we would spin it out into a pitch by phone, then during a meeting several months later, to be commissioned months after that. If commissioned we'd chase presenters, then interviews, then days editing and scripting... we were high maintenance. We felt we created radio and the others filled it. It's true, I admit it, but then Radio Scotland had space to fill, and the networks, well they had space to compete for, and better money to pay for it.

So Marc, who had a shoestring budget to populate seven days of music, news, drama, religion, culture and features... didn't really have time to indulge us. But Jennifer did. So it was she who had meetings with the hysterical Sarah who knew Swedish folk music like no one else and wanted a little piece poked into every programme, and Beverley who could write a PhD thesis on every doc she produced, but couldn't quite deliver it to schedule. She indulged Andrew's lunch expenses, Chris working from home because he didn't want to use the office software and Beverley's assurances that the networks were wrong on what they were expecting from the pitch. We were an eclectic bunch, and perhaps it was wise to try to keep a distance between us and the Russians. But it wouldn't work forever.

In the meantime I remained vigilant around my home. Mr Silence didn't break form. I saw him twice on the step where he looked at me in a way that I took as acknowledgement and twice on the pavement where he very much ignored me. Maybe he wasn't Russian, I told myself. Maybe I was paranoid.

On the national front a flooding crisis had shunted the Russian problem to the later pages. The clever political soothsaying and massaging of the Russians had turned it into a technical story for the political enthusiast, the only people who might be able to spot the sleight of hands.

After the minor riot the George Square tank incident eventually produced, the Russians were playing it more low key. You could hardly tell they were here.

The guy Aleks was about, though. You could sense him. When his staring eyes appeared in the office a hush came over the place. He was like a Harry Potter dementor, just sucking life out of the place. I saw that guy Grigory too a couple of times. He was a hand shaker. I saw him shaking hands by the lift, in reception and outside while having a smoke.

I'd just convinced myself that my imagination had embarrassed me, and that above me a hard-working Presbyterian silent type was renting, when on a Sunday morning I threw open my security door lycra clad and ready to start my run, and nearly jumped on Grigory himself.

He stepped back in surprise, his body tensing. His hands reflexed as if to grab something from a holster. He was broader than I remembered now I saw him face-to-face.

'Oh sorry,' I spluttered. I had no intention of speaking to this man but my politeness reflex overruled me.

'I'm very sorry,' he replied, in that funny Russian-

American twang. 'I didn't mean to startle you. I was just ringing for my friend. He lives at the top floor in this block. I guess you're neighbours?'

I was sure he didn't recognise me. I couldn't resist. I had my hair scraped back, and I had been sitting at the back of the conference room when he'd spoken to us, so... 'Yes. And I guess you must be from Russia. Part of the diplomatic consignment here to negotiate on the Rockall disagreement. I guess you're interested in the media? And your name is Grigory.'

His jaw dropped. I smiled and bounded down off the stoop and ran away along the pavement. I resisted the urge to turn and look at him, but I could feel him staring after me. Small victories.

The feeling didn't last, though, because my exchange with Grigory confirmed that I had a cuckoo in the nest upstairs. I kept telling myself not to panic. Maybe the Russians really were here to foster relationships between us and them, and that the chap living above me was just a simple civil servant enjoying life in Edinburgh.

Who was I kidding?

Winter applied itself halfheartedly that year with lazy attempts at sleet and wind that left shrivelled leaves dangling from branches, before finally knuckling down to some serious frosts when the wooden huts of the German Christmas market in Princes Street Gardens were long flat-packed away.

The newsroom was adjacent to our office. The Russians had made themselves comfortable there, and being a small base altogether, we'd squeeze past them in the corridor and weave through them in the hallway. I started recognising a few of them. The guy Aleks in particular would hover around and glower at anyone in his path. The man Grigory I saw in passing. He would take interviews. He was a public-friendly face of this soft invasion, solid and reliable in his assurances.

He'd stop to say hello to people in the corridor, who would say hello back. I'd duck into the tea room and avoid his eye, not wanting to be ensnared in his net.

Journalists became a more common sight in our radio feature office having whispered conversations and sneaking glances towards the door. I saw Jennifer take meetings with a couple of them in our glass-walled meeting room which she'd never done before. Yet it was all very indirect and cloak and dagger, and the news broadcasts remained unnervingly cautious. Items that I knew had been taped were dropped. Trusted commentators were sidelined. The SBC news team was slowly being suppressed from above and beyond, their oxygen being cut off to the point of suffocation, but the valve was being turned too slowly to notice.

It was business as usual with our department. We always had monthly catch ups. We'd be given any news about future commissions and network changes. Jennifer would tell us how great we were doing then remind us that things were still tight when it came to convincing Marc we were worth the investment. During one of these Jennifer did her slow painful cautionary delivery, which always precipitated bad news, as she outlined her plans for us to have a brainstorming session about a potential Russian-themed season.

'As in,' asked Andrew, 'a sort of morale boosting anti-Russian propaganda season, but a bit more delicate than that?'

'Noooo,' Jennifer eased out, 'it's a season, really to explore the vibrancy of the people and culture we might not necessarily be aware of, and to, eeeeh,' she glanced down at her notes, 'bust the myths that are swirling around them.'

An unimpressed silence filled the room.

'Well, there's lots we can work on there,' said Craig, a senior manager whose main role in the department was to smooth over cracks and keep morale up. He nodded, 'I can definitely chair a few meetings on that.' He smiled round at us. I don't remember anyone smiling back.

...

We had a meeting. Generally in these things we would sit around a table and throw some initial ideas out in the hope that putting our heads together brought new angles and takes on things. Craig would appear delighted at the most pathetic attempt at creativity, encouraging every word association attempt and dreg of memory. We'd come away with a couple of ideas, which were generally ones the producer had come in with anyway. Normally two Russians wouldn't be sitting there with us.

The first was introduced as Viktor. He gave a nervous smile before concentrating on his notepad. Beside him was an older, podgy, balding chap who introduced himself as Boris. He appeared very much at ease in this role.

'Tell me what you think you know of Russia?' he asked, as Craig took an intake of breath to lead the session.

Andrew ventured the story of the tsar, the revolution, communism... and was interrupted.

'Tell me something about Russia that you think is impressive, or should I say pretty cool.'

Boris looked around. We studied our hands or the wall or the table. Viktor scribbled notes in a pad.

'Chris,' he pointed at the producer, 'what are you thinking?'

Chris sat up a little taller, startled by the name recognition, and flicked his pen from side to side.

'I, well...' honestly: Chris never had any decent ideas, or numerous other ones. He just plodded along. 'Like Andrew I thought about the revolution, obviously.' Boris managed to look both encouraging and unimpressed at the same time.

'And?'

'...and mountains!' Chris stabbed his pen towards Boris in jubilation, this thought just coming to him. 'The Caucasus. Mountains. What's there?'

There was silence. 'What is there,' stated Boris, less a

question than pointing out that none of us knew. I guess he was rapidly getting the picture that we were unexpectedly lame sometimes at coming up with ideas.

'Okay, Miss Facebook, what about you?'

'This is Anna Aitken, she's one of our producers.' Craig was trying to change the tone back to friendly. I was wondering how he knew of my Facebook addiction.

'I know who she is. Tell me Anna, something you know about Russia which you think is an interesting story.'

I hesitated.

'You were briefed about this meeting, weren't you? You all were?' There were a few shifting glances and I nodded.

'Yeah, but I sort of started with treatments and was working backwards. Or formats.' I was always rubbish at being put on the spot in meetings. Hopeless at pitching. Too much crap running around my brain. He wanted more.

'...and?'

I was put out by his assumption of authority, his expectant silence and demanding answers when he shouldn't have been in the position to demand them in the first place.

'I thought about a series of assorted stories of random Russians called Russian Roulette. Not because anyone gets shot, but because it would be recorded as a sort of pot luck journey.'

'Pot luck?'

'Yeah, it's when you're at a fair or something and you pay money and stick your hand in a bag and it's luck whether you get a great prize or a not so great one.'

'Anna,' Andrew had his look he reserved for me of affectionate amusement, 'a pot luck is when you have a gathering of people and everyone brings a different dish. I think you're thinking of a lucky dip.'

'Oh right, yeah. That. So it's a series of chance recordings.' My face was red. This wasn't going well.

'And that was your one idea?'

'No,' I replied and sighed. Time for the idea vomit. 'I

thought about doing some sort of archive piece about the Russian space mission. I didn't know if you wanted to link it to Scotland in any way, they talk about a space port coming here so that could be the in. I did wonder if most Russian astronauts could speak English we could do an interesting soundscape recorded on a space mission. I thought about doing readings recorded from space, about space, read by the people in space....' I tapered off. I'd thought space but not much more. Viktor was scribbling away. 'I thought about doing something about fictional detectives. Pitting the best of Scottish against the best of Russian. Rebus versus Fandorin. Have literary people say how they'd go about solving a sort of case, and who would come up trumps first. Have it all about the culture of crime writing in Scotland and Russia, as it's having a resurgence over there, isn't it?' No response. That's as far as I'd thought on that. 'I thought about doing something on snowdrops.'

'Snowdrops?' Boris looked bemused. Well he did ask.

'Yeah snowdrops, the little white flowers. You know there are such people as galanthophiles, people who are nutty about snowdrops here? Certain bulbs get sold for thousands at big snowdrop festivals. Well,' I said, cutting off his obvious follow up question, 'they come originally from the Crimea. So it's the rise and rise of the mighty snowdrop type thing. It could link with our gardening series, or could be a special. I thought maybe we'd be taking that route with the commissions. If there were any.'

'Okay,' he said it slowly, looking around.

Beverley was nodding in a patronising way. She obviously thought the ideas were rubbish but still wasn't being forthcoming on her own. Chris was twitching like he had an urgent meeting with the loo. Andrew was studying the window.

'What we tend to do...' Craig started.

'It's alright, I'm getting a sense of the ability here.'

There was a commotion occurring outside the meeting

room in the main office which was instantly recognisable to us locals as Sarah arriving. Sarah, as I mentioned before, was an expert on Swedish folk music. She was slightly eccentric, supremely highly strung, and liked to work irregular hours. It was almost lunchtime, and this was her first appearance.

'Who is this?' Boris pointed out the office.

'That's Sarah,' started Craig, with the tone a doctor might use to break bad news, 'she...'

'She knows there is a meeting that the whole department was to attend?'

'Well,' started Craig. The truth was that a few producers were not in attendance. Brainstorming meetings were not compulsory. I was at a bit of a loose end, and Chris was likely there because he was in the office on the off chance. Bet he regretted that now.

The door burst open.

'The CD player isn't working in the studio and I can't get an engineer down. They say I have to phone SOMEBODY!' Sarah shrieked at us, not caring what kind of meeting we were holding, hysterical at her workflow disruption.

'Sarah,' Craig explained, once again, 'you know you have to phone the central engineering line...'

'I saw Marcus walk by the studio.' She stared, goggle-eyed at Craig, annunciating slowly so he understood the full scale of the treachery, 'I waved at him,' she demonstrated, her underarm giving a little extra waggle in support, 'and he walked by As If He Hadn't Seen Me.'

'Well he might genuinely not have seen you, Sarah. He might have been working with something else. You really must phone the central line to book him.'

'Sarah, this is an ideas meeting for the forthcoming Russian season.' Boris was blindly wading in without appreciating what he was dealing with. 'Do you have anything to contribute?'

'WHAT?!' screamed Sarah. 'I HAVE A STUDIO WITH A BROKEN CD PLAYER. WHAT HAS THIS GOT TO

DO WITH THAT? I HAVE A PROGRAMME TO MAKE THAT IS DUE FOR DELIVERY. IN. TWO. DAYS'

'Why don't you try one of the smaller studios?' Andrew was quite good at dealing with Sarah. 'They can't be fully booked, Sarah. We're all in here.'

Boris wasn't giving up. 'I'd like to ask you a question, Sarah.'

'I DON'T HAVE TIME.' She grasped the sides of her face with hands that were already full of scrunched paper, then turned and ejected herself back into office.

She left a noise vacuum in her wake. We sat awaiting permission to leave, eyes roving from Craig to Jennifer. Then the door burst open again,

'Is your question about Swedish folk music? I can help you with that quickly. Right now.'

Boris gave her a straight answer. 'No.'

She vanished.

Boris stood up.

'Right guys,' clapped Craig, 'some great ideas there I thought.' He looked at Boris for agreement and saw that none was coming. Boris stared back at us all with a look of disdain. Viktor was gathering his notes. 'Let's keep in touch with it all and I'll chat to Jennifer about how we want to go forward with this.'

We all left, gasping at the turgid office air.

CHAPTER 3

The next day or so I was procrastinating in the tea room by making a precise cup of tea. More than just tea had been brewing that day. The news department was scrabbling to substantiate a recent unverified leak of a Russian document outlining the drilling potential of the seabed around Rockall, all denied by the Russians, but the source was shrouded in uncertainty, dominating nationalist press and opinion blogs but not national newspapers. The stage was finally being set, it seemed. I stepped out into the corridor and nearly slopped the hot liquid all down what looked like a rather expensive shirt being worn by that smooth muscovite chap Grigory.

'Hello Anna Aitken, radio producer, Oxford graduate and weekend runner.' He smiled, his eyes studying me from behind those lenses. The specs gave him, I realised, a more academic appearance than his bruiser colleagues, and his smile wasn't leery either. But it was controlled.

'I don't just run at the weekends.'

'Ah, my mistake. I should apologise. I'm sorry I didn't recognise you last time. I'll make sure I pay attention in future.'

'No worries at all, please feel free to totally ignore me, and hopefully we won't have cause to see each other much, if at all, soon.'

He smiled again. Frustratingly it was quite an attractive smile and not as contrived as I'd first thought. 'Maybe you're right, but I think we will be seeing a little more of each other. Your politicians are being a little stubborn.'

'Or simply defending our land.'

'Your land? If you like I can show you the map that I carry around with me. If you can pinpoint the location of Rockall on this, which has been discretely removed, I'll be impressed.' He propped his foot up against the wall and balanced his briefcase onto his thigh and started fiddling with the combination.

Boris suddenly popped up beside me. He'd been hanging around a lot recently. 'Hello, Miss Facebook.' I glared at him. I'd been very strict with my use lately. 'You have a meeting now.'

'No I don't,' I replied. It really annoyed me that he was here bossing people about. He wasn't in the SBC, he had no right to tell me what I was doing.

'Yes you do. Ah, here is Jennifer. I was just telling Ms Aitken that we were expecting her in the meeting room.'

Jennifer was bustling through into the tea room. She had that distracted look she carried as if she was still finishing off her last conference call before rushing into the next meeting, and we'd just interrupted. She smiled. 'Yes, please, Anna. Are you free for a moment? In the meeting room.'

I tried to avoid Boris's smug look.

'Oh well,' I said to Grigory, who was shutting his case, 'next time,' and went to grab my note pad before taking my place at the table, only then acknowledging a wave of unease as I questioned how Grigory knew about my academic background.

I was joined shortly by Jennifer, Craig, Boris... and then Grigory smiled as he joined the party.

'Now Anna,' Jennifer started. I liked Jennifer, admired her. She was obviously very smart and efficient at her job. 'Marc has asked Features to make a contribution to the coverage of the Russian activities in Scotland right now.' She looked at Grigory and Boris. 'One programme to begin with. I've spoken to Craig about your work load and we think he can shift Shetland Song back to June, which would likely happen anyway as we rejig slots to make way for this new commission.' She looked at me. 'Is that ok?'

Well, it wasn't. I didn't understand what was going on, but didn't like it. I didn't want to be entering the quagmire of Russian shape shifting and passing it off with the confidence of the SBC, and I certainly didn't want to have to interact with any more Russians than I had to. Unfortunately Jennifer was my editor, and therefore my boss.

'What content are you looking for in the programmes?'

She gave me a look of appreciation. 'It's shedding a light on how the Russians are currently interacting with people in Scotland. The recording will be mainly focusing on the diplomatic efforts and how the Russian party is engaging with us as they do it.'

Well, that was as clear as mud.

'There is going to be a series of meetings on Islay next week,' explained Boris, 'and an opportunity for some colleagues to explore a little more of Scotland. Distilleries... the seaside... and so on. This material can be used for the radio programme to dispel some of the false rumours that we have unfortunately noticed circulating.'

'What rumours?' I asked. Boris shifted in his seat. He looked to Grigory.

'Russia, as I am sure you know,' Grigory explained, 'has been having extensive communications with Scotland, not only about the dispute on Rockall, which after the UN review I am sure will be rightfully passed over to Russia, but also about how Scotland could benefit from an improved relationship with our country. There is a myriad of benefits we could provide each other now Scotland is a little more isolated on the world stage. Only benefits. Of course, those of a more regressive persuasion are still blinded by the historical associations of the Cold War. Luckily the majority of Scots exist in the modern world, and appreciate that we are no longer a nation of communists. But for those who retain such prejudice, it is easy to sow seeds of doubt in their mind. The role of the SBC, surely, as the national broadcaster, should be to give an accurate representation of what is happening in the country.' He gave me an intent look. 'So that is your role, and next week is an opportunity to gather some good recordings of us 'in the field' as you might say.' I wouldn't, but I didn't bother correcting him. I looked at Jennifer. It appeared she too was trying to see through Grigory's smooth delivery. Then she nodded.

'We can chat through the editorial line for this once you've gathered some material and have more of a feel for the subject.'

'We can help you with that,' interjected Boris.

She didn't shift her focus from me. 'Are you happy with this, Anna?'

I gave her a look that I hope conveyed my confusion, but I decided the trip might shed some light on it all.

'Well, I can see how things go and then meet up with you afterwards.'

Jennifer smiled. 'Good idea, let's do that.' She picked up her notes, phone and cup, and left.

'We leave on Monday. Eight a.m. from here. You can be briefed in the car. You will return on Thursday.' Boris too felt the discussion of content, slant and tone was at an end.

'You want me to travel with you?'

'Yes. We have made all the arrangements. You just need your microphone and recording devices.'

Grigory had been checking his phone. 'I'm sorry, I have to go somewhere.' He flashed his smile. 'I will see you Tuesday.' He left. I grabbed my notebook but Boris wasn't finished.

'What further work have you done on your space idea? Or any of the others?'

In truth those half thoughts had been tossed in the corner, like so many others, to be recalled if necessary, but Craig had moved onto more pressing broadcast crises and there hadn't been any follow up about it.

'Nothing really,' I replied, thinking it was none of his

business.

'I think you should develop the space idea, focusing on exactly what dialogue you think would work best in the programme and how that would interact with the sounds. Russian Roulette – the name is catchy but misleading. If you can find stories you want to cover in that format, however, that is worthwhile. And find out a little more of how the snowdrops travelled from Crimea to Scotland. That could be a good tale.'

'And what do I do with all these developed ideas?'

'You email Craig, Jennifer and me.' He spelt out his email address. An SBC email address. He'd become part of the organisation.

CHAPTER 4

We gathered outside the office in the cold for eight. I wasn't the only media minion being dragged along for the ride. A freelancer, Colin, stood smoking and chatting to someone called Rachel from the Scotsman. I'd exchanged pleasantries with one of the newsroom cameramen who was now standing with a look of zen as someone who is used to standing and waiting manages to do. And as a minivan drew up and Viktor stepped out, Graeme leapt out of a coffee shop that had just opened, large cup in his grasp.

'We can stop for coffee!' Victor declared. He appeared more relaxed than when I'd seen him in the meeting. Sort of human-like.

We piled in and embarked on the long journey west.

I think my companions viewed this as a free jolly. It seemed that normal strict SBC rules on expenses were not going to apply as the whole thing was a treat from the Russians. They were at pains, Viktor explained, to give us the opportunity to see the 'real' side of them. Not the intimidating superpower taking advantage of a tiny evolving nation, but this jovial bear who was on holiday. We did indeed buy coffee and the chat mostly centred around which football team Viktor was going to select to support (probably Kilmarnock, maybe Hibs) and which pub he thought best in Edinburgh (The Queens Arms). Viktor really was quite affable when he wasn't acting as a diplomatic underling, with a buxom laugh that erupted from him, taking me by surprise the first time I heard it. I thought the Russians were actually a little daft to not push him further forward.

'I love the cannon,' he was saying, 'at lunchtime. Boom! I nearly drop my soda.'

Between fun anecdotes about getting lost and the wonder of Irn Bru, I pressed Viktor to explain that we'd be present on a series of outings with various diplomats and we'd be able to interview some governmental personnel. He assured me 'it will all be very good'.

We reached Tarbert by lunchtime and ate sandwiches and soup together overlooking the hibernating boats in the harbour before driving down to the ferry terminal. We queued behind some male-populated cars and then we all rolled on to the ferry and piled out. I delved into my bag to fish out my recording equipment, but Viktor stopped me with a hand pressed over the top of the microphone.

'No, no no. Not yet. Everyone is relaxing. You should relax now.'

'Gathering material while people are relaxed is actually a good thing,' I replied, my hand still gripping the mic.

'No, no no. Let them relax without that. You will get plenty of opportunity later on.'

I let him push the microphone back and trooped upstairs with everyone else to the passenger lounges. I didn't like this control. Sometimes I was used to having an over-zealous PR person hovering and being irritating when it was a high-profile interview, but if you're asked along for the ride... usually it's fine. The SBC don't generally pull fast ones. Editorial guidelines and all that.

I entered the bar to see a room of Russians embarking on the start of their drinking for the day. I found myself a cup of tea and decided to brace it outside. It was sheltered enough behind the funnel and I stood and watched the view unfold.

I was only alone for a few minutes before someone came out speaking on his mobile. It was Grigory. He wasn't wearing the same coat as everyone else, but what looked like a more expensive version. I looked out over the water and heard the sound of footsteps on metal as he approached me. He was holding a cigarette in one hand and a lighter in another.

'You mind if I join you?'

'If you stay downwind.'

He nodded, not bothered by my brusqueness and stepped further away from the funnel.

'You like the fresh air.'

'I did,' I said, glancing at the cigarette, and then realising I was being too rude. 'It's a bit crowded inside.'

Grigory ducked to peer through the window and saw the gathering at the bar. He turned to the receding West Loch Tarbert.

'It's very beautiful.' He waved his fag towards the rocks and collapsed orange ferns. 'You're very lucky. Have you travelled here before?'

'Yeah,' I admitted, 'cycled. I cycle a bit.'

'Ah. That's nice. Good place to cycle.' He gave me a tight smile, studying me. 'Are you looking forward to this trip?'

'Not really,' I shifted my stance. He could be quite disconcerting. My tea was half drunk and cold already, the fresh breeze was becoming biting. 'I quite liked where I was.'

'You don't like to travel?'

I shrugged. My brained whirred through a kaleidoscope of images ranging from snowy Alps to wide plains, but I didn't want to hand over my personal history.

'You don't want to tell me. You don't like me? I've done nothing to you.' Yet.

'I don't dislike you.' It felt like every conversation with this man was a game.

'You don't like Russians?'

'I don't dislike Russians. Per se. I'd just prefer you to stay in Russia at this moment in time.'

'You think everyone should stay where they come from?'

Urgh, my move. 'No, of course not.'

He heard the exasperation in my tone. He leant against the railing exhaling smoke into the wind. 'Don't you think there is some hope that Russia and Scotland could become closer countries?' I scrunched my face up. He continued. 'We are both proud northern nations with strong creative histories and a fondness for our national drinks.'

'I don't really think that's a foundation for a healthy relationship.'

He tried again. 'We are both nations steeped in proud military histories, we've fought on the same side many times...'

'I don't think we are the same in that respect.'

'No?'

'No. I think the Scots are rightly proud of how we've fought. We disproportionately sacrificed in both World Wars. We've stepped up to the plate when we've been called. We fought, and beat an English army grossly outnumbering ours to claim our independence. I think all this is lingering in the DNA of every Scot.' He nodded. 'But I think Russians: I think you guys are scarred by the wars you have fought. I think the desperation of Stalingrad and the horrors of your own revolution, I think they simmer just below the surface. War isn't a distant romantic notion for you, in the way I think it resides in the spirit of most Scots. I think it's omnipresent for you people. I think it makes you more volatile, more dangerous.'

He took a last draw on his cigarette and stubbed it out on the railing before turning his gaze towards me, the smoke coiling around his face and then darting away towards the clouds. 'Maybe. But I think we can still be friends. Don't you?'

I shrugged. I didn't want to concede anything.

The hotel was small, dug into the side of a hill, and we took up every room. Mine was under the eaves and jutted out over the bins, but it gave me a little view of the water and small harbour. There were about eight Russians staying in the same hotel. The press was called for coffee and tea and a briefing in the lounge.

The briefing was held by a tall, broad-shouldered woman called Marina. She barked louder than necessary for us to listen and gave out the impression that she expected us to misbehave.

'Welcome to everyone. We are very much delighted that you have come to join us here on Is-lay. Now I will outline the agenda for the next few days and the strict access the press will have. This must be adhered to at all times.'

As she rustled some papers Grigory jumped up to address us. 'Hello everyone. Before Marina does her very important job of outlining the calendar for the next 48 hours let me give a little introduction. A few of us on this diplomatic process in Scotland have been lucky enough to have spent several months mostly in and around the major cities, with some of us enjoying even further travels within this beautiful country. As we take the opportunity to explore more of the sights, we felt it was an ample opportunity for the media to get access to speak and understand a little more about what we are trying to achieve here.' He then went through introductions: Us, the press from Edinburgh, plus other reporters from such papers as The Herald and The Press and Journal and a freelancer.

Ignoring a bristling Marina, Grigory outlined the Russian contingent, but the names washed over me in a fug of foreignness. I didn't know who I was going to interview, or what this programme was about but I wasn't going to let myself be entirely dictated to. Grigory was trying to put a good spin on how they were going to give us time to record, washing over how they might dictate to us too. Then Grigory said, 'this is Anton.' A slender man stood up, looking late thirties, wearing a more casual attire of slacks and jumper. 'Anton is here for you as a translator if necessary, of course I and Viktor will do all we can to help you with that too, but Anton can be of use to you, in particular, Anna, if you'd like some description or interview questions to remain on tape.'

He looked at me and I looked from Anton to Grigory. 'Like a contributor?' I asked.

'Like a presenter.' Grigory replied. He saw my look of disbelief. They're selecting presenters too? He raised his hand up towards me, 'we can talk about this in a moment. Okay, let me pass back to Marina and then we can do a little exploring before dinner and you will have an opportunity to do some filming and recording and question asking.'

Marina took over, outlining the touring plans for the trip, then handed out a contact sheet for us. We broke to refill and digest the plans, and then Grigory came over to me with this guy Anton.

'Anton, this is Anna.' He waved his fingers between us. 'You haven't met before, but I assure you that Anton has much good experience of interviewing and is very competent. I think you will find him very useful.'

'Right.' I said. 'I get to choose ultimately who presents this programme. It will probably be a Scot. If I'm making a programme about what a bunch of Russians are doing in our country then I think we want the reassuring tone of a Scot.'

'Yes, of course, of course,' said Grigory, 'but you will need someone to translate maybe some of your more local words, and you might find him useful.' He patted me on the shoulder. 'It is up to you. Anton is here for you.' He went to charm someone else.

Anton smiled at me and we made small talk before Marina burst in thrusting another piece of paper at me. 'Here are your guidelines. There must be NO recording unless sanctioned by myself or another member of the Moscow party. You understand?' I nodded and took the paper. She went to yell at someone else.

I felt like I was in the trenches unable to see above to get a clear shot. Without seeing ahead how could I outflank them?

...

There was an outing around Bowmore where we were staying. A wander up to the gates of the distillery, which were now shut, and a look out to sea. I asked to record a little wild track of the exploration, which was granted. It's easier in radio just to blend into the background without a camera pointing at anybody, but I still noted people taking steps away from me. It didn't matter. Microphones are powerful things. I didn't use the mics like they use to interview footballers after matches, say. These microphones pick up everything – a door closing in the background, a whisper in the corner... so I was hearing the crunching on gravel, and the shrieking of distant seagulls, and the hushed conversation in a language I didn't understand. Viktor came over to me, and nodded.

'Hi,' I said.

'You are recording now?'

'Yes,' I replied. I had no reason to conceal. 'When there's a light on here,' I pointed to the recording device, the size of a TV remote control with a red dot shining out of it, 'then you know I'm recording.'

'You have recorded a lot already.'

'Well, you never know what might be useful, plus it's likely I could use background material like this under, say, narration of some sort. And whole chunks won't be useable, say if someone is speaking in Russian and it's distracting, or there's a big lorry. And there are moments that you can't tell when you'll get a little bit of detail. For example, bursts of laughter, or someone saying 'look, a dolphin' and that's exactly what you want. So, you record lots and pick out small bits to get the best colour for your programme.'

He nodded. He seemed genuinely interested.

'You must get a lot of material. Is it all stored in there?'

He pointed at the machine. I shook my head. 'Memory cards.'

'Ah, so you've brought a lot of memory cards?'

'Yeah. A few.'

Then he said, 'some people don't like you recording when they are just walking around.'

'Then why did they invite me?'

He shrugged. We were going in anyway. I switched it all off.

We had dinner together in the hotel. I suspect this was intended for mingling purposes, where the Russians would woo us with their warm humour and great chat. In reality us journos stayed at one end and the Russians the other. In the buffer zone was Viktor who would instantly seize upon any object or place related to Scotland and declare that he very much liked it. Grigory sat nearby, sometimes engaging in chat with his fellow countrymen, sometimes gazing over at us with that calculating look on his face. Marina came over between courses to inform us we were having a good time. We all exchanged glances, stifled mirth, and told her we were. To be fair, they were very generous with the booze, and the meal was a perfectly tasty cliché of scampi, salmon or venison.

After the meal we split into two groups, the bar and the lounge. There was a Scotland football game playing on the TV in the bar, so most of the Scots decamped there. Unsurprisingly Viktor declared a great admiration for our tactics. It was a comment too far for Colin. 'Don't talk shite,' he said over the froth of his Deuchar's.

I was ready to retire, but I stood by the bar and had an orange juice, watched a little of the game and had an interesting chat with some local fishermen who were sure they'd seen a hint of a Russian submarine while out, and weren't too impressed by the swell in foreign numbers that night. Soon, though, I went to bed.

My aim, I had decided by the next morning, was to take as much recording as possible and edit away later. The agenda being pushed by Marina was to allow us interview time in the morning and then give us access for recording some outings in the afternoon. I did as bid.

A succession of bored military and diplomatic men were sat in front of me and batted away my, or Anton's, broad questions of their intent, impression and experiences in Scotland. One man, Mikhail, denied having any interest in the Rockall issue at all, just saying he liked whisky and birds of prey. He had no interest in engaging with me, only making eye contact with Anton as he translated.

A quick lunch, and then we were off round some distilleries. It was banal stuff but I recorded it all. There was a brief stop at Finlaggin, a historic base for the Lords of the Isles which required a little imagination, which they evidently lacked, taking a quick turn of the island while smoking cigarettes then jumping back in the cars. It wasn't until the trip was almost over that things got interesting.

The chap, Mikhail, did, as it turned out, have a genuine interest in birds. He requested a walk around the Loch Gruinart nature reserve in the hope of a decent sight of the waders. I went too, thinking it would give me some interesting sounds to contrast with the echoes of the distilleries.

It was just me, him, and another diplomat who didn't want to visit the Bruichladdich distillery. We trudged for a bit, me getting some lovely bird and farming sounds, and passing the occasional fellow bird appreciator.

I was standing and listening to the breeze and the birds, my headphones on and my microphone well covered with fur to protect it from wind interference, when a distant conversation was picked up. I turned to see it was Mikhail about ten metres away starting a chat with someone whom I hadn't seen approach. He could have been a local, it was polite, but then it got heated. The man knew they were lying, he insisted, that he'd seen the boats for himself. He knew about the survey. They might think they could pull the wool over McCulloch's eyes, but they wouldn't do it to the rest of Scotland. They were liars. Mikhail lost it. He grabbed the man by the lapels, who baited him, telling him to 'do it', 'show his true colours'. There was a bit of a scuffle, the other Russian ran over and dragged his companion away, shouting at him in Russian. The Scot shouted that he knew they were all wolves in sheep's clothing. The truth would out. The Russians walked away, Mikhail breathing heavily, trying to control himself, sweeping his hair back away from his face, shaking his colleague's hold off. The Scot walked on round the loch. My brilliant microphone picked it all up. I kept my distance, then when I was sure the action was over I switched off the mic and followed them back to where we were to meet the car.

As I waited Mikhail finally made eye contact. His companion translated. 'You record that?'

I gave him wide eyes and shook my head. 'No,' I said, 'Too windy.' Editorial guidelines could wait.

The car arrived shortly and we returned to the hotel. When I got into my room I pulled out the memory card from the recorder. I tucked it into my pillowcase and went to join the others for dinner.

CHAPTER 5

The next morning I got up early with the sun and went for a run. The audio I'd gathered at the nature reserve was by far the juiciest I could have hoped for. At dinner I was sensitive to glances from Marina after she'd spoken to Mikhail, and I knew her repeated questions about how much recording I had done were symptoms of her nervousness.

I greeted the fishermen and ran for over six miles, breathing in the unfurling gorse flowers and sea air. The island was quiet and I doubt more than a few people saw me on my route through road and path.

I pulled my muddy trainers off at the front door and padded in past reception. Breakfast was in full flow. I paused at the door. The waiter, an older, genial man, greeted me.

'Good run?'

'Yes thanks. How much longer are you serving for?'

He checked his watch. 'Cooked breakfasts for about another forty-five minutes.'

I thought. 'Would you mind if I grabbed a cup of tea and a sausage roll and took it up to the room?'

'No problem.' He noted it down.

'Just a mug for the tea, thanks,' I called after him, stepping into the room.

As he disappeared into the kitchen I turned and noticed who was eating. Five of the Russians were there, with Grigory facing me. He nodded at me. Some others turned and followed his look, snorting at my sweaty, muddy, dishevelled appearance. Marina appeared by my side, making me jump.

'Are you happy with the material you have gathered these last two days?' Not this again.

'Yeah. Yes, I guess so. We can see what we can do with it when I get back to Edinburgh.'

'Did you get material on your walk yesterday?'

'Yeah, eh, not really. It was very windy.'

'Did you record anything at all there? I would be interested in what you recorded. I have interest in the recording for radio and I would like to listen to your walk recording so I can understand better what will work for you.'

Thankfully the waiter appeared with a mug of tea and a filled roll for me.

'Thanks. Yeah, of course you can listen to a little of my recordings if you like. It's not up to much and I deleted any distorted stuff I gathered.'

'I would like very much to listen to the material. Can I listen to it here today?'

Handing over recordings can end in you handing over editorial control. I wasn't planning on doing that.

'Eh, yeah. I haven't got access to a computer here, but I can upload some samples to you when we're back.'

'No, I would like to listen to them here. Particularly the recording from the walk.'

She was seriously invading my personal space. I wasn't tiny, but I was pretty wiry. She was taller, and broader, and I suspect she could pick me up and throw me across the room if she wanted too. She was standing tall and her eyes were trying to lock down my shifting gaze. Despite that, I had no plans to give her the material she was sniffing around for. Why not the Bowmore wander? The distillery tours? The interviews? This other stuff I didn't care about and I knew she didn't too. She must have heard about the scuffle and was desperate to find out what I got on tape.

'Well, there's not really anything to listen to there, but you can have a flick through all the memory cards if you like.' I glanced over at the men at the table. Grigory was watching, then he looked away.

'Yes, I will come with you now.' She gestured towards the stairs and stepped aside so I could lead the way.

We trooped up the stairs. I hoped I was generating enough of a sweat stench that it wasn't pleasant for her. She followed close behind me into my room, her eyes scanning around as I went over to the bag and grabbed the three memory cards I had there.

'This is all of them?'

'Yes,' I replied. She stared at me in challenge. 'Right, do you mind if I jump in the shower?' She studied me. 'Cheerio,' I emphasised.

'Good, as long as this is all the material. There is nothing else in your machine?'

I rolled my eyes and showed her the empty edirol.

She gave a curt nod and left.

I took my time. I showered and ate my breakfast. The roll wasn't enough to sate me after the run so I went downstairs. Rachel was there, reading a magazine while drinking tea and picking at some toast. I greeted her and went to scavenge something from the buffet.

I had downed some cereal and was heading back for some yoghurt when Marina reappeared.

'You have another card for me. There is more material?'

I shook my head and tried to look innocent. 'Look Marina. It's actually borderline unprofessional of me to hand over that material. I'm starting to get a little put out that you're demanding to listen to it. I deleted the walk material.'

'You did not record at the sunken island?'

Bollocks. The Finlaggan material was on the Reserve memory card.

'I think it was windy there too. I deleted a whole bunch of material.'

'Which memory card was the Finlaggan material on?'

I sighed. I looked around the room for inspiration. Grigory saved me.

'Hello, Anna. You feeling refreshed now?' He smiled at me like a benevolent uncle at a wedding ridding me of the drunken advances from another guest.

'Yes, much better thanks. I like fresh air. Could do with some right now.'

'No problem, good idea. Hey Marina, how about I take Anna out for a little trip to see Dunyvaig Castle and we can chat about some ideas for the programme?'

I walked right into that one. She stared at him as if she'd been slapped. I almost wanted to help her with it. Offer her my room key so she could search it.

'Sure,' I said. I gave them both a full beam smile. 'Let's do that.' He beamed back at me. Marina looked angry. She trailed me a fraction too close to my room and stared at me from across the landing as I popped in to grab my jacket. I jumped out, slammed the door shut and bounded down the stairs before she could make up some nonsense about inspecting my equipment.

Grigory was waiting for me at reception, looking up as if we were going to the prom together and I looked ravishing. I climbed in his car, the door shutting with an expensive 'chunk'.

'Nice car. Is this a company car, so to speak?'

'Yes, I like it too. I am very lucky.' We cruised around the corners and paused for a van to pass.

'Doesn't Boris have a three-door car? What's the hierarchy of vehicles for you guys? What do you get if you are a General? A Rolls Royce.'

'A helicopter.'

'Well, that's pretty high spec. What about if you're a government minister? A private plane?'

'A space shuttle.' He smiled.

'I see the attraction.'

We visited the castle and made small talk about the building when Grigory ran out of his loose questions about what I was thinking for the programme. We stared at the views and were getting back into the car. I thought that would be plenty of time for a search of my compact room.

He asked me to wait a moment while he made a phone call. I sat watching him as he dialled up, spoke, then rubbed his forehead, before returning to the car.

'Everything ok?' I asked.

'Yes,' with forced enthusiasm, 'it's all good.'

We drove back towards the hotel, but then pulled up into a small car park that had a sign pointing towards a path.

'What are we doing here?' I asked.

'I thought you might like to see one of the famous beaches before we all leave.' Ah, all wasn't well with Marina then, Mr Smoothy.

He looked at me. I looked at him, he wasn't bad looking with his intelligent dark eyes, then scrunched up my nose. 'Why?'

I saw a flicker of nerves, and it pleased me. 'You mentioned it yesterday, and I thought we could talk about the role of everyone here. You had a few questions.'

'To be honest, Grigory, I think my time with you and your colleagues has cleared everything up for me.'

'Ah.'

'I'd be quite happy to return to the hotel, unless...'

'Yes?' His eyebrows were raised in attention.

'Well, I've been really keen on those sea life trips. Don't suppose you want to go on one of them?'

I gave him my best effort of an innocent look. He looked satisfyingly side-stepped. 'Or do you want to just go back?'

'No, no, let's go get a boat. Sounds like a great idea.'

I guessed they were very thoroughly searching my room now. Hopefully it would take them some time. If they were going to play it this way, I was going to milk it for all it was worth.

We drove over to Port Ellen. It was pretty quiet, in between ferry sailings, and Grigory had to call the displayed number to have someone drive down and get things going.

'Will you be warm enough?' he asked me. He was wearing his smart coat. I was wearing my windproof jacket. Annoyingly, I hadn't thought of this before I left my room.

'I've got blankets,' said our boatman, Doug, yanking back the canvas and untangling thick ropes.

We clambered on and Doug started the engine before reversing us through the stinky fug and we chuntered out of the harbour. 'I can't promise anything,' he announced over the engine, 'it might take a little time to get a sighting.'

'I think that's ok,' I said. Then looked over at Grigory perched on his bench frowning into his phone. 'Is that okay with you?'

He looked up and smiled. 'Yes, absolutely. Take as long as you want.'

'We don't want to miss the ferry.'

He shrugged. 'We can get a later one.'

We swung out to sea and the boat lurched over some waves. 'A puffin!' shouted Doug triumphantly. We gave a dutiful look then Grigory settled down to chat, the conversation more flowing now there was activity going on.

He asked me about myself: how I got into the SBC; what I liked about my job; what other programmes I'd made. I was curious about him. This Russian gentleman.

'So Grigory, what is it you do, exactly?'

He considered me, not the question.

'What do you think I do?'

'You're, like, the PR for this.'

'The PR?' He shifted forward. 'You think I do PR?'

'Yeah,' I wasn't so sure now. 'Well, you're not in the army or the FSB…'

'You don't think I'm in the army?' He fished for his phone.

'Well, you aren't in the army.'

He turned his screen around and showed me a photo. Yellow light, tired faces, helmets and guns. Him one of three.

'Is that an outward-bound trip for the office?' I asked.

A flash of annoyance washed over his face. 'No,' he

replied, and he replaced his phone.

'Your English is very good.' I thought a compliment might smooth things over. He knew what I was trying, a cynical smile playing over his lips.

'I did some high school in America.'

Doug leant away from his wheel and shouted back. 'We'll head out over here. I think I saw a fin. Maybe...' It was starting to rain. We shifted further into the boat under the solid perspex and wood shelter. Doug was scanning the horizon.

'So, my question is even more pertinent. Why are you back in Moscow with these dudes? And Marina.'

'Marina,' he repeated, and glanced at his phone. He looked at me. 'I love my country. I want to serve. It's my home.'

Rain started splattering onto the cover above our heads. The boat was rolling over every wave now. Doug was concentrating hard. He kept pointing out imaginary sightings, trained to keep hopes up against impossible odds. We weren't even looking out.

'Look guys,' he said finally, 'I hate to break it to you, but I think we'll have to turn back.'

'No problem,' I shouted over the engine, then I looked at Grigory, texting away. 'Yeah?'

He looked at me. 'Yes, of course.' He shrugged. His phone flashed. He glanced at it and sighed. 'Is there anything else you want to do?'

I shrugged. 'Not really. I don't have any money with me or anything. Everything is in the hotel room.'

'Everything?' he repeated, his face perked up with interest.

'Everything,' I emphasised. I held my palms to him. Then I fished in my pocket. 'Except, of course, I have a rather important...' he leant forward, 'old tissue here. And my room keys. And my phone.' I made a great show of emptying out my pockets. 'Everything is in that room. Shall we go back? I'm keen to go back. Getting cold'. He was forming an answer. Thinking. His phone started flashing, an insistent silent ring. 'In fact, the only thing that would stop me from going back to my hotel room would be a proper slap up meal at the Port Charlotte Hotel.'

He smiled at my impertinence. I'd pulled out the name of Islay's poshest eatery. He received the call and gave a short Russian answer, then said to me, 'Absolutely. That's the only thing that would keep me from going back too.'

We berthed, refused Doug's offer of a refund, and drove to the hotel. We were early for lunch and had to wait five minutes before they would take our orders, but we went to town. Three courses. I jokingly suggested champagne, he ordered it. 'Marina would like us to have this.' We guffawed, toasted her. Ordered coffee. He received phone calls where I could hear a shouting female at the other end. He started laughing when she called. I realised I was drinking most of the booze. Finally, during coffee, she called again. He rolled his eyes, holding the phone away from his head.

'Anna. Marina is concerned she might have lost one of your memory cards. She thinks you gave her four, but she can only find three. I'm so sorry.'

'Oh don't be sorry Grigory. There were only three.'

'Really, there were only three in the first place? You are absolutely sure? Marina thought there might have been four.'

I shook my head. He spoke English into the phone. 'It is good news, Marina. Anna has categorically informed me that there are only three memory cards.' I nodded at him, my movements exaggerated by the champagne bubbles. I held up three fingers. He smiled at me, then said something in Russian before hanging up.

I laughed. I suddenly couldn't stop laughing. I leant over the table and giggled. He laughed a little too. Both of us laughing at crazy Marina who thought I'd hidden a memory card somewhere.

I started to speak then I stopped myself. 'I'm going to pop to the loo,' I said, pushing myself up from the table.

The restaurant had filled up since we arrived. I swerved past an elbow and brushed past a waiter and made it to the other room. I started laughing again. I admit I was pleased with myself. I'd called it just right.

That morning on my early run, I had made a quick call to a freelancer I trusted in Oban and passed the memory card with a small token of financial gratitude to the fishermen who carried it across to the mainland for me. My phone had also flashed while out in that boat: it had told me that my material had been transferred online and emailed to me and several other BBC colleagues asking to be locally downloaded. It was safe.

We finished up shortly after that and returned to the hotel. I entered my room and gazed around. It looked only slightly ruffled, almost as if a window had been left open and a breeze had blown through.

We left on the afternoon ferry as planned. Marina handed me back the memory cards with a glare and a curt 'very interesting'.

I stood out on deck, this time because I felt a little queasy after all that champagne. Grigory popped out to have his cigarette. We stood admiring the view, then I saw a movement.

'Look,' I said, 'porpoise.'

'You don't miss anything,' is all he said.

CHAPTER 6

I had a meeting with Jennifer not long after returning to Edinburgh. We sat across from each other in the glass meeting room, the goldfish bowl, we called it. Jennifer had listened to my recap of the days away and had heard the controversial clip.

She was across the rumours of a suggested Russian naval base, but Angus McCulloch had snorted in derision at the prospect of Scottish waters hosting anything. There was a fine political line for Jennifer to balance between the pressure on her from above to be hospitable to the Russians, but to prove our department could represent this story with authority to the London media who were showing a keen interest.

Jennifer did her professional usual. With authority and reassurance, she palmed it off to me, the producer.

'You do what you feel is editorially right. Don't feel any pressure. Run anything you want by me.'

'Do you think I should use this Anton as a presenter?' I asked, desperate for more guidance.

She paused. 'Marc is keen that we use him. I don't know what interaction he's had with Anton in the past, but he wants to have a genuine Russian voice heading this, and I think, to be honest, he is in agreement with the Russians that he's got the credentials.' I don't think either of us were happy with it, but it seemed to have been settled for us.

We went with a textured piece, mixing music, news and interviews. I created a potted history, using archive news material and political commentary I picked up from the usual garrulous subjects, of the Rockall disagreement. I gathered more material, taking discrete recordings from the street, of Russians passing and snatches of conversation, of people muttering to me about what they'd seen and heard. I tried for an interview with Angus McCulloch, but the Holyrood press office weren't biting; News next door said he'd been increasingly cagey giving any comment these days.

I wasn't happy with the ending though. It was simply the start of some hazy worry about Russian influence, with some nice texture in news and a decent delivery in fairly lame scripting from Anton, but no real justification and conclusion. Then the day before my final edit, a political storm arose when Jean Kelly, the Interior Minister, stood up in parliament and offered her resignation, saying she'd let the country down in an 'optimistic oversight based on trust and naivety' and by sleights of hand and Angus's enthusiasm, we now found ourselves in a position where a foreign country had undue influence and physical presence in our land and she could not agree with the proposed Russian naval base at Scapa Flow in Orkney. Why resigning helped the position, I didn't know, but it meant all the whispers and worry I'd been atmospherically whisking together finally had an end point. And the man accosting Mikhail on Islay was spot on with his accusations.

Jennifer listened to the final edit. She signed it off. It broadcast.

After several years of producing I still felt a little frisson when I knew my work was on air. That day, as Islay broadcast, I watched the seconds tick imagining the music and introduction, Anton's warm explanation for the Russian presence and then the descent into controversy. I had slightly misled him. I'd intentionally handed him a script that was light on detail, giving me flexibility on the content I fitted around it, and also keeping him in dark about the actual tone of the programme. I knew whose side he was on.

It transmitted, and the world kept spinning on its axis and there was no change in the office rhythm for a couple of hours. I had my earphones on, which always dulled my spatial senses, so I got a fright when Jennifer tapped me on the shoulder. 'Can we have a chat?'

I followed her into the goldfish bowl, my nerves beginning to jangle. She closed the door after me and we sat down.

'Marc's given me some feedback on the programme. Now, this was really a mistake on my part and I want you to know that I acknowledge this and have told Marc so.' She laboured over her word selection. 'Marc feels we didn't achieve what he expected us to set out and achieve. I think he might also have been in touch with someone from the Russian office too, from what he said. He mentioned some Islay material being used that we shouldn't have done. Do you think that's the bird reserve material?'

'I thought we'd discussed that material?'

'Yes. He gave me the impression that perhaps we had misled the party out there. Did you give them any guarantees about the material we would use?'

She squeezed her lips together and peered at me.

'No!' I answered, 'They insisted on hearing some of it. I didn't let them hear all of it.' Slightly economical with the truth.

Jennifer shook her head. 'Of course not. I have full confidence that you have acted appropriately. You are across the editorial guidelines and we discussed the material beforehand. I felt it was a balanced and accurate programme.' She nodded to herself. 'And I think it was a good programme. A very good programme.' She smiled and got up. 'Good. I think we can leave it at that.'

I returned to my desk with a fluttering in my stomach. I'd picked a fight. I hoped not with the wrong people.

I wasn't aware of any more of a fuss. Graeme paused outside the tea room and gave me a compliment, but really, the timing made it a background piece. The fact the Russians had embedded themselves in Scotland was now old news. Questions were raised in Westminster, hackles raised in the media, and Angus McCulloch was egged en route to an engagement. But this agreement had been struck behind closed doors and the Russians amassed in our waters without constraint. Back at the office one morning I was horrified to see their name being entered on the list of companies by the door buzzer.

'Why is their name going up' I asked Sam, dreading the answer.

'They're starting a prayer group here, what do you think?' I glared at him. 'They've got the third floor now. We'd all better behave.' He shrugged. 'Management need to pay the rent same as you or I, I guess.'

From then on, we'd pass them even more frequently. They smoked a lot, and I'd get a nod from Boris, a glare from Aleks and a shy smile from Viktor. I'd feel Grigory's gaze before I saw him and he'd give me a knowing smile with his greeting, as if he held a secret about my future.

CHAPTER 7

I settled back down to work and got myself busy on a history of science series. Then the Snowdrops From Heaven programme was commissioned in an email, signed off with a quick nod although we weren't sure whether it was going to justify its own thirty minutes which made me think there was Russian involvement. The space programme too was a goer, it seemed, without even a proper pitch by me. Odd how fast things were moving along.

Jennifer was holding the monthly meeting, with a general catch up about workloads and forthcoming seasons, when Boris sauntered in. He just sat down at the back and pretended it wasn't a big deal. We producers glanced at each other and pretended to ignore him. Jennifer didn't pause.

We were producing to the high standard we always did. We were working well under the financial constraints. We would be told as soon as she knew whether there was going to be a tightening in the department.

Then: Radio 4 had commissioned its own series of Russian-themed programmes. Contemporary and exploring the current relationship between the two countries and their commonalities. So this was a big deal.

'And who is going to be making these, Jennifer?' asked Andrew, leaning back across two chairs, legs crossed, twitching his upper foot. 'Obviously I'd be happy to, but I'm all tied up with the Tartan Noir project. Completely tied up,' he emphasised, looking between Jennifer and Boris.

'We were thinking Chris would be a suitable match for this,' Jennifer said, 'Anna did a wonderful job on the previous

Russian programme,' I felt Boris's glare, 'but having studied workloads we decided on Chris, who is coming to the end of his Estuary Life programmes over the next few weeks, and his diary is the lightest going forward.'

She gave me a look of reassurance, as if I might view this as a slur on my production values. I felt like I'd dodged a bullet. I wasn't the only one. There was a collective sigh of relief. Nothing from Chris, however, who didn't work Wednesdays and so would be blissfully unaware of this poisoned chalice heading his way when he arrived tomorrow. 'We did think,' added Craig, nodding and smiling at Jennifer and Andrew, 'that you could act as senior on the programme.'

Andrew held up his hands. 'I'm rather brimming over with work.' He gave Jennifer an intent look. 'Truly. I am.'

'It does not matter,' Boris spoke for the first time, 'I believe Marc will be personally overseeing the programme. Is that not right, Jennifer?'

Jennifer looked at Boris, then she said 'I believe Marc will be having a listen before broadcast, but this is all detail we can discuss with Chris. Thank you everyone.'

We stood up and shuffled out, making space for Boris who inspected us as we passed. I avoided eye contact and made a wide berth. Definitely dodged a bullet.

I dodged too soon. Two days later Craig sidled up to my desk. 'Have you a moment for a chat in the meeting room?' he asked, both nodding and smiling, so I knew I was in trouble.

We sat down. 'There's been a bit of to-ing and fro-ing with the Russian series.' I held my breath. 'Chris, in fact, isn't as available as we thought with his part-time status, and he has children....' He tapered off. I imagined Chris standing over Craig haggling and hammering his points home about pick-ups and meals and family and pressure until Craig lost the exact reason why he couldn't do the programme. They always pick on singletons. 'Well, your schedule could be rejigged to accommodate this production and you generally have more flexibility with travel, with no... without the family commitments that people like Chris have. Okay?' He looked down for his notes and realised he hadn't brought any, so forced himself to look at my face.

'Won't the Russians be pretty unimpressed with me producing?'

'No. Why? You did a sterling job last time. You are a very strong producer with a good track record of delivering a high standard of programme, and regardless of any pressures you might feel we think you will be strong enough to maintain SBC editorial values.'

'Pressures?' I repeated. Of course this was pressured, but maybe I was missing something more concrete than just the feeling that something sinister was happening behind the scenes.

'Well, it's been agreed that eh, well, Boris, and Marc, are very keen to extend the collaborative process, and so Marc, well we, have agreed that Boris might be able to give some input on the direction of the programmes.'

'Like, he's an executive.'

'No. Absolutely not.' Craig gave me his concerned frown. 'And if you have any further questions on that point you should not hesitate to speak to myself or Jennifer. Or Andrew. He is always happy to guide. Regardless of how busy people are you should always feel supported.'

'So is Marc exec'ing in some way?'

'No. Well, he is keen to hear the programmes before they get sent to Network. This is quite high profile. Yes. But don't you worry about that.' He patted my hand. 'Just you do your normal high standard of work.'

He stood up to leave. I wasn't quite ready. 'Do you want to chat about the content?'

'Yes, of course. But,' he leant out the door and looked around, 'I don't think Boris is around today. We could check his diary and try tomorrow.' He smiled at me. His bad bit of work all done. Then he left.

I sighed and rubbed my eyes with my fingers.

'Alright?' asked Andrew, standing in the doorway. I rolled my eyes. 'Craig given you the good news?' Then he laughed and walked away. That's how you dodge a bullet.

I have to admit, that despite him being a sneering, invading, imposing arrogant mis-handler of people, Boris did know how to get things moving in an SBC meeting.

We had a get-together. I was handed the paragraph pitch with the feedback, and the producer at the top clearly stated as Andrew Coulter. Craig said Network knew he was too busy to commit to this fast turnaround, but they were delighted with me. I said I'd be amazed if commissioner Tom Worthington knew who I was. Boris said we should move on with the themes for the five short programmes and how they could assist me to get useful recordings. Then he glared at me for a good full minute. 'We would like to help you, Anna. We would like a good relationship and help you make your good programmes.' He must have registered my, probably frightened, face, so he held up his hands, 'and of course, you can use the material as you like.' I nodded in relief.

'Right.'

'But all programmes will be listened to in full by Marc before delivery to Radio 4.'

Craig nodded. 'Yes, Marc would like a listen. But that's nothing to be concerned about. Marc is simply keen to be kept across the content.' I pushed that oddity to the back of my mind.

We moved onto what that content would be. Radio 4 had been won over by a series that was snapshots of different aspects of the Russian involvement in Scotland today. It meant location pieces around Edinburgh, at the political hub; Orkney, at the new naval base; Lossiemouth, where there was now a presence of Russian fighter planes officially just parking at the former air base for the moment; Glasgow, where there was a lot of chat of new Russian-Scottish enterprise links being forged; and a concluding programme, assessing what good could come from this relationship.

It was going to be a busy few weeks for me, so I got to work.

CHAPTER 8

Boris was true to his word, and I was immediately given access when I expected prevarication. Flights were booked, cars hired and hotel rooms reserved. I had a list as long as my arm of interviewees, and Anton, of course, was booked solid for a fortnight. The story being fed to me by Boris and his crew was of a growing friendship, a northern alliance where both parties would benefit and a small newly independent country like Scotland would thrive and get to punch above its weight. By hosting Russian forces in its waters and on the ground, Scotland had greater protection from potential threats. By collaborating in enterprise, new markets would be opening up, both for business working abroad and our own tourism industry. I spoke to Graeme, who said the whole thing stank, but the SBC couldn't quite put its finger on why and so couldn't, in full confidence, report it. He'd heard of arm twisting at a political level, and overheard roughly translated jokes about Scotland being transformed into a Russian satellite state. I also put in some calls to journalists who had been monitoring the situation without the weight of SBC compliance leaning on their shoulders. Russia was definitely pushing it, they said. Exerting its weight, taking advantage, and it was going to be solely to our disadvantage as they dredged us for what we were worth.

Some of my interviewees would be happy to talk about this. Some locals and commentators around the country were first or second hand witnesses to the manipulation and discussions which belied the smooth amicable relationship being presented by Boris. It was going to be a tricky one, but

I was building up an idea of how to do it.

The phone call was unexpected, and unprecedented.

'Anna Aitken, SBC radio,' I trotted out.

'Anna, it's Marc here. I thought I should give you a call. About From Russia with Love?' It was officially a working title, but it was starting to stick.

'Okay,' was all I could muster. Marc never interfered in Network business.

'I wanted to make sure you understood where we are going with the programmes. The tone in particular.'

'Right, yes, I think so. I've been chatting to Craig, and er, Boris, about it.'

'Good. I know you were a bit tricksy with the last programme you did, and I don't want any hijinks with these. The BBC is watching us, and I don't want some sort of embarrassing cock-up with either them, or our relationship with Moscow. We're working on a lot of collaborations with them, Anna, and it's not up to you to throw a spanner in the works.'

'Absolutely, I wouldn't dream of disrupting anything. I'll double check for accuracy.'

'I know you will, but it's beyond that. The Russians don't like to be messed around, Anna. They don't like dusting off criticism and soldiering on. I don't want to hear a series of Moscow bashing and anecdotes that don't stand up to scrutiny. The official stance is that we are friends. Do you understand that, Anna? You don't unnecessarily upset a friend, do you? Do you?'

He'd repeated the question as I stared into space. He was asking me to tiptoe around the situation. To present something that could potentially be biased. He was breaching the editorial code. I understood that.

'I understand.' I said.

'Good. I hope so. Get the programmes to me as early as possible, and leave time to make edits after I've listened. Okay?'

He hung up. I slowly replaced the receiver and leaned back. In the SBC and the BBC before it, we were always trained on balance, on accurately representing people, and on pace, and narrative and pitch and tone. Never had I been told to tread lightly as to not offend when I was supposed to be exploring a topic. I needed to talk to someone.

Andrew was in one of the small studios – DAWs we called them, Digital Audio Workstations. I knocked and opened the door, which didn't have the illuminated red light over the door to signal there was a live mic on. He was playing out some speech and stopped when I came in. He sighed.

'Eight minutes over. Go on, Anna. Help out an old hack. Have a listen and tell me where to give it the snip.'

I smiled. 'Sure.' I sat down. 'You know From Russia with Love?'

He smirked and nodded while shifting the cursor along the wiggly lines of audio. 'I'm sorry about that. They wanted something. I gave it to them. I didn't have time. Chris said he didn't have time... obviously you were my first choice, would have been, if you hadn't already pulled a bit of a fast one with them.'

'Yeah, so, Marc just called me...'

'Really?' I had his attention now. His focus snapped on to me and he swivelled round.

'Yeah. He was saying that I had to tread lightly with the Russians and keep them on side. Like, how much on side do I have to keep them? They're dodgy.'

Andrew nodded. 'Bunch of second-hand car dealers if you ask me. Selling their knocked-off whisky to us.' Then he shrugged. 'But Marc's in charge. There's something going on there. Wonder if the Russians are giving us something in return. Don't know.'

'But I can't give Network some gushing rubbish.'

Andrew seemed to wake from a dream. 'No you can't.'

He thought. 'I should have a chat with Tom.' Tom the commissioner at Radio 4. 'You should have a chat with Tom.'

This worried me a little. Speaking to commissioners was rather tricky and involved a little diplomacy. Andrew saw my face. He slapped my leg.

'You'll be fine. If you can take on Marina and win, well, Radio 4 is nothing. Leave it to me.'

Later that day I had a tap on the shoulder from a colleague and turned to be pointed towards an Andrew gesturing for me to come to him. He had a phone to his ear. 'Here she is,' he said and passed it to me. He vacated his seat for me. I sat down.

'Hello?'

'Hello Anna, it's Tom here. Andrew has just been outlining the editorial hurdles you might be having in Scotland. What are your thoughts on it?'

I wasn't entirely prepared for this. I didn't want to misrepresent Marc, or our department, or imply I wasn't up to the job. 'It's quite tricky, Tom, to be honest. I'm not entirely sure, with the final programme, how to...'

'Are you worried about being pushed into taking a line that you wouldn't believe to be accurate?'

He got it. 'Yes. Afraid so. No real, proper, solid justification for feeling that just now, but I have a worry that it might be the case.'

'Okay. That's fine. I'll tell you what – I'll sign this off.'

'Instead of Marc?'

'No, you're missing the point. You let Marc listen to whatever he wants to listen to. The script. The interviews, whatever. You run the final version by me.'

'Marc is insisting he listens to the final version.'

There was a pause. 'Right. Well, I'll tell you what. You stick a final version in the system to Marc. If you want to change anything, you tell me. You let me listen to the unofficial final version. I'll tell Presentation that only a version signed off by me goes out. Stick my initials at the end of the file when you deliver. Do what you know is right. Anna, we'll support you. If it all goes Pete Tong with Marc I will make sure the top hears about it. The BBC still carries weight with you, but make sure what you broadcast is watertight. I want stories, but I don't want apocryphal third-hand anecdotes.'

'Yup,' I said, feeling galvanised, 'sounds like a plan.'

'Good. Keep in touch.'

He hung up. So did I. This could be fun.

CHAPTER 9

Making a series for radio can be like assembling a series of jigsaw puzzles where the pieces have been all mixed up in one box. If you've done it right, you'll end up with five cute pictures all neatly fitted together. If you haven't gathered all the right pieces then you might have to force bits together so they look a little twisted, and some pictures could end up missing parts altogether.

I had to interview people in Orkney about the Scapa Flow base, but also there was someone in Orkney who would be useful for the background to the programme in Glasgow, and academics in Edinburgh would be informing on the situation in Lossiemouth, as well as others talking about Holyrood. The politics affected the whole country, of course, so there would be interviews whose content might bleed through several programmes and others who would pop up in one. The trick was to spot the pieces that would fit best where, and cut them out of not just the interview, but try to imagine that cut as they were being captured in situ. This was a test, but it also made it easier to carry out my plan.

Without a proper set script, I was making imaginary snips where I heard good material and imagining deleting other bits. It came automatically. Sometimes I would get a presenter to give me a spontaneous introduction, or try out a few sentences that would work if I guided the listener in that direction in the final edit. So it was natural for me to ask for little pieces of speech, or for questions to be tried out at the end of an interview. All I had to do was sneak in a few phrases that I could use in an alternative edit, alongside an official script, which I knew would be monitored. That was my plan: to produce two programmes if need be, but only let Marc know about one.

Anton was his normal, enthusiastic self. He took direction well, and did seem genuinely interested in the subject. I started to like him.

It was in Lossiemouth that I saw Grigory again. We'd just arrived, weary from the overnight ferry from Orkney, loaded with damp luggage and hopefully dry recording equipment. He was in his usual sentry position, smoking outside the front door of the hotel. It seemed we had chosen the one the Russians favoured.

'Hello,' I said. No point in being rude.

'Hello!' He seemed pleased to see me, or maybe just pleased at the acknowledgement. 'How are you? Getting good material?'

He stopped and stubbed his cigarette out and tossed it in the communal bin.

'Mostly, some,' I paused by the door. 'Are you on the base today?' I found myself hoping he was.

'Yes, part of the job.'

'Is smoking part of your job?'

'No, smoking is a prerequisite for Russian citizenship.'

'Oh what a pity, I'll have to stay British.'

'That is a shame. I can highly recommend it.'

He held the door open for me, and I passed through for yet another check in. Anton stayed behind, and I heard the Russian brogue start up as the door closed behind me.

We were allowed on base, and I recorded a lot of distortion with the explosive sounds of the aircraft, as well as some blatant lies from the Russian staff as Grigory lingered somewhere in the background. That night, in the hotel, there was a very rowdy Russian table, and to my dismay, we were invited to join the revelries. Anton persuaded me to sit with them and I sat as they downed vodkas and I refused, and watched the staff as they struggled to remain polite towards these thuggish drunks.

I chatted very briefly to a Russian, but his accent made it difficult for me to discern whether he was speaking Russian or English and a bloated, inebriated Russian called Sergey kept on nudging me and laughing, so in the end I gave my regards and retired for the night.

I went to my room and flicked through the TV. After the 7am dock of the ferry and a long day I was pretty tired. I gave up and got ready for bed. I could hear someone passing in the corridor every so often as people retired for the night. There was a knock on the door.

I sat up, thinking I'd misheard. Then it came again: knock, knock.

'Hello?' I called out.

'Hello!' called out a brash thickly-accented voice. 'Will you let me in?'

'Eh, this is Anna's room. What do you want?'

There was a husky laugh then, 'I have something to show you.'

Yuck, it was Sergey, I was sure of it. This was not what I needed. I sighed and put my book down then rubbed my face. 'What is it?' I called out. I had climbed down to the end of my bed and peered around to the door to check that it was indeed locked.

'I have a wonderful bottle of champagne for you. Will you open the door?' He sounded a little put out.

'No thanks. I'm in bed already. No champagne for me. Thanks though. 'Night.'

He laughed again, thick with cigarettes. 'Being in bed is a good start. I could show you something else there.'

I decided to ignore him. I'd said no. He wasn't to be dissuaded. After a long pause he tried again.

'Anna. Open the door. I think we could have some fun together.'

'Will you go away please, I'm quite tired.'

'I think we can have a nice time. If you let me in I will give you a good time.'

This was not fun. And despite it being a locked door, if it was indeed Sergey I didn't want a man of his tall and bulky stature trying to get in. Who could I call to get rid of him? The hotel staff themselves wouldn't be keen to move this lump on. I reached for my mobile and selected Anton's number.

He answered in Russian.

'Anton? It's Anna here.'

'Hello yes, are you ok?'

'Not really actually. One of your pals is outside my bedroom door trying to get in, and he's freaking me out.'

'Someone is trying to get in your room?'

'Yup. Sergey, I think. I don't think he wants to play scrabble. He's being quite rude. Can you get rid of him please?'

There was a pause. 'Eh, he is an officer, Anna. It is not my place. Eh. Have you asked him to leave?'

'Yes Anton. Come on. The guy's drunk. It's not unreasonable that you help me out here.'

I'm sure I heard him groan. Then he replied. 'Okay. I'll try something.' Then he hung up.

I could hear Sergey was still at my door, knocking softly and singing my name. Anna, Anna! Come on Anton, I thought, find some balls.

There was the sound of footsteps, and the singing stopped. Someone spoke in Russian in a stern voice, it might have been Anton, but the tone wasn't him, then two sets of footsteps retreated.

All was calm.

I lay back in bed and sighed. Thank goodness.

The ring of my phone made me jump. I picked it up.

'Hello Anna?' It was Grigory.

'Hello.'

'Sergey has gone now. I am very sorry about that.'

'Okay, thanks, cheers.'

'Goodnight.' He hung up.

I stared at my screen for a moment then it went dark. I leant over to switch off the light. I felt a flutter within me. My hero. Then I pushed that thought away. He was just doing his job.

CHAPTER 10

The next morning the hotel was quiet and we carried on as if nothing had happened. I didn't see Grigory as we loaded the car up to continue the recording trip.

By the end of three weeks I had a decent amount of material and plans for a series containing docile, optimistic coverage of how my beloved country was being slowly infected by Russian expansionists. Anton was very compliant at interviews, agreeing to every 'final question' I asked him to put out, but afterwards he would ask innocently as he stirred his tea at the service station if I would be using 'that point about the negotiations being heated' or the anecdote about 'the pushy Russians roughing up an oil manager' and I would smile and shake my head.

'Probably not,' I'd say. 'I can't see it adding anything.'

'Good,' he'd reply. 'I thought so.'

It was all getting fed back, I knew. I had an email from Marc asking when he could hear material. It was just after we'd interviewed a retired navy man who still lived local to the new base, who gave a highly critical but measured appraisal of what was at risk. Marc dropped into his email that he hoped I wasn't using anything from David Coleman – he had some information that he wasn't reliable and it would devalue the programme if we featured him. Hmm, I thought. I dug further. Nothing came up. In fact, he had been used in recent SBC TV series about Scotland's naval history, and the producer of that programme had nothing but praise for him. I made my call. His name didn't appear in the script that Marc asked to see. I was right to exclude him on that draft – anything remotely probing about the Russians had scores and annotations in the scanned version of the script he returned to me. I sighed and rewrote.

The time came for the recording of the scripted links. I booked Anton and the requisite studio and sent him the official scripts. I received a polite reply confirming he would be there, and I was prepared to squeeze in the few extra sentences I needed to weave the secret pieces into the unofficial programme.

The phone call came through saying Anton had arrived. I jogged down to reception. He had, but when he stood up Boris did too.

'Hello Anna,' he said, 'Marc felt it would be helpful if I joined you for the script record, therefore if you have any questions I can immediately assist.'

I stared at him open mouthed. My plan of getting Anton to bend to my will wasn't going to work. I nodded. I had no option but to let him come up.

'How are you today?' asked Anton in the lift.

I could feel my cheeks burning, but I forced the reply, 'I'm well thank you.' I glanced at Boris. He looked at me and smiled.

With three in the tiny studio it was a squeeze but Boris didn't care. He wedged himself by the door and I readied the mic and checked levels. He already had his own copy of the script.

'I think this will be a very interesting programme for your listeners,' he said without invitation.

'I hope so,' I replied.

We began. Anton delivered. He could read well. People usually take a little bit of time to warm up when they read, but he hit the ground running. We skated through the first few links. A retake here, a rephrase there. I listened closely, noting levels, hesitations, emphasis. And I listened for where I could get him to say something that I could use.

I needed a 'not everyone agrees'. Just that. Or something like that. I had the name in my location recording already, but not an easy link to get to it. I also wanted a 'it depends on how happy you are for that change...' or again something along those lines. And a final phrase. An ambiguous phrase. How could I get that with Boris staring and listening?

Boris's phone rang. We were twenty minutes in. He said something to Anton and stepped out.

'We must wait,' Anton said. 'I mean, he's very interested and would like us to wait.'

I think he was expecting me to argue but I nodded. 'Okay.' I kept recording.

'Would you like a cup of tea?'

'Eh, yes, maybe. But maybe in a little while, when we are half way through.'

'Okay,' I replied, then tried, 'I find it funny you don't take milk. I thought everyone took milk in their tea.'

He laughed. 'Not everyone likes the same thing.' He smiled.

Bingo. It was enough. A snip, a merge, a fade. Enough.

We sat in silence for a moment. He glanced down at his next links. I racked my brains. Boris's jacket brushed the small window at the door.

'Are you missing the Russian weather?' I asked. 'Do you miss snow?'

He smiled. Shrugged. 'I could do without the long winter. It gets tiring.'

'You're not missing it?'

'I'm not missing it.'

'Do you get to February, and just yearn for some warmth?'

'Yes. You look forward to the better weather, definitely.'

'You can't wait for it to change?'

'Everyone looks forward to it changing.'

Not good enough. Boris was finishing his call.

'Do you think most people think like that?'

'That they want Spring? Yes, of course. Everyone has

65

enough of it by then. A long hard winter can get you down. You want a change. Everyone wants a bit of sunshine.'

The door opened. It was enough, I was sure it was enough. A cut. A slice. Not everyone wants a change.

I took a deep breath and stared back at the screen to check whether the levels looked okay. Boris said something to Anton. Anton shook his head and said something back.

'Okay,' said Boris, 'we go from where we left off, yes?'

'Yup,' I said. 'The levels should be fine. When you're ready Anton...'

We continued. Through stories of improved international relations, boosts to rural communities that suffered under the domestic military cuts, and jovial Russians complementing our country. Back slapping. Joke telling. It was propaganda of the highest order. It made my skin crawl.

He stuck to the script. I made tea and they remained in the studio. I chatted and Boris ushered me on. I didn't know how to get this to work.

We ran through to the end, then I got Anton to deliver the first couple of links again, in case they seemed relatively relaxed now he'd been in the studio for ninety minutes. Then it was almost time to go. He stacked his pages neatly together and smiled.

'Okay. You happy?'

'Yeah,' I said, realising my time was up. 'Is your tea all done?'

'Yes,' he lifted his cup. Boris stared into his phone.

'I'll take it,' I said. Then I saw the bottom. 'Look, some tea leaves. Your bag must have burst a little. Sorry.' Then I tilted the cup towards him. 'Want to read them?'

He laughed. 'I don't believe in that.' Then he shrugged. 'Or maybe it's just that I can't.' There was something here, I knew it. I made a show of examining the leaves as he watched.

'You think you can see the future in your tea leaves?' I shrugged back at him, careful to stay silent. He bit. 'You can't predict the future. No one knows what's in store for us.'

Boris looked up.

'This is over?' he demanded. I nodded.

I had it.

I had experienced tough edits, but this was tougher. I didn't even know where to put the material I was going to broadcast.

The SBC had a centralised system whereby the editing software used material held on a server, so that you could go to any computer and access it. Anyone could listen to my programme at any stage. Marc. Craig. Anyone.

I got hold of Tom and had a frank conversation with him. Radio 4 would be sent through the raw audio recordings and a bounced copy of my roughly edited official programme for Radio Scotland. An engineer was assigned to me to listen to the official programme to understand where I was coming from, then through my direction edit the programmes as I dictated over the phone.

This was tough. I'd only ever edited a programme by making the cuts myself. Listening and relistening to them, taking tweaks here and there. Here I would be telling them what to do and hoping it sounded right at the other end. At my end I was making five similar, but significantly different, programmes.

And then it got even trickier. I was chatting to an engineer, Bill, as I inputted some material when he asked how things are going. He'd heard, he said in a lowered tone, that the Russians were elbowing their way in strongly at the Aberdeen office. They had an actual physical person with a desk in the actual same office as our producers. Then he leant forward, while the VHS chuntered along inserting its archive, and whispered 'they're rumoured to be tapping phones. Definitely in Aberdeen.' He nodded at me. 'Definitely.'

He waved a finger at the walls then waggled a thumb and pinkie towards his mouth and ear as a pretend phone. 'Look after yourself.' Then he disappeared out of the studio.

I watched the space where he'd been standing then I cast my eyes around the walls, nooks and crannies of the studio. Surely not. Then suddenly I felt watched. I finished my dub and got out.

I sat staring at my phone receiver, innocently asking me to tell it all my secrets, then I got up and walked round to Andrew's desk.

He was reclining in his chair, one leg crossed, reading the Telegraph like he was sitting in the lounge area of the Crieff Hydro Hotel.

'Andrew?'

He tilted back the corner to reveal an eye and smiled at me. 'Can I help?' He nodded to his screen. 'Keeps crashing. No point trying.'

I sat in Chris's vacated chair beside him.

'Have you heard…?'

'What?' he asked, leaning forward. I had been pretty much whispering.

I hunched forward and rolled the chair a little closer.

'Have you heard anything about,' and I pointed to the phone, 'about having to be careful…?'

Andrew flicked his other newspaper corner over to examine what I was pointing at, then he flicked it back to attention. He folded up his paper and tossed it onto the desk. He stood up. 'Come,' he said, and gestured for me to follow.

I followed him back through to the hall, then further on to the newsroom. There was more activity here, and a TV screen showing BBC news on constantly. He stood in front of it.

'What have you heard?' he asked.

'Just Bill mentioned to be careful with what's said.'

Andrew looked around. He shrugged. 'I don't know. I don't know if people are being hysterical or sensible, but we've been told to try to speak face to face and if we feel it's necessary, to meet in public places for important conversations. Happily wine bars fit the bill nicely, and

68

expenses are being more tolerant about it.'

He gave me a smile.

'Right,' I said. I saw him frowning at me.

'Got a problem? Can I help?'

I shrugged. 'I'm sort of editing... remotely... this latest piece directly with Tom.' I gave the phone gesture.

'Oh Christ. Yes. Don't do anything like that here.' He snorted, gave me a pat on the shoulder, and gently shoved me aside to greet a visiting literary news guest.

I wandered back to the office. This was going to be even more challenging if I couldn't do this at my desk.

I spoke to my assigned London engineer that afternoon, having headed home a little early. He was a pretty sound guy, no pun intended, and was happy to accommodate what was going to be a rather unusual bit of direction. We agreed he wouldn't take my calls. Instead he would let me go to voicemail each time so my message was recorded at his end. Then he could replay it as many times as necessary to get all the edits I would list.

I admit at this stage I did get paranoid. It was disproportionate care taking for the time, but not with hindsight. I decided that since I was sure these people were out to control me, I wasn't going to slip up anywhere. If there was an open understanding that our phones in the office were at risk of being tapped, then why not my phone which sat beside me on my desk during the day? I left my mobile out all the time; when I went to the loo, meetings, sometimes lunch. It could have been fiddled with so often I dreaded to think how sloppy I'd been. I resolved not to use it for this.

I was preparing for a triathlon then. That Saturday at our 8am meet I handed out to any other cyclists who would take them a short list of edits. It was amazing how obliging people were. Just the very mention that it could be something resisting this lightly malevolent pseudo-invading army meant I had my own volunteer resistance force. The notes were a jumble of numbers – programme numbers and insertion times.

As we separated in our different groups – the stronger going down to Melrose, some along the coast and others practicing sprints, these edits were taken and calls were made to London describing chunks of programme to be cut and knitted together by police officers, surveyors, accountants and a dentist. These snippets of notes on my programmes were tossed into public bins, set alight and flushed down loos in a thirty-mile radius. Nothing went through my phone.

I sat through the official programmes again and again at my desk, cutting them neater and neater, and precisely to time. I sat again with an engineer, polishing them to professional smoothness. I then sat at various phones at various friends' flats and listened to a different version of each and marvelled how they had managed to turn out coherent, and intoxicatingly provocative.

I signed off the London programmes, and sent the Scottish ones to Marc. He came back with a couple of tiny adjustments, but I stayed so far from controversy that I imagined he too would think them dull. So then I pretended to deliver them. With Boris watching in the studio, pretending he was keen to watch the process, and me carefully labelling them as I'd discussed with the network such that they were to be discarded at their end.

Then I went on holiday. There was a shitstorm forecast here.

CHAPTER 11

Eight years earlier my parents had moved to Norway. My dad worked in gas and oil and an opportunity had come up that they felt, with me away at university, they shouldn't pass on. They left behind my older sister and me, and a small cottage on the west coast of Scotland, by the Kyles of Bute. They bought a flat in Edinburgh that became my temporary then permanent pad when I moved back to the city from Oxford, with the condition that they stayed with me whenever they returned. My elder sister had spent the last six years in a bog of gestation and birth, so she and her husband had got themselves a decent space in the suburbs. The situation had evolved that my parents would only pop into Edinburgh from time to time, and mostly when they came they liked to return to the Kyles of Bute.

The bad thing about Shore Cottage is there's no mobile reception.

The great thing about Shore Cottage is that there's no mobile reception.

So the first I realised I had a barrage of BBC people trying to get in contact with me was when I was on my way back to catch the Dunoon ferry and my phone buzzed excitedly as it got up to date with missed calls and messages.

I expected at least one message. I have an enthusiastic aunt who likes to let me know when she's heard my name stated at the end of a programme, which I appreciate, and I thought Jennifer might check in.

The majority (eight) of the missed calls were in the aftermath of the programmes on the Monday, then five on

71

the Tuesday, then it was a steady four a day as the callers realised it was futile.

I stood up the upper deck as we launched into the Firth of Clyde and called up my answer machine. Marc was asking me to call him. Then: Marc was telling me to get in touch. Now. Then: Marc said he knew I was on holiday but I couldn't just switch off. Get in contact. Now. Then it was a stream of Jennifer, then Colin, then Boris wanting a chat.

I glanced through my texts, and they were of the same vein. And a lovely text from my aunt saying she'd heard a programme and thought it very provocative. I suddenly felt extremely nervous.

I spent a fairly jittery Sunday clearing out the final paperwork left by my ex-boyfriend. We'd been together five years then he'd got a job in Dublin, I didn't want to follow, and despite a heart-wrenching goodbye and promises to make every effort to see each other, we found the 200 miles didn't make the heart grow fonder, and three months later we'd admitted it was over.

I'd been dreading this job, but it was better than checking my work emails. Finally I decided I wouldn't sleep, so I logged into webmail. There, amongst the usual cascade of upcoming broadcast information and departmental news, was a rather feisty selection of emails related to the Russian series. Jennifer had rushed out a congratulations in the minutes that followed the broadcast, then in quick succession Marc, then Boris, both asking for an urgent word. Andrew noted that he thought the programme very strong, and to 'keep my head up' when I got back. Then Chris gave me the thumbs up. The following two days continued that pattern. Day three also contained complimentary emails from a few other BBC people – the Head of Radio 4 (!), another producer I hadn't met but recognised the name from Manchester and, very nicely, Pick of the Week letting me know they were going to be using me.

Friday's email contained an order from Marc for me to

see him in Glasgow on Monday at 2pm. No other comment.

Checking my emails wasn't going to help me get to sleep. I got the train through the next morning. I drifted around for ten minutes until I found a free desk, then I skirted around further afield for another ten when I was sure I'd identified Marc's coat slung over a chair nearby. Finally, I asked the radio bookings team if I could hide out in a small studio all day. They readily agreed. Maureen gave me one of her knowing smiles and said she'd heard I'd made something worth listening to, even if some particular people weren't very happy about it.

I'd almost made it there and was passing the windows of the TV editing suites when the broad figure of Boris stepped out in front of me, hand clamped to his ear. It took him a few seconds to click who I was, and I thought I might have made it past, when he quickly finished his call to speak to me.

'Ms Aitken,' he said, a light but unmoving hand placed on my shoulder. I turned to face him. He studied me, not showing emotion, anger or otherwise. 'We have been trying to contact you. With some urgency.' His hand was slowly removed from my shoulder, now he knew he had me. 'We were surprised to hear the programmes. I do not believe they were the programmes that I saw the script for.' He cocked his head, then lowered it to engage my avoiding eyes. 'What do you say to that?'

Having feared one of these encounters, I was suddenly emboldened by his audacity. 'The programmes were what was agreed with the commissioning network. My feedback has been very good. Sorry, I've got to go.'

I turned and left.

I heard him call after me. 'Make sure you are not late for your meeting with Marc. He is very keen to speak with you.'

I scuttled off to my tiny studio and hid there for a few hours, replying to emails and doing a little digging for a future programme.

I stuck my head out for ten minutes to run up to the

canteen for an early lunch, hoping I'd avoid the rush and therefore reduce my chances of seeing anyone in particular. There were a few TV people gathering coffee, and the mid-morning radio show team having their noisy adrenaline-filled debrief. Someone tapped me on the shoulder. I jumped.

'Sorry,' Nigel Shott, Exec in Factual. 'I wanted to say hello, and to congratulate you on your series.' He performed the little smirk I remembered from my short stint as a researcher in his department when I first joined the then BBC. 'I hear you've ruffled a few feathers. Might as well be hanged for a sheep as a lamb, eh?'

I hadn't decided what to do with my face, which I'd just realised was frozen in surprise, when the server saved me by asking me what I wanted done with my baguette. Sometimes it's easy to forget the whole country can hear your programmes. The whole world.

On the way back to my hidey hole Stephen from News gave me a wave and a thumbs up from across the concourse. I gave a mock salute back.

I only managed a bite of my baguette before nerves filled my stomach. Soon an email came from Jennifer asking me to get in touch if I needed any more support from her. My talent manager dropped me a line to say if I needed to speak to her just to pop by her desk. She heard I was about. That wasn't reassuring.

Then finally it was just before two. I gathered my notebook, then my handbag, then I decided just to grab my coat in case I was about to be fired, and I made my way to the meeting room.

It was empty. I stood by a flip chart with the words Audience Hungry? scrawled on it in green and pretended to ponder the question.

As in Edinburgh the meeting rooms in the SBC are also all glass walled. It's to give a sense of transparency, to let the long rows of the call-centre-like creative space merge seamlessly into these pockets of power. It also means you can easily have a nosy as to who is in where. I heard people walking by and sensed them peeking through the glass.

Marc came in at five past. He threw his jacket over the chair, which slid onto the floor in a heap. He chose not to notice and pushed the door shut. 'Sit down,' he said to the table. Marc was a notorious eye avoider.

I sat, feeling like a child about to be berated in the headmaster's office.

Marc stayed standing. I suddenly remembered old stories of him having a temper that I'd never paid attention to.

'I thought I had made it clear that I was to exec these programmes. Did I not make that clear?'

I looked to the wall, wondering what the safest answer was. To lie and pretend I didn't realise what I'd done, or to admit it and get the bollocking over and done with? 'I did make that clear,' he answered for me, 'but you went ahead and ignored it. You defied me. You made me look like an idiot. Oi!'

I looked up. 'Don't stare at the wall. Look at me.' He leant closer, eyeballing me now. 'I'm your Head of Station and I asked you to do something. I was exec'ing those programmes and you deliberately went out to make me look like a fool. You think you're so smart,' he started stabbing his finger towards me. 'Your department think you're above the football and the music and the banter, don't you?'

I try to remain silent when I'm not sure of the best choice of action and this was definitely a dubious situation. Marc didn't care.

'I'm in charge of your department. I'm in charge of you. You could be out of that snobfest making jingles for sport, like that.' He clicked his fingers. 'You think because you make pieces about DNA and architecture you can do what you want?' My silence was a relief, as I knew my voice would not have sounded as resolved as I was starting to feel. Suddenly I knew why I'd gone ahead and defied him in a whim. Now I felt justified. Deep down within me, behind my eye rolling in response to the technology issues, the enthusiastic work experiencers, the tedious trawl for programmes to fit into themed seasons and the self-righteous crusaders amongst my work colleagues, I did actually believe in my job as a public broadcaster to defend liberty in the press. This man didn't. This guy was compromised.

I sat there as his voice rose in level and I felt spittle fleck my check when he shouted at me to do exactly what he said in future. And I felt calmer. Mostly calm in the inside while my fingers trembled. Finally it was over. 'Get out,' he said. 'I mean it. Any more stepping out of line and you'll need more than the unions to bail you out.'

I grabbed my coat.

The air that met me felt cool as I opened the door. The space felt quiet, although I knew there were banks of people facing computer screens in rows that I was passing. I made my way to the concourse where the stairs spread their way across and down in stages through middle of the building. Tiers of balconies stacked up around me. I felt some people looking. I took a few steps. Then I heard a clap. A clapping. I glanced up as I crossed a mezzanine and saw Nigel from Factual there, leaning over and clapping and nodding at me. His claps echoed across the huge concrete and metal space. Then others were clapping. I kept walking but I glanced up and saw people I knew, people I'd seen before and people I didn't recognise, gathering by the balconies all around me and clapping. Some whistling and a few shouts, but mostly clapping. My face reddened and I concentrated on my steps down, taking one final glance up as I reached ground level and the security doors, to see tiers of colleagues looking down at me and cheering me as I left the building.

CHAPTER 12

Once, during my early days at the BBC, I blundered into a national story. While doing some routine interviews in rural Wales, within a mile of me a man was settling a long-simmering feud by shooting to death his sister-in-law, niece and going on a shoot-on-sight rampage along lane and across field until he completed his task and killed his brother. While I was on the hunt for a sandwich and scone, the village and surrounding area were put in lockdown. I did make a few phone calls, and picked up a few interviews to help the Network News lot, but I can't claim to have contributed to the manic coverage that sprung up within minutes.

However, by simply being at the epicentre of a news earthquake on my return to the office I received pats on the shoulders and sympathetic emails. I got a reputation as being a bit of a survivor, when my only survival achievement was making it to three o'clock until I found somewhere to give me lunch. I was now a newshound, when I simply switched on a mic to someone I'd bumped into. It was only in hindsight, when I recognised the buildings on the news with sheeted bodies in front of buildings I'd passed, did I realise what I'd been part of. But I wasn't part of it.

You can live through something and not appreciate the significance of what you saw or did until long after.

I think so much of what happened then was like that. Sometimes I think I was mad, or perhaps arrogant, and I could be painted as a lone resistance fighter, but in reality I took it each person and each day at a time. I had no idea how history would paint that period. So when I write 'then we had the Aberdeen Agreement' and some of you will feel a weight of sadness descend upon you as you recognise the severity of that day: I didn't. It was just another obscure meeting between Scots and Russians that was tediously documented in banal language as a trade agreement that I glanced through then went to buy a coffee because I had to cut two minutes, three seconds out of a bulging programme, and I knew it was going to be a long day.

I can't say that I brushed off the meeting with Marc with ease. The fury of the dressing down had shaken me.

Aleks had eyeballed me with contempt as I passed him into work most mornings. Conversations in corridors were stopped and stares hard behind Slavic features. But it passed. Still the whole soft invasion felt like a temporary sideshow to the rest of us not battling the broadcast news censorship.

I passed Grigory one morning, the cold morning air turning his breath to mist which mingled with the cigarette smoke. He gave me that sly smile as he said hello.

'Hello,' I went to walk in.

'Anna.'

I stopped and turned to him. He leant in to me. 'Don't pick too many battles.'

I didn't need to answer him, but it felt like a confrontation. 'Surely it's my job to do my job properly, and for you to do your job properly, which means, since we're on opposing teams, we have to clash.'

He nodded. 'But you're just a Scottish terrier and you're baiting bears. Don't bait a bear: it will rip your head off.'

I rolled my eyes and nodded. 'I've no intention of baiting any more bears, Grigory, I just wish I wasn't being put into the ring with them.'

He stubbed his cigarette and pulled the door open for me. 'Take care of yourself,' he said, and followed me in, splitting off to reception. He needn't have said. When my father found out, God knows how, about my deception, I'd been forced to promise him too, that there'd be 'no more messing around'. I was on my best behaviour.

Then we had the Aberdeen Agreement. News had been shady. The battle of censorship was working on both sides – neither the Russians nor Holyrood wanted the extent of the invader's presence, a huge mass submerged and flying around our coasts as well as significant embedded personnel, to be a terrifying common knowledge. Our warehouses couldn't support a stockpiling of goods; our financial districts couldn't survive a mass exodus south of the border; our banks couldn't afford a war. England were haggling for a NATO troop movement from Poland to Northumberland, and were saying a line had already been crossed whether Holyrood believed it or not. We had to talk, and the Russians thought this was delightful.

The Aberdeen Agreement was on the surface a mutually beneficial confirmation of the Russian bases on Scottish soil. It had already happened, and no one really noticed any difference to themselves, particularly. Buried in the agreement, however, was an acceptance that there would be an ongoing reception to the Russian negotiations. We did not accept that Russia owned this rock peeping above the ocean, but we were going to let them come aboard and chat to us about it. And until we resolved it, officially we accepted that in addition to a lease to use Scapa Flow as a naval base and Lossiemouth for their planes, that the Russians could have their submarines in our waters to protect what they believed was theirs, even if we believed it wasn't. And if we believed that that piece of rock was ours, and we ruled that from Edinburgh, yet they believed it was theirs, until it was resolved through the UN, the Russians should have a foot in the door at Holyrood, in order to be party to all discussions on the cartography and access to the region. There would be no fighting over this rock. That was integral to the Aberdeen Agreement. There would be no war. That's what they promised us then. We could talk this through like adults discussing a grown-up principle and maybe something good would come from it.

The battleship appeared within a stone's throw of the Forth Bridge within a day of the Aberdeen Agreement. The bombers landed in their tens at Lossiemouth the same week. Opposition parties shouted that we'd been betrayed. Grigory Rancovic haggled in the news room that they were sticking to the Agreement to the letter, and the Agreement itself stated that both sides were being explicitly permitted to defend their side of the argument. The military presence was simply to reassert that. There would be no war. No invasion. He shrugged, a well-practiced nonchalant shrug. How could it be called an invasion if we were invited in?

'But you are, to an extent, occupying us,' our newshound argued, 'Your people are walking in the corridors of Holyrood. Your soldiers are standing in our roads. If I look out my window I can see a Russian boat in the Clyde.'

Grigory would start looking bored, but he remained calm, carefully explaining as to a child: 'We are not occupying your government. We are not telling you how to teach your children or run your trains. In our view,' he said for the hundredth time, pointing his finger to the desk of whatever journalist was testing him, 'you are occupying our territory. We have a right to defend it.'

'Maybe you are not putting us under a full military occupation, but you have performed a soft occupation.'

Grigory acknowledged the point with a twitch of a smile. 'There will be no war. We can work together on this. The main thing,' he would say, leaning forward to set his message across, almost, but not quite, a threat, 'is that no one gets hurt.' He held his hands out, 'us Russians are not afraid of fighting, I think we all know that. We can solve this amicably, but we need to be here to make sure that it is sorted to both our satisfactions.'

CHAPTER 13

Things moved apace after that. The Russians now had their own broadcast and communications unit ensconced in the floor above us, and Boris prowled around between meetings giving disapproving looks to anyone not busy digitally clipping audio away, jotting down ideas or interviewing and researching down the phone. My parents would ask me, down the line, how things were going on. From their perspective it was just the kind of thing they expected would happen when the Yes voters reeled with joy in George Square after that second referendum. It was inevitable that some international diplomatic cock up would occur when placed in the hands of naive incompetent politicians who had never run a country before. They would sigh, and paint me familiar pictures their friends had told them – rude Russians in restaurants, the Orkney ferry filled with soldiers, brawls at the harbour in Lossiemouth. It was a temporary blip and when this political winter was over they assumed the Russians would go back home and they'd have the weather to complain about again. I didn't tell them that in many circumstances I was directly answering to a Russian now as commission after commission was approved that had a Russian slant to it, and that they didn't see these reports on the BBC News because the Russians vetted everything being broadcast, citing the argument that they were avoiding bias.

People still had a commute to grapple with; kids who needed to pass exams and be picked up from choir practice; house prices to consider and diets to embark upon. Life went on, and for some people nothing changed when we became occupied by stealth. It was like a retrovirus snuck in our cells, blended into our DNA, and every time we turned our backs, it multiplied and hid itself somewhere else.

I tried to boost my own politico-immune system. I started Russian language evening classes. If learning a little of the language stopped them pulling the wool over my eyes in any way, then it would be worth it.

I'd wade though the tide of Europeans and postgraduate students at Edinburgh University and sit in a small classroom, still filled with a musty warmth from its daytime occupation, and plod through the Cyrillic alphabet and the sounds that used to seem so alien, but which started to decode themselves.

I very much wanted this to be kept under the radar, no matter how pleased I'd bet Boris would have been if he knew. I kept my text books discretely hidden away and didn't mention it to anyone. They had plenty of cards held to their chests too.

Outside the office it did seem most of the trouble with the Russians was them enjoying themselves raucously as opposed to any direct intimidation. These soldiers were like the American cops eating in the local diner. Their presence just reminded you they were there. What they did no one really knew.

I knew. They were there to add bulk to what was happening around me. Grigory and his multiple meetings; the pressure to tilt news and documentaries in a slightly more generous light, so subtly done you were sure you were still sticking to guidelines. I'd see Grigory infrequently in the office, but what was more unsettling was when I'd see him outside around where he must have stayed near my own place. A couple of times returning from my run, making the last approach up the hill on the adjacent street. Once, he stepped out in front of me from his hedged gate so we almost collided. One evening I heard him call as I was starting my run going down the hill. I turned to look and saw him enjoying a cigarette out the window. He gave me a cheery wave. I waved back, a funny feeling in my stomach of being watched, and perhaps slightly liking it.

...

I was going to bed. It was approaching Autumn, and we were a week into the fuel crisis with Grangemouth at a standstill while the workers striked in protest at the crude oil supply switch from Norway to Russia. Cars were scattered along the motorways in Scotland. Buses were running on half their schedule. All fuel had to be retained for the emergency services and our own highest priorities. I'd discovered a few new running routes, along roads which had been unpleasantly busy before. Like Edinburgh when it snows heavily and the town is forced to slow down, the lack of petrol was making us all pause and take in our surroundings.

I had replaced some dirty cups to the kitchen and was retiring for the night when I heard the security door clunk shut and the steps being climbed up above me. I climbed into bed, switched off the light and lay down, then BANG, THUD THUD SLUMP THUD!

I froze in my bed. Was that in my house? Did someone just break into my house? Was it on the stairs?

I got out of bed, pulled a sweatshirt over my top and peered out my room. No one there. I went to the front door and peered out the spy hole. Nothing there. Was something just hurled down the stairs?

I heard a groan.

I opened the door and looked up the stairs. I could see a hand. I leapt up. It was my neighbour. Sprawled head down on the stairs, still in his military uniform. Blood splattered on the wall.

I panicked. He couldn't be dead – I heard him groan but he was completely still. His head bleeding, his arms twisted around him, his legs bent awkwardly.

I ran back downstairs and phoned an ambulance. I'm not

good with blood at the best of times, and when it's a foreign invader lying unconscious on my stairs, I really panicked. I was told to check he was breathing, not to move him, and to stay with him.

I ran back up. I was still barefoot, clambering over him to get to a point where I could check his face. He was breathing. It sounded raspy.

'Hello?' I asked.

His phone lay three steps beneath him. Maybe he'd been carrying it and flung it away. Maybe he'd dropped it and slipped on it, propelling him down the stairs. I had an idea.

I picked it up and scrolled through it. No lock on it, but it was all in Cyrillic. Grigory might be on there.

I flicked through the recent calls then clicked on a number that looked the right one. It rang.

'Anno?' A woman. In Russian. I hung up. Maybe this was a bad idea.

My hands were shaking now. The man let out a moan. I tried another number.

'Anno?'

'Hi, Grigory?'

'Hello?'

'Is that Grigory?'

'Yes, hello, who is this?'

'It's Anna. I live below your friend? He's unconscious lying on the stairs. He's fallen. I've called an ambulance. I don't suppose you want to come and take care of the situation, and eh, him?'

'Yes, I'm coming. I'll be there in a moment.' I could hear him shifting as he spoke. If he was home he would be minutes.

I was relieved that someone else could take care of this. I stepped over the body again, watching its laboured breathing and perched beside him on the stairs. 'Sorry,' I said to him, 'I've been told not to move you, and you're breathing okay, so let's wait for the ambulance.'

He gave out a groan. Seconds later there was a bang from the door. I leapt up and opened it. Grigory.

'Where is he?' he asked while seeing him and jumping up the steps. I stood on the ground level and watched him lean over him, speaking in Russian, saying Vladimir! Vladimir! He started lifting his body.

'They said to leave him in case his back is bad.'

'His back is not broken,' he replied with a confidence I viewed as unjustified. I could hear a siren approaching. I opened the door and stood n the pavement to let the paramedics in and then, leaving my door ajar, I went back into my flat and got a drink of water just to get out the way.

One of the paramedics came in to ask me about the circumstances of what happened, then they lifted Vladimir onto a stretcher. He was gaining consciousness, groaning in Russian. I couldn't say if it was coherent or not, but Grigory leant over and spoke to him in a reassuring tone. I stood by the door, ready to shut it finally when I knew I was released from my duty.

'I'll go with him,' Grigory said then turned and straightened up, looking at me properly, 'thank you for helping.'

I think it's the first time I heard his real, genuine, tone. 'No problem. Do you want to check his flat is locked? I don't know if he opened the door or anything before he fell. He might have put the oven on, although,' I tried to remember the timings of what I heard. Whether he could have made it into the flat or not, 'I don't know.'

'Yes.' Grigory ran upstairs then quickly came down. 'It's locked. I'll go now.'

I said good night. Then added a good luck, because it seemed appropriate, and I closed the door, before going to stand at my window to watch them depart.

It was exhaustion. Grigory came to my desk late the next day and pulled a chair over to tell me. Vladimir's body had decided he had been working too hard without enough sleep, and decided to make itself heard by letting him know at the top of the stairs in no uncertain terms in the form of a seizure that propelled him backwards. 'It is quite a private thing,' he said, giving me an intent look. I nodded. I'd already told Andrew about it. He hoped if all the Russians worked too hard they might all spontaneously collapse too.

'I might have mentioned it the morning after. A little bit, non-specifically.'

Grigory sighed then shrugged. 'It's okay. You must have got a fright. He will be fine, after a little rest. So it's nothing to worry about.' He gave me a reassuring smile.

I was relieved. I won't lie. Mainly because I'd formed a fear I could somehow be blamed for it and accused of attempted manslaughter. Totally irrational, but you know what these Russians are like around the truth, right? It's whatever they want to see.

The fall had taken place after an intense time at work for me. One day the previous month I'd come in to find my desk empty. Aleks came up to me looking satisfied.

'You are upstairs now,' he said, jabbing his finger towards the ceiling.

'What?!'

He laughed.

Craig wasn't in. Anyone who could find an excuse to work from home would do it these days. It was only us people without home editing suites or flexi time that were at the mercy of the occupiers. I went upstairs out of curiosity and found my notes and my phone at the far end of the office. There was a central grouping of four desks surrounded by glass, and I was on the outside of this fortress. Boris was inside, his desk sat within the glass partition opposite me.

I found Viktor and dragged him into a DAW. 'What the fuck is this? I can't work up there. I work down here. I work for the SBC.'

He shrugged. He even looked a little apologetic. He might even have looked a little scared of me. I tried to impose myself. I slapped the desk a few times. I channelled all my powers, but it did nothing.

'We all work together now. You are next to me!' He gave me a weak smile.

Jennifer came in to work. I cornered her, pointing out how I'd been moved. She looked surprised, and told me she'd speak to Marc to see what the situation was. A few hours later I got this from her: 'we are indeed merging as a department and the desk allocation has been approved by Marc. Please don't hesitate to ask me any further questions.' Craig later told me with a smile to view it as a secondment.

So I was now upstairs, constantly supervised, and working at a pace I'd never done before to satisfy my new, more demanding, editor apparent. My programmes were generally anchored to some Russian topic, whether discretely or overtly, and I was less an SBC employee than a stooge of the new, belligerently emerging, Russian-run Broadcasting Corporation that was dominating Holyrood. Being upstairs now, it wasn't just my content that separated me from my peers. I was isolated, physically and topically, and heavily monitored with my work. Every day at some point I'd hear a knock on that partition and feel my shoulders tense before I looked around to see Boris beckoning me.

He had access to all the shared folders, so I knew he could monitor my research list – which he insisted was kept on there – my scripts, my ideas. He constantly checked on me and pushed me. It was exhausting.

Despite the relentlessly nitpicking Boris and simmering mistrust, we did produce some decent work together, and I'd produced three feature programmes in three weeks, efficiently cajoling various Russian recordists around the country over the phone while recording interviews in studio from Edinburgh, all of which were World Service-worthy depictions of the modern Russia Boris and I haggled over. I'd become adept at conversing with my reporters, and the country's scroll was unfurling itself to reveal the depth of text and recording opportunities available. I was working hard. I was tired.

This leave had been long booked off. I needed to make use of this time, and not just slob around Edinburgh. An idea had formed in my mind, which I knew was a bit nuts, but made perfect sense. I decided to try it out.

CHAPTER 14

I walked up the stairs to the top flat and knocked on the door. Maybe Vladimir wasn't back, but then I heard a shuffling and the door opened. He looked awful. Sort of yellowy, matching his overgrown hair, and gaunt. He leant against the doorway.

'Hi,' I said, all jovial as if this was normal. A stale smelled diffused towards me.

'Hello,' he replied without any enthusiasm. 'Thank you for your help.'

'Yeah, no problem.' There was an expectant silence. 'So, I was wondering. My parents have this cottage over on the west coast. I'd promised to paint two rooms before they visited in October, and I'd leave booked to do so next week. But with the oil strike I can't get a car across there. So I was wondering if you might like a little bit of fresh air and a free holiday, but in exchange I wondered if you happened to have access to a car with fuel in it we could use to get there and back?' I gave him a smile. He stared at me. Then blinked.

'Okay,' he said. He opened the door further. I could see into the corner of the kitchen where mugs lay precariously close to the edges of piles of plates. 'When you go?'

I could understand his keenness. 'Well, tomorrow if we can. Go via B&Q. Can you get a car? Or fuel?'

'You have car? We use your car and my fuel.'

'Okay, great. But,' I pointed my finger at him, 'you are going there to rest and I to paint. You do not go near me.'

He scoffed and looked down at himself. 'I can do nothing but rest now.' He shook his head, and muttered something in

Russian. 'You...' and he knocked on his door, '...tomorrow?'

'Yeah,' I took a step down. 'We'll get food on the way too.'

'Okay,' and he shut the door.

He delivered his part of the bargain okay. He told me which petrol station to go to, showed some ID, and there we were with a full tank and a clear road ahead of us. The M8 was great, and he was a good passenger. It was Radio 4 until the reception went, while he slept like a baby.

I left him in the car to get the paint supplies, but he woke before the supermarket and unfurled his long limbs from the seat. I don't know whether it was him or the seat that creaked. It was like his body had aged forty years from the proud erect soldier I was used to seeing, or he was just so exhausted he couldn't hold his own body up. He shuffled around the shop and then returned to the car.

We took the Loch Lomond road to Argyll. He wasn't too impressed by the deer I pointed out, but smiled at the highland cow. We made it to the cottage by early afternoon, the sun shimmering on the loch, a light breeze blowing the clean air into me. I instantly felt relaxed.

It was an indulgence keeping the cottage. In theory we all used it, and we did, but not really enough to justify the expense and time required for the upkeep. I think my parents still believed they might enjoy a retirement where they would summer here, but Dad showed no signs of slowing down. There'd been a loose tile which had led to a leak into the main bedroom, and costly repairs. I'd promised to get the room back to its bright and neat state, and had thrown in a reckless bonus to brighten up the shower room too.

Vladimir wasn't joking when he said he wasn't up to much. He collapsed in the back bedroom and slept for thirteen hours straight the first evening. I got cracking with the sugar soap and the masking tape then went for a stroll.

I love the west coast. I love how the rain feels soft and the tea tastes better. I love watching the skies shift and the light change. I love how I feel there. I feel enveloped in a loving home.

The cottage itself is rather compact. A kitchen, a sitting room, and upstairs a main bedroom and a back bedroom and small shower room. There's no real garden, just a little patio on the far side of the porch and steps down to the road. You don't need a garden. On the other side of the quiet road is the beach with a bench on one of the upper rocks. I do some of my best thinking there.

I got to work early the next morning. I had a quick breakfast of toast and tea while resisting the urge to check that Vladimir hadn't died in his sleep. I threw some of the old sheets over the bed and furniture and started rolling on the paint. I always find painting to be really satisfying... for an hour or so, then it becomes tedious, exhausting and very annoying.

Vladimir gave me a pleasing distraction when he stuck his head in the door after two hours to say hello. I'd been standing on the bed rolling on the slanted ceiling.

'Help yourself to food.'

'Yes,' he said. 'Good sleep here. Very quiet.'

'Yeah, you should get some fresh air. You could lie outside for a bit. Actually, that's a good idea. I bet some sunlight would be good for you. Do you want a sun lounger to sleep on?'

'No, it's okay.'

Now, I've been told I can be a bit bossy, and reflecting on moments like this I admit it might be a true. I became fixated on Vladimir getting a bit of vitamin D as he lay about. While he brewed himself a coffee I lugged the rusting sun lounger out and set it on the little patio garden.

'There you go,' I said, coming in, 'you can sleep there. It's much better for you.'

Vladimir stood with a buttered knife in his hand. 'I have choice?'

91

'No,' I replied, and starting to feel the first nip of embarrassment, I dodged back up the stairs into the bedroom.

I heard the scrape of the door a while later and leant over to see him peer outside. I think he went for a stroll, then a while later I noticed him reclining on the seat. I gave a smile of satisfaction. I was sure he was starting to look a little better.

The man must have been seriously sleep-deprived. I stopped for coffee at about 11 and saw him asleep, then a couple of hours later when I sat outside for lunch, he still hadn't stirred.

I'd been pretty efficient at the bedroom, so post-lunch, I got cracking on the shower room. I had to get out for Vladimir to do his business, but I was in the swing of things, listening to some music on the radio while at the top of the ladder when a voice startled me.

'Hello?' I spun round, swaying more than was comfortable, and Grigory leant in to steady the ladder.

'What are you doing here?'

'I'm sorry,' he laughed, rude git, 'I have come to see Vladimir. He's here?'

I stared at him for a few seconds. 'How did you find out where we were?'

'We had a text conversation. I was in Oban this morning.'

'Why were you in Oban?' Everything about Grigory just whiffed of contrivance.

'I was speaking to people. Is Vladimir here? I'm sorry, I did knock.'

I got down off my ladder, having noticed the paint had now slid off the brush onto my arm. I started wiping at it with kitchen roll. 'If he's in he's likely in his room. If not, in the sitting room, but I guess you've looked there...' Grigory stuck his head round Vladimir's door and shook his head, 'and if not there he's probably back in the garden around the other side of the front door. And if he's not there, well he's a big boy and he can go out without my permission.'

Grigory smiled. 'Thank you. I'm sorry for surprising you. I'll go find him.'

He trotted downstairs. I turned the radio off and heard foreign chatter coming from the front of the house. I looked about me. Just a bit more, then I was going to take a proper break.

A while later I emerged to get myself a drink. I looked out the kitchen window and saw the men on the beach, Vladimir perched on the rocks and Grigory standing tossing stones. I sat and ate a yoghurt then threw on a heavier top and shoes. The guys came in, Vladimir taking slow, heavy steps back upstairs. Grigory came into the kitchen and stood looking at the stairs until the footsteps retreated. He looked at me and said in a low voice,

'He's been sleeping much?'

I shrugged. 'He's been in his room, or on the chair. I haven't monitored his brainwaves.'

'He looks... tired.'

I nodded. 'I think he must have a virus or something. You know when you work really hard then you stop and your body lets you get everything you've been fighting off when you wouldn't let yourself rest?'

Grigory thought for a moment then nodded. 'Yes: maybe. He says he feels better. He needs to eat more.' He looked quite contemplative.

I studied the view out the window for a moment, then after what I thought was a reasonable time I said 'you off then?'

It shook Grigory out of his reverie. 'Yes. I guess so. It's a pity, the weather is so nice. I wanted to talk to him more. He's got to... he's too tired.' He kept staring at the stairs.

I decided he wouldn't do anything stupid. One semi-conscious Russian in my house I could deal with, another, in full health and mental capacity, I felt was changing the odds a little, but Grigory seemed reasonable, at least on the surface.

'Well, I'm going out for a walk. You can stay here and have a cup of tea or something, if you like. If you want to wait to talk to him.'

He looked uncharacteristically uncertain. 'Yes, thank you. That would be nice. Actually,' he looked around him, 'would you mind? Can I walk with you?'

I actually wanted a little company after all my solo work, so I agreed.

We set off along the road then cut down onto the beach once past the last set of rocks, watching our footing and walking in silence. There was a sand spit near us, I explained, and it was almost low tide. It would be fun walking out.

Razor clams spat water at us and we squelched on seaweed, until a strip of sandy beach met us.

'Do you come here often?'

I'd been distracted scanning the shells and listening to the sea.

'Yeah. Well no. I've walked this so many times it's familiar, but I haven't been here for months.' I looked at him. 'I've this new nightmare of a boss.'

He smiled. 'I'm sorry to hear that.'

I realised then something that I'd experienced without actively noticing: that Grigory had a drier British sense of humour than his compatriots, so you could be sarcastic or understated and he didn't flare up with it. I would have never criticised Boris to any of the other Russians I knew- Viktor or Vladimir – they might take it the wrong way, add too much intent to a remark set as an aside. I realised I'd been living with heightened awareness of everything I said about people in front of these guys. Not that I was an angel in the office. I would turn up in Glasgow huffy that I'd been summoned to another stupefying meeting. I still didn't entirely trust Grigory. You could see him slotting away everything, but he acted like he got me.

'You know he likes you?' I'd drifted away again.

'Who?'

'Boris. He rates you very highly.' I rolled my eyes and stuck my hands in my pocket. I felt a finger on my arm. 'Let's not talk about work.'

'Good idea,' I said. 'Although you are dressed for it. Do you always wear a shirt?'

'I was working this morning! If I was painting I would wear a t-shirt. Or running: I wouldn't wear a shirt then.'

'Swimming?'

'Swimming, no. Well, you never know who you might bump into at the pool, so maybe.'

I nodded in appreciation at the joke. We walked on a little more in silence.

'You can see the big house from near the end. It's very nice. You can't see it from the road.'

'Ah, nice. Does your family have a history with this part?'

'Not really, just sailing. My dad loved it, still does sort of like it, but he got rid of his boat when we were young. It was small and he said it was too scary with kids on it when we couldn't swim. I think he always thought he'd get another one, but we were always doing other stuff so he knew he couldn't just cram us into a boat every summer.' It occurred to me then how much I didn't see my parents as the people they'd always been, just as parents. They would never get a boat now.

'I love sailing.' I looked at him in surprise. He pointed at his neck. 'You can wear a shirt.'

I laughed then.

'But I do sail. We have beautiful lakes in Russia that are great for sailing, and you can sail at St Petersburg.'

'Is that where you're from?'

'I grew up in Moscow, but my family were mostly from St Petersburg. Although before that half were from what is now Kazakhstan.'

'The seal is here.' The head had bobbed up and was

watching us five metres off the narrow shore.

'You really do see everything.'

I looked at him in surprise, and then recalled the Islay ferry trip.

'So,' I decided to let him in on a childhood tradition, 'There are three rocks up here that you have to run and jump along without falling.'

'So you don't get wet?'

'No, so you've passed the spit test.' It sounded nonsensical to my adult self. 'It's a family tradition.' I added.

I ignored his bemused look and picked up my pace, jumped onto the first of the rocks, still a miniature pool of water cupped on its surface, sprang onto the second and leapt off it onto the third. Seaweed had formed there in the intervening years since I'd competed with my sister, and I suddenly slipped, spun, and partially regained my balance in order to jump onto the far side. I laughed and looked at Grigory who was laughing too.

'You have to pirouette?'

'Yeah!'

He took a slight run up, and with his longer legs, jumped along the three with grace, making a little turn as he jumped onto the shingle at the far side.

'Very good,' I admitted.

'That was a challenge.'

'It is when you're eight.'

The jumps had broken the ice, making us comfortable in each other's company. We crunched through the shingle together, lapsing into conversation about dinghy sailing and midge repellent before reaching the green warning marker. It loomed over us and I stepped onto its concrete plinth and walked around it, Grigory following me. We paused, looking out over the short channel to the other side.

'The current is so fast.'

'Tide's changing.'

He looked back where we'd walked. 'How long before

that's all covered over?'

'About six minutes.'

'What?!'

'Joke. About two hours. This bit will cover quickly, but you can walk it. We should go.'

The seal watched us return to the shore as the loch hid our tracks. I gave him a wave but he looked wary. It's like he knew something I didn't.

Vladimir was awake when we returned. I painted, they chatted. Grigory even got Vladimir to go for a short stroll and sit on the rocks with coffee, then he came in and asked with uncharacteristic hesitancy whether he couldn't possibly stay the night, sharing with Vladimir of course. It seemed rude, and pointless, to say no.

At that moment, away from the political epicentre of Scotland, we were friends. It was like we supported opposite football teams, and it wasn't match day, so we just wouldn't chat about sport.

The next morning I went out sharp for a run, climbing the back hill, following the sheep tracks I know and meeting the forestry road. The loch gleamed in the sunshine. A sail was already riding the water, almost luminescent. I returned refreshed, ready to throw the second and final coat of paint on the rooms, and to Grigory sipping coffee in the sitting room.

'Hello,' he said with that knowing smile of his. 'Did you have a good run? It is a beautiful morning.'

'Yes thanks.' I was conscious of my sweaty beetroot features.

'I wondered if you would like to go for lunch today? Both of you.'

I paused from drinking my water. I likely only needed a couple of hours to finish my tasks. Don't look a gift horse... 'Okay, yeah. There's a good place on the way back with a short detour.'

'Perfect.'

I showered, dressed, and got back to painting.

He even offered to help, Grigory, dabbing paint on the patches where it was lacking. Vladimir had regained a little colour in his cheeks (apparently telling Grigory it was sunburn from his enforced outdoor snooze) and was dozily mooching around the cottage, staring out of this window, then another, before sitting on the doorstep and drinking his coffee.

He was happy enough to come to lunch, certainly seemed to find his appetite on presentation of the steak and ale pie followed by sticky toffee pudding. We had a nice time. Okay, it was fun, really pleasant. Vladimir didn't say too much, I think his English wasn't so fluent, but Grigory flitted between English and Russian easily. We talked of Scottish words that amused him 'shoogle', a favourite, and the grammar that infuriated him 'amn't I?'

'Don't ever correct my grammar, Grigory,' is all I said, 'that would be a step too far.'

We drank our coffee.

'So, do you guys just know each other from work?' I asked.

Grigory and Vladimir exchanged glances. Grigory nodded as he brushed some crumbs from his hands.

'We did some training together.'

'Vladimir worked in PR?' I teased. Grigory paused his brushing and looked at me.

'No.'

He didn't appreciate the joke.

'So why aren't you still in uniform?' I asked.

He considered his response, scratching his face to buy time. Vladimir looked out the window at the seagulls in the shingle.

'I was injured,' Grigory said, 'quite badly injured. I nearly left the service but decided to return in a different role. I told you: it's my home.'

'So were you in the infantry, or where?'

'No,' is all he said, and he asked the waiter for the bill. Conversation over.

CHAPTER 15

I didn't mention Grigory dropping by the cottage to my work colleagues. Or anyone. Of course, me zooming off to the west coast while everyone else was fuel rationing immediately begged questions, and I answered them honestly. I took my Russian neighbour, but he slept pretty much the entire time we were there, which suited us both fine.

I don't think Grigory told his colleagues either. I couldn't imagine Aleks not sidling up to me and making some comment about it. Certainly, Boris was as demanding as ever. As I pulled my jacket off while my computer zapped into life I heard the tap on the glass.

'Hi,' I said, once round the glass barrier. Boris sat in front of his computer; Aleks stared at me from behind his.

'Hello. You have a nice time?'

'Yeah, it was very pleasant being away from here.'

'This project here.' He pointed to a project in the server listing. 'I want a 28-minute edit by end of today.'

'Sorry,' I was confused. 'I have two questions. Firstly: are you joking?'

'No.'

'Well, secondly... isn't that Beverley's material?' They were marked, as was protocol, with her initials.

'Yes.'

'So, is she ill?'

'Edit the programme by end of today. Go. You are wasting time.'

I wandered out a little bewildered and turned to look in the studios for a bit of peace and quiet. 'Anna!' Boris was jabbing his finger at my desk. 'No hiding.'

I sighed and went to my desk. In theory we can all edit at our respective desks, removing the need for expensive editing stations. In practice it's rather distracting, and the sound quality with limiting headphones means it's never as easy as in a studio. Plus, you can't waste time on Facebook unnoticed when you get bored, or make private phone calls. I hated working at my desk.

So straight back in it, hacking back five hours of material into one and a half in the first swoop. I didn't even know what the brief was for this but I knew Boris would say it was irrelevant if I asked. Viktor twirled around on his chair at one point – I was actually concentrating so hard I hadn't noticed him sitting down – to ask if I needed any music for the programme. Boris had evidently sent him onto the case to cajole me on.

By lunchtime it was at 45 minutes and pretty slow. The scripting isn't what I would have done, and most of the on-location material was pretty stilted, but I guessed it was an emergency job if I was called in last minute. With some well-chosen music (selected by Viktor under my guidance) and some archive material pulled quickly from news, I walked out at 5.45pm.

'Hey!' shouted Boris. I do like to give him a little bit of a fright.

'It's in the system,' I said over my shoulder, and carried on.

The next day I was at the CD copy machine downstairs in the main office when the door to the goldfish bowl swung open and Beverley burst out. She was crying. I turned my attention back to the machine, not wanting to gawk at her, but she came right up to me.

'We all know which side you are on, traitor.' Her eyes were swollen and snot was oozing from her nose. 'I suppose you like hiding away with your friends upstairs, you bitch.

Do anything to get ahead.' She marched out of the office.

It must be the programme. I cursed myself for not asking more questions. I saw a few people staring at me from their computer screens. Craig rushed over. 'Are you alright? What did she say? Is she alright?'

'Eh no, I think she's a bit upset, Craig. Do you want to go see her?'

He looked flustered. He went out, and I heard him knocking on the ladies' loo door, calling out Beverley's name. Boris came out of the goldfish bowl, unperturbed. I hurried out and up the stairs after him, stopping him in the doorway the upper office.

'Why did you make me produce Beverley's material?'

'I got you to prove there was a better way to make it. Thank you.'

'Boris, you can't do that. It was her programme. I decided maybe she was ill or something. Oh God, you can't do that.'

'But you did. This is not a popularity contest. We are supposed to be making the best programmes we can. Beverley underperformed.'

He brushed past me. I put my head in my hands in horror, imagining the humiliation if another producer was brought in to create an 'improved' version of my programme. I'd hate them. She'd hate me now, and I didn't think she liked me much in the first place.

As I should have expected there was a sense of being ostracised in the office. Heads that would usually pop up with a smile and a word went almost imperceptibly down as I passed, or maybe everyone else, too, was busy. I searched out Jennifer as soon as possible, several days later. She knew. I don't know who from, but she looked tired and told me that whole situation was barely tolerable. The unions had been informed of what they termed Beverley's bullying. Not by me, thankfully, but Boris, who they were apparently building a dossier on as he pushed and shoved producers into a higher yielding and tougher state. Some of the more robust in us thought maybe a bit of tough talk was needed in the department, but Boris went in for the lowest end of diplomacy.

In addition to this tension in the office, it looked like we might, finally, be going to war over this stupid piece of ocean floor. The date was starting to creep closer for a set of general elections, and the opposition parties had finally found their balls. A new party was forming – the Scottish Democratic Party – mainly from some disaffected SNP stormtroopers plus a fair few pissed-off young men who were willing to make a bit of noise in the street. There had been protests, the participants only protected from Russian soldiers' violent barbarity by the heroic behaviour of the Scottish police. No Russians were charged.

Further afield, countries were waking up to this latest example of Russian expansionism. Norway was furious about the Russians parading through their waters and undermining their oil markets. Westminster decided to stop asking if we wanted advice and instead took it upon themselves to stick some troops north of Newcastle, and Germany had decided it was a threat to European safety and remiss of them to not interfere in the business of an applying EU member when they were so blatantly being bullied around... Well, finally, the world was taking notice.

Within the SBC it was a tale of two cities. One morning I had an interview to record in Glasgow. I walked out of the studio to get back to Edinburgh for a meeting. I routed through the edge of the news room, passed hushed reporters trying to sneak in conversations while Russians circled, along the rows of TV teams now quieter than I'd ever seen them, down the stairs where directors and producers exchanged silent nods instead of conversation and a soldier stood surveying the scene, and out the main doors where a fug of smoke surrounded another bunch of Russians, and the SBC workers stood further away in smaller groups in the rain.

Then I got to Edinburgh. Walked through the doors where Grigory stood smoking, chatting, laughing with some reporters and shouted hello, up the stairs and through the news room where one Russian stood distributing a collection of fresh coffee to lots of smiles and thanks, and across to the main office to clock in with Craig where Viktor stood bantering with producers as they talked radio. If Glasgow was under siege, we were hosting a party and the Russians were our honoured guests. No wonder it was so easy for them.

That day it was a fairly typical departmental meeting for the new normal. The monthly meetings headed by Jennifer had become more sporadic as she roamed the bases around the country fighting fires and confronting the elusive Marc while trying to keep the Russians to toe the line they kept shifting. Instead Boris chaired invitation-only meetings where programmes and ideas were discussed. The main difference to the old days was firstly that people arrived on time, and if they were late Boris stopped the meeting to ask why that person was late and then rated their excuse; and secondly, if Boris thought your idea wasn't too strong, or 'needed development' as we might have said in the past, he would phrase that as it being 'lazy', 'boring' or sometimes 'shit'. It's always a little nerve-wracking giving ideas an airing and it would have been avoidable in the past, but then it became apparent that we wouldn't be allowed to leave the meeting room until we gave a decent input. Initially they were scary, but then increasingly productive. I found after being told the first few times that various contribution I was giving were 'underwhelming', 'lazy' (he loved saying things were lazy) and 'bullshit' (admittedly one I did make up on the spot) I did make more of an effort to prepare. And my ideas did get better. When they were good, he would give praise.

'That's a good idea.' he would say, looking around the

table to make sure everyone knew what a good idea sounded like.

But some people just crumbled with the pressure. Daft maybe, considering we were in the idea-selling business, but that was the cosy culture at the SBC. Eventually Boris consigned them to more menial production jobs, branding, small news packages, a new magazine strand strictly produced by the Russians, where they were heavily supervised. It meant there became a smaller group of us regularly called in and told our ideas were lazy and shit, and then pushed to improve the better ones. There was me, Chris – who came across from Glasgow for them – Andrew and Julian from online. Sometimes someone beaten down by the banality of the magazine programme might tap on the door with an idea, but that became rarer and rarer. After the Beverley incident she never showed her face at one again. Sarah found she could just about squeeze in enough lute music into the arts programme to satisfy herself so she stayed there. All in all, we were a department within a department now, controlled by the Russians.

Another day I was walking in to the lower office, coffee in hand, where the goldfish bowl meets were still held, to have a chat with Andrew about some gossip. There was an opaque strip across the goldfish bowl at my head height, so I would never get a full view, but I saw Russian soldier legs, and then I thought I saw Julian's. 'Oh crap,' I thought, 'was the meeting this morning?'

I took the risk to duck down slightly to peer below the strip and locked eyes with Viktor. I mouthed:

'Should I be in there?'

He nodded. Oh God.

I knocked on the door and went in. Boris broke off and looked up.

'Ah, Miss Facebook. Why are you late?'

I thought for a second. 'If I answer with 'is this a meeting I should be in', does that answer your question?'

'That is a pathetic excuse.'

'How about, I was walking into work when suddenly a horse galloped passed me with its tail on fire. It was whinnying and screaming and I...'

'Shut up and sit down.'

He finished telling Julian to come back to him with a better outline. Then:

'Right, so in two weeks Anna, you are going to Russia.'

'What?!'

'In two weeks you are going to Russia to do some recording. Lots of recording.' Viktor and him exchanged nods.

'I'm not going to Russia.'

'Yes you are. You will be pleased to hear that Viktor has sorted your visa, you can thank him for that, and it is time for you to go. You have spent too much time and money sending reporters around the country at your beck and call. You will record for Russian Romantics there and anything else you can motivate yourself to do.'

This was a horrendous proposal. I'd cooked up Russian Romantics in one of these meetings with Boris as some series blending the people who wrote about the Russia spirit, with stories from Russians, recorded around Russia in a mosaic of Russian soundscape and music. I didn't think it would work. The Russians I'd spoken to didn't have the English to fully give themselves in their stories and the whole idea of the thing was weak. My plan was to pass it off as fully researched, set my freelancers off on their hopeless task and then shrug my shoulders and say they all did as best as they could but this was all the material I could get, sorry, maybe it won't work. Now I'd be sending myself on a quest for banality, and it was all my fault.

'I can't do all that. I've never been to Russia. I can't go on my own and get lost in bloody Siberia.'

'Of course you are not going on your own. You cannot be trusted with your material and so that must be fully monitored and you are too lazy to get it all done in time. You will have two companions. Viktor will go and help you with your recording and editing, and he will solely control the access to the editing software...'

Not Marina, I thought. Oh God, not Aleks.

'...And Grigory Rankovic has kindly agreed to give up some time to accompany you too.'

Oh.

'Viktor has made a start on the schedule.' He pointed his finger at me. 'Viktor is in charge of the schedule and you do not agree to meet anyone else. He will talk you through this and then we will meet next week to go over the recordings. Good. I have to go.'

Boris didn't care that I had a race over those weeks; that I had a dinner date; that I was getting my car serviced: I was going.

'How could they get you a visa without your passport details?' A training friend asked me one night as we got changed after swimming.

'I don't know, the fuckers. They've probably stolen and replaced it. You know they read all my work emails?'

'No?!' That stopped people mid-towel down to stare in horror.

'Yeah. I got pulled into the meeting room once to be told I wasn't working hard enough and that a 'routine check' of my work email account showed that over a two-week period two thirds of my emails were triathlon related content. And fourteen were a conversation about what people were wearing to a party. I didn't want to break it to them that the party in question was also tri related.'

'Do you use your private email?'

'No. I thought about trying to change it, but who says they don't know that one? Plus, if they have the audacity to read through all my emails they deserve to read though endless conversations about car shares, race stats and PB times.'

We had a meeting the following week. Viktor had presented the full horror of what was in the initial plan, with nights spent sleeping on trains, remote industrial towns and long car journeys. I'd been setting up potential interviews thinking I'd be sending some other Russian keen bean reporter out to do the legwork while I awaited the .wav files to drop in my lap. What a sap I was.

Grigory was on the phone in the meeting room when I walked in with Viktor. We took seats and he finished the call.

'Hello.'

'I can't believe you've agreed to go on this nightmare of a trip.'

'If that's your way of saying thank you for agreeing to take Aleks's place, then you're welcome. And we're going to Russia. That's never a nightmare. It will be very much enjoyable.'

'Shall we go over the itinerary?' Viktor had been all glowing eyes and smiles when he kept bringing the trip up, he must have been looking forward to it. 'Anna has managed to make some good additions to what you have seen, but it will be tight.' I'd been on a salvage mission since the last meeting, to make sure we'd get at least some good material. He handed out three annotated maps. 'We fly into St Petersburg, record there, drive to Moscow with some recordings before a long driving loop to visit Pushkin and Chekov's estates, then we make our way back to Moscow to catch the train to Perm with some additional recordings here and there. We fly back to Moscow for the final date – there is a conference in Berlin that a few people we wanted were on, so we have to delay that to the morning of the last day, then we fly home. Anton will be with us in both St Petersburg and Moscow, but he isn't going on the overnight to the country estates, he has TV commitments in Moscow he has to stay for. The timings of the interviews are such that on occasion I will conduct an interview at the same time as Anna, and on those occasions you will accompany Anna.'

'I thought we were going to try to do three at once in...' I looked at the now familiar map of Russia, but whose names I still struggled with.

'No, only two. Three is not possible.'

'But there are three of us, and doesn't that then save us half a day somewhere?'

'But only two of us can record.'

I looked at Grigory. 'So why is he coming?'

Grigory did his Grigory face and answered for Viktor. 'You must be accompanied at all times, Miss Aitken. You and a microphone on your own make some people very nervous.'

I suddenly got it, but it was ludicrous. 'What does Boris think I'm going to do? Run amok in Russia taking interviews that I can't understand and then what, email them to London?'

'I don't think our imaginations stretch to what you might do. You've done it before.'

So first impressions were sticking despite my recent obedience. Maybe it was because general tensions were increasing. It was only three days earlier that a young chap had run up to a group of soldiers in front of parliament and lobbed a grenade in their direction. Two serious injuries, including one amputation and the protester hadn't been heard of since. The press reports noted that Russian soldiers would 'no longer tolerate behaviour they viewed as potentially threatening'. Things were rather serious so I wasn't going to mess about.

I listened to Viktor outline the stopovers and what he'd booked. 'Where do we eat here?' I asked. I hate scavenging around for food after a long recording, and some of these places were pretty far from civilisation.

'I don't know, probably McDonalds if we can't find somewhere.'

'Book something,' Grigory ordered.

'We will bring the big wind-shielded mic, and three

edirols...'

'I'll bring a nagra as back up.'

'No,' said Viktor, 'you bring nothing. You bring no flash cards, no memory sticks, no computers and no recording devices. I bring everything. Okay?'

I nodded. They must really have thought I was a renegade, and inwardly I was quite pleased about that.

We agreed meet times at the airport and returned to our desks. Before the stairs Viktor stopped me.

'Anna. You don't mess about here, okay. If something goes wrong I will be in deep shit. You understand. I don't want to be in deep shit.'

It was the first time I saw him look moderately aggressive, but when I looked into his eyes I saw a little fear.

'Yes of course, Viktor. We'll go out and get some good recordings and make some fun programmes.'

He smiled. 'Okay, good' he said, and patted me on the shoulder.

CHAPTER 16

The trip, in the beginning at least, went according to plan. We hit St Petersburg hard, with a list covering the interviews on Dostoevsky, Gogol, Pushkin, Nabokov and building a picture of the public readings and cultural set that enlivened the city. Viktor was still paranoid, however, and I was subjected to a bag search and a pat down before we pressed record, where I stood with a raised eyebrow looking at Grigory who found the whole thing very amusing.

'Just imagine what would be happening right now if Marina were here? You should be grateful.'

'I don't think I want to imagine how Marina would search me.'

Viktor went off to Pushkin's old flat to record a tour with Anton prepared to pose pertinent questions and gentle observations. Grigory and I roamed through the market streets, recording and soaking in the hubbub by Sennaya Square, managing to squeeze in a coffee before attempting to persuade some locals to read out some of Crime and Punishment in its own environment. I made Grigory do the talking, seeing him pull up to his full six-foot Russian height, and flatter and cajole before escorting the men – all men, the voice of the novel is very male – towards me. It was interesting to watch, this bartering. A much more formal and masculine affair than it would be in Britain.

I sat on the edge of the steps outside a metro station, away from the streams of people marching up and down, the traffic horns and engines brewing in the background, and wound up the microphone cable to put it away (to be carried by Grigory, obviously). 'I can imagine this place being pretty rough at night. Pretty gritty 150 years ago.'

'150 years?' Grigory scoffed. 'Try... 80.' His eyes scanned left and right and he perched beside me. 'My grandmother lived in Petersburg most of her life. She was here for the war.' He shook his head. 'They ate rats. They ate each other, some people.' He rubbed his hands; inspected his nails. 'You can reduce anyone to behave like vermin if you starve them.' He looked at me. 'You know, sometimes, on occasion, some idiot will want to tell me in the street in Scotland what he thinks of the Russians. They'll shout at me.' He jabbed his forefinger into his chests. 'I've been called a Nazi. In Edinburgh, more than once and at different times, so it's not a unique thought: I've been called a Nazi. We fought the Nazis. Millions of Russians died fighting the Nazis, and if we hadn't fought them, like you and your people, you would be speaking German. Never mind what the Americans eventually did.' He stared up at the lights of a huge shopping precinct. 'It reflects badly on the Scots that they are so ignorant. And here, it was the worst. You know, you said to me, that time, on the ferry, that you thought there was a toughness just under the surface of the Russians.' He waved a finger around him. 'It's because of places like this. We are survivors.' He smiled and leant towards me. 'We are the cockroaches of the human race. Nothing will kill us.' He patted me on the shoulder. 'Okay, a little serious. Let's go see a little more culture.'

We stood up and crossed the canal, where I pulled out the mic again to record a little, and made our way to Pushkinskaya 10, the great former artist squat, now studio, where we hoped to get a little more potentially bohemian wild track. It turned out to be fruitful, followed by an enjoyable stroll around artworks and crafts that I cooed over only to be reminded we had to move on.

We had a couple of academic interviews booked in the afternoon. I'd planned to place them over soundscapes derived from our own tours, so we rushed off to the university to get the facts from the people who knew. By the time it was dinner, I was exhausted. The flight had been early, we'd travelled far, and my head hurt from attempting to understand fragments of conversation while attempting to conceal that I could.

Viktor was upbeat with his material. Sometimes I felt he'd finally found his niche in life, and it wasn't in the army. I ordered a beef stroganoff, in the local tradition, and munched away on some cheese bread while we waited. Grigory returned to the table after having a cigarette outside.

'Do you ever think you will give up smoking?' I asked.

'No. Why should I?'

'Because it kills you; because you stink.'

'I stink?' He looked amused at my impertinence. I realised I was so tired I hadn't moderated my response.

'You don't stink. Well, you do stink of cigarettes. Do you never smell it?'

'In the morning I do, but I like the smell. You hate it.'

'Yeah.' I fingered some more bread.

'Are you exhausted? You look exhausted.'

I leant back in my chair. Viktor was chugging back his drink, buoyed with enthusiasm, gabbling away to Anton. 'I am very tired. It's an information overload, when you don't know a place, and the language is different. You have to concentrate...' I petered off. I'd said too much.

'Russian is difficult.' Those bloody eyes sparkling. 'It's not Germanic.'

'No it's not. It seems completely impenetrable.'

'I think a smart girl could learn it.'

I shrugged. 'Maybe.'

'Do you not think we should do more interviews on location?' Viktor was oblivious to Grigory's subtle probing. 'It seems a waste.'

'Yeah, maybe. I don't know. I think the more theoretical stuff will be more pliable to play with if it's got a blank canvas behind it, and then we can blend it more easily and chop and change from interview to interview if we keep it clean. Then all the readings and Anton's musings can be on location. Have you been musing well, Anton?'

'I muse as directed. You'll be surprised how many spontaneous musings by me will sound familiar to yourself.' He gave me a wink.

'Jolly good. With a few inspirational surprises in there too, I hope.'

'Of course.'

'We'll do Dostoevsky's place and interview there tomorrow and then Nabokov together, I record atmos while you do interview with Anton.' Viktor reeled it off from memory.

'Yes, God, Dostoevsky is so depressing. I don't know how I'll make this programme upbeat.'

'Well, he was in prison, and poverty struck.'

'Yup, cheerful.' Our food arrived. I tilted away from the plate as it was put on the table, and inhaled the aroma. Very welcome.

Grigory was having a pie, stabbing his knife in to release a swirl of aroma. 'Sometimes I don't think you like to face the serious side of anything.'

I considered this, my brain rejuvenated by the prospect of glorious food. 'I don't see why you would ever unnecessarily make yourself depressed. You only have one life. There is so much about life that can be amazing, and beautiful and funny, and all these things enhance life. So why would you seek out to wallow in depressing stuff?'

'Maybe it can make you a better person. Make you understand the world better.'

I leant back in my chair, and studied him. Grigory, with his fancy watch and nice car, and hazy background.

'Do you seek out the harsher side of life to understand ourselves better?'

'No,' he took a sip of wine. He only ordered good wine, 'but I don't hide from it with jokes, or actively avoid it.'

'I don't actively avoid it. I've had my fair share of pain.

I've experienced disappointment. I've known people who have suffered, and tried to support them, but I don't then hoist this suffering on my shoulder and drag it around with me, like some martyr, to improve my understanding of the world. Why would I? Why would anyone?'

'I'm not wanting to be a martyr. I'm not saying you have to carry the world's pains on your shoulders, but it's good to click on those news articles too, alongside the showbiz, from time to time.'

'You think I read and watch crap?'

He smiled. 'I have the data to prove it.'

Looking at my browser history now, were they? We stared at each other, and I became aware of Anton and Viktor tentatively eating their dinner, while watching us closely.

We changed the conversation. To the weather.

The next day we bagged the interviews we needed in the morning. I started to build that pleasant feeling of having material, even if I didn't know quite what I was going to do with it.

We had a quick, Italian, lunch, and metroed it to the grand Moskovsky railway station to make our way to the capital. I was happy to relax and let the views wash over me, but with a bit of enthusiastic prodding by Viktor, I listened back to some of the material he'd gathered. While doing so an attendant popped her head in and asked if we wanted tea – I understood, but pretended I didn't – and Grigory ordered us all some. He told me it was obligatory for me to have some proper Russia tea. It was okay.

We arrived. Grigory was from Moscow; Viktor from one of the soviet mining cities. We were due to interview someone at the city's biggest park about the chap it was named after, Gorky, before going on to his museum to do even more.

'And this is where I leave you,' Grigory said, as we staggered on stiff legs through Leningrad station. 'I have family to see and meetings to attend.'

'Is this stage actually a free jolly home for you?'

'Yeah, see you in a week! No, I joke, just today. Viktor says he will be fine today. It was part of the agreement that I come. You behave.'

I rolled my eyes and got out. Comments on my behaving were getting a little tiresome.

It was day two and I was aware that we needed more colour. In the UK I always knew I could conjure up someone to breathe life into a programme, but I had a more limited choice in Russia.

Then it turned out our Gorky woman, Kat, was great. A little dry at first, admittedly, but then towards what was looking like the end of the interview I asked Anton to ask about her own life in the city, and whether she could still feel any of what would have inspired Gorky there. She paused and then gave a very personal answer about growing up in the Moscow, in the tower blocks, with damp, with the cold, and feeling that she could be one of millions who might live and die as a nobody. She felt Gorky understood her, and this gave her power amongst the poverty. As she spoke, I could hear the spark of a programme forming, the flavour brewing, of a parallel world of the folklore living alongside the industrial and revolution of this country. She gave me anecdotes of her life set as a backdrop to stories she'd been told and read, and a blend and tone started to reveal itself. This could work, even with the interviews we'd done already. With a nod of my head Viktor switched off the mic and we shook hands. Maybe I could relax and enjoy myself now.

The next day we met up with Grigory, who took the driver's seat as we journeyed. We were driving south of Moscow, in a sort of loop, to visit two writers' country estates, and to interview some reclusive retired writer who, I hoped, would be a good catch. I'd heard horrendous stories of the condition

116

of the Russian roads, but they were pretty smooth. We entered the old dacha country house region, with the collections of more ramshackle older buildings being outnumbered by grander new builds. Patches of birch tree forests, as they had between St Petersburg and Moscow, padded out from the roadside. Alongside the narrow hard shoulder, people stood by buckets of apples, and sometimes mushrooms, waiting for cars to stop and buy. I don't know how they could bear the cold but I guessed they were used to much worse. Suddenly the tyres started buzzing, and the car lurched a little.

'You feel that?' asked Grigory, looking into the rear-view mirror.

'Yeah. The road?'

'Yes. You have now officially left Moscow.'

First up was going to be Tolstoy's lush pad. I'd been resisting having the walk-and-talk type interviews, but I'd been told, and photographs corroborated, that Yashaya Polyana would definitely be somewhere you could soak up the atmosphere within an interview.

'Did you read War and Peace?'

We were driving by the city of Tula, two hours in, and I was watching some morose trams trundling alongside us. We'd been sitting quietly, in a very pleasant manner and I'd been observing communist architectural brutality clashing with neighbouring vintage quaintness.

'Yes,' and then I couldn't help myself, 'Almost. Sort of. Wikipedia is very helpful.'

'You didn't read any of it?' I could see his eyes in the mirror, a frown joining his eyebrows.

'Well, it depends how you define reading it. I feel like I've read it.' I wasn't letting him off that conversation at dinner. 'It's pretty rough going for someone who has things to do in their life, like cooking, and sleeping, and reading the showbiz column. I only had a week.'

'You've had more than a week.' We braked suddenly. I lurched forward then swung back against the seat with a thump. Viktor turned to study me.

'Okay, maybe, ten days, two weeks, two months when I knew I was making this, I suppose.'

'Did you read Crime and Punishment, or lie about that?'

I laughed. 'I read both of them, of course I did! And Lolita. The Brothers thingy. The Seagull. Well, I concede, I scanned the last hundred pages of War and Peace. I was wilting.'

He turned, us stuck at lights, not appreciating my teasing. 'Well, good. Did you like it?'

'Not really. I have to say I subscribe to the 'show, don't tell', philosophy of writing.' He snorted and turned back. 'Why are you going on about this? You know I read books. You've seen me read books. I was reading a book on Islay. In Argyll. Of course I'm going to read the books if I'm making a programme about them.'

'I know. Yes, I know. I find it odd that you read a Booker Prize winner one day, then read about some famous woman's hair the next.'

'It's not mutually incompatible. It's possible to enjoy a decent book then crash in front of drivel. Do you never go low brow?'

He drove off as the lights changed, then he considered it. 'No.'

'You never get tired and think you want to watch some trash on telly, or flick through a magazine?'

He wiggled his head a little. 'Sometimes I might watch something, but I think my threshold for watching something like that is significantly higher than yours. In fact, if I am honest, and you won't like this, I think you are very much under-stimulated in the way you apply yourself to your job and so you mess about online as a way to fill your day.'

That was kind of true. 'I don't see why it should bother you.'

'It's a waste.'

'Of what? Worker output comrade?'

'Of your life.'

A short while later he parked the car outside a little wooden restaurant, apparently sited for this purpose, and we made our way up the long drive, lined with trees clinging on to the last of their withered leaves and a pond covered with water lilies. The house was beautiful, our contributor suitably passionate, and I gathered some readings from Anna Karenina and War and Peace by the lake and in the woods. It was all very reflective.

Then we got back in the car to drive the back roads to our next stop. Grigory turned to make our way back towards Tula.

'No, keep on the same way,' I heard Viktor say in Russian. Grigory replied something I couldn't understand – I was still at the stage when I would have to hear everything slowly and well enunciated – and they had a brief chat about the route, and we kept on our way. For a very long time.

The plan was we were to drive on to our next location, do a quick interview, then head to our lodgings and have a meal. I didn't think it was going to be that far, in Russian terms, about an hour and a half, but that time passed and we were still driving.

The snatches of conversation taking place in the front became terser. The sun was low, and I was getting hungry. Often, when I reach a point with hunger, I get pretty grumpy, and I could feel that blight starting to stir in my stomach.

'Are we nearly there?' I asked.

Grigory sighed and rubbed his eyes.

'I think so,' said Viktor. 'The signs aren't good here.'

'The signs are fine, it's just that Viktor is ignoring them.'

'One was wrong,' Viktor stated, his finger pressed against a specific point in his crumpled map.

We drove on.

'Can we stop and grab something to eat, do you think, before the interview? Stop at a petrol station and just get some sweets or something? I'm rather peckish.'

'We are late,' is all Grigory said.

'We should be there soon,' Viktor fingers splaying across the map as we lunged across a pot hole. As he recalibrated himself I'm sure he placed it somewhere different.

'Should we phone this guy Ivan and tell him we might be late?'

'Yes, we should,' said Grigory while Viktor said 'No, we are almost there.'

I looked around at fields merging into more fields. I leant over. The road surface was making the car grumble and throb inside.

'What time are we supposed to be there?'

'It's fine, Anna, we will be there.' Grigory sighed and rubbed an eye.

'I'm actually really quite hungry. Has anyone got any food on them?'

Viktor shook his head. Grigory asked if I wanted a cigarette.

Another half hour passed with touches of pithy comments from Grigory, one turning, but no sightings of any progress, and no more roadside apple sellers, which I would have been very keen to see.

'Guys, do we actually know where we are?'

'No,' said Grigory.

'Yes,' said Viktor. 'I cannot concentrate on the map if you keep interrupting me.'

'She wasn't interrupting when we set off in the wrong direction,' replied Grigory.

'Well, if you see any more people selling stuff on the roads, can we stop?'

'Yeah,' said Grigory, his elbow propping up his slumped chin on the car door.

Another ten minutes passed. Viktor told us to turn left, down what looked like a track. It ignited a terse discussion between the pair, which I assume was Grigory asking him if he was intentionally trying to annoy me, all delay at this point was concluded in my mind as some deliberate ploy to prevent me from getting some food. We took the track, and bumped our way down it for five minutes, the low sun peeking through the tree trunks.

'Grigory, I'm in a really bad mood now. Look,' I shuffled right forward to lean into the front seat where I could smell the stale smoke off Grigory's shoulders, 'I know your grandparents were in Stalingrad or whatever, but I'm fucking serious, I'm literally starving. Seriously hungry.'

'We ate about five hours ago. Come on.' He slapped his hand against the steering wheel.

'I'm really hungry. I don't care about what's happened, and we shouldn't be in the car right now.'

There was no response, so I leant back again. Viktor just stared at his map. Grigory at the road, with the occasional glance to his right. Then he said something and Viktor replied.

The car stopped suddenly. We didn't pull over, we just stopped on the road. There was no one else here. There was a moment's silence then we all got out. Grigory progressed to the bonnet where he started fumbling for his cigarettes.

'Well, Miss Aitken. We are totally lost.' He pulled out his lighter. I climbed out the back.

Viktor was spreading the map out on the car roof, then he chuckled and said something to Grigory, looking like he was going to join him for a contemplative cigarette. That's when I lost it.

'Why aren't you looking at the map Viktor? Why aren't you on the phone? Why aren't you sorting this out? This whole fuck up is entirely your fault, yet you don't care. You're fucking useless as a researcher, and fucking worse as a tour guide. What are you doing?! Do something.'

'Anna,' it was Grigory, 'let's have a break and think about the best thing to do instead of driving in what seems to be the completely wrong direction. There's no need to get angry. It won't achieve anything. Viktor has messed up and he's going to sort it.'

'Are you going to sort it, Viktor?'

'Yes Anna,' said Viktor, straight faced, 'perhaps you are on your period and you are finding this difficult?'

I snapped, and ran at him. He braced himself, partially crouching, partially turning towards the car as I swung my leg, but I connected, my foot against his tailbone. He yelled and collapsed.

'I fucking dare you to ask me that when I actually have my period.' I stabbed my finger at him as I leant over him, 'I fucking dare you.'

I spun round and went to confront Grigory, but he stood frozen in surprise, cigarette poised in his hand. I marched into the undergrowth, pushed past some branches, and kept walking.

It took me ten minutes before the red mist thinned then I felt a bit of a wally. I was still hungry though, and angry, so I decided to keep walking until I felt sorry, then I would return. I came across what looked like blackberry bushes. After a minute of consideration, I picked handfuls of the berries, which although an unripe red colour, were very sweet, then I strolled back.

Grigory was still leaning against the bonnet smoking. Viktor was in the car, map in hand.

'Ready to go?' is all Grigory asked.

'Yes, and I'm not apologising. He deserved it.'

He flicked his cigarette away with a smile and got in. I sat in the back in silence as Grigory turned the car around.

'We are heading straight for the hotel now. We've delayed the interview until tomorrow.'

'Okay,' I replied, 'do we know where the hotel is?'

'I hope so,' is all Grigory said, 'I'm getting hungry too.'

'Well I'm okay. I had some berries,' I stated as I snuggled into my seat.

They both started laughing.

I don't know if Viktor did know where we were going, or whether we went the right way, but three hours later we arrived somewhere bleak, dark and unattractive which he declared was our intended location. We pulled up outside what looked like an abandoned shop front.

'This is the restaurant,' said Viktor, sounding not entirely convinced himself.

It was raining now, and thinking of sleeting. The night had brought a Siberian wind with it, and the roads ran slick with water beside us as we decanted from the car and peered in the windows. I can't say, even if it had lights on, that it would have really whetted my appetite. We stood for a moment, the three of us, staring into the darkness, then Grigory muttered something. Viktor said something back, then Grigory snapped.

It was a low roar of a dressing down, lashed across Viktor, who stood looking dejected. It was too fast for me to understand, and too angry for me to want to. After a minute of that Grigory stomped to the relative shelter of a wall and lit a cigarette. Viktor was rummaging in the car for something so I approached Grigory.

'I take it dinner is in jeopardy then?'

'Evidently. Our shit researcher is an even shitter tour guide, as you say.' He shook his head. 'I should have had some of your berries.'

'Well Grigory, it's only been eight hours since our last meal. It's hardly Stalingrad.'

He huffed at me and paced to the edge of the road, staring down at lorries and battered jeeps spraying their way through the concrete. 'Not funny. Not funny now.'

I could feel my hands stiffening in the cold. Viktor approached. 'We can go to the hotel now.'

'And where do we eat, Viktor? There is nowhere in this dump. We need food.'

I did feel sorry for Viktor at this point, he looked so

dejected with rain running down his nose and his hair plastered against his face. He looked like one of my aunt's westies after a forced walk in the rain.

'Why don't we go to the hotel, Viktor, and see if we can get any food there?' I suggested.

'There is no food at the hotel. It is very basic. Only breakfast.'

'Can I ask: Why are we staying here? In this town.'

'The contributor is only a few miles away. I thought we'd be tired...' He lifted his hands up to his side, admitting his failures.

'Okay. Is there a supermarket? Or a not supermarket? Yeah, I saw lights when we drove in. It was that, or a petrol station, maybe that would have something.'

Grigory brushed passed to get in the car. 'Let's move,' is all he said.

We drove around a while, and Viktor called the hotel and confirmed they would let us use their oven. I heard him saying something like it was okay, that we would sort it. So we found a shop and Viktor and I went in and I bought pasta, and cream, and some cheese and some veg, and some sweets, while Grigory wallowed in his misery at the wheel. We then went to the hotel and checked in.

It was pretty basic. A bathroom in the hallway. Three small rooms, although the men nicely gave me the biggest as they wanted me to have a view in the morning. We assembled down in their kitchen, a very modest affair, while the owner lavished tea upon us. I conjured up a pretty good creamy pasta dish which we ate around a small, chipped Formica table. Then we were offered vodka, which for once I felt like enjoying, and we moved through to a small sitting room. Our hosts refused to let us clean up. Slowly Grigory recovered although Viktor remained a little sheepish.

I was given permission for some supervised editing of the material we'd gained. Viktor sat staring at the map, he was intent on getting it right tomorrow, and Grigory flitted up and downstairs, watching the news and using his phone.

About ten o'clock I went upstairs and got ready for bed. We were interviewing Ivan tomorrow, then off to Chekhov's country pile, before the long drive back to Moscow and a catching of the train east. I reopened *The Cherry Orchard* as I made myself comfortable against the pillows, which I planned to use the following day.

There was a knock on the door. 'Yes?' I said, tilting the book down to look over it from my lying position. I realised I hadn't locked it – they were normal doors, not modern hotel ones. Grigory opened it.

'Are you warm?' He stepped in and put his hand on the radiator. Muttered something, apologised to me then disappeared, the door clicking shut behind him. I heard him pacing around the corridor, his voice elevated as he said something to Viktor then he knocked and opened my door again in rapid succession and felt the radiator again.

'I have no heating in my room,' he said as an explanation, and gave me a wry smile. He gestured out the door: 'this side of the corridor has heating, this does not. But this radiator out here is fine.'

The owner appeared, holding a wrench with a familiarity that led me to think that perhaps this wasn't the first time. The door shut again and there was much talking and clanging and doors shutting. Then I heard talking outside my door and silence. Then a sigh.

'Are you alright, Grigory?'

My door opened. He looked really tired. 'My room is freezing. It's snowing now. I don't want to sleep there. There isn't another room. I can share a bed with Viktor.' He gave me a look that told me he was at the end of his tether and glanced at my cosy double bed then closed the door.

'Grigory?'

It opened again. 'Can you put your mattress on the floor of Viktor's room?'

His mouth tightened in consideration and he turned

to go to Viktor's room. There was a bit of chatting then he returned.

'No, his room is tiny.' He sighed. 'It's okay. I can sleep downstairs on the sofa. I wouldn't mind, but I've done my share of sleeping in the cold, you understand.'

'Grigory, just grab your mattress and sleep on my floor.' I wasn't offering him the bed but I thought there was space beside me. 'Is it a double mattress?'

He stared at the floor. 'No, two singles. You don't mind?'

'No, unless you snore. Do you snore?'

'No.' The door swung shut again and I heard a bit of thumping and some chat, then my door was thrust forward by a mattress and it was dumped down, then wedged between the radiator and my bed. 'Are you sure?'

'Yeah.' I sat up. 'But you stay down there. You come up here and I cut your balls off.'

'I wouldn't expect anything less, Anna.'

He disappeared again and ten minutes later, as I put down my book and curled up to go to sleep, I hear him enter, and with the rustling of bedding, he settled down.

'Light off?' he said.

'Yes please.'

He flicked it off.

'Are you alright now, Grigory?' I asked in the lull of night, backdropped by a distant train and revving engines.

'No. This is not how I like to travel. Good night, Anna.'

I resisted the obscure urge to lean over and stroke his head, then went to sleep.

CHAPTER 17

I slept well. A car horn opened my eyes and I could hear water dripping off the windowsill. Then the starting up of what sounded like a distant, but huge, piece of machinery.

I leant over the bed. 'What is that noise?'

Poor Grigory's whole body jolted. 'My God you gave me a fright.' He wrestled his hand out from under his twisted sheets and looked at the time. 'Too early,' and he pulled the sheet up to his neck and closed his eyes.

I looked at him for a second, how cosy he looked and how his hair was so uncharacteristically ruffled, then I got up and trotted through the cold corridor to the bathroom to examine the situation. There was a shower. I returned and, as quietly as I could, pulled out clothing and toiletries before grabbing two towels and using the shower.

In the corridor Viktor, wearing tracksuit bottoms and a t-shirt, was exiting the loo.

'Are you going to breakfast soon?' I asked.

'Yes, I'll take a shower. Look,' he shrugged, 'I'm sorry about my mistakes yesterday.'

'Dude, it's ok. But you'll check stuff today, right?'

'Yes. I'll check the map. We are close now.'

'Well, I don't know how Grigory will be, but don't worry about it.'

'He is angry I didn't bring sat nav.'

'Yeah, that was a bit dense.'

'It wasn't supposed to be far!'

Grigory was sitting up rubbing his face when I returned. 'Shower okay?'

I told him it was nicely toasty and left him to get himself sorted. We ate breakfast and got ready to go. The owner was full of apologies which Grigory pretended to dismiss as unnecessary.

We were indeed close to our next contributor. He was great – a cultural historian who talked of history, the people, the climate, the changes... and tied them up in literature and stories. He read for us, and recited for us. We trooped back into the car and visited Chekov, the rather ugly industrial town, but also the nearby estate the author owned which was anything but. Devotees showed us around and explained us their passion for the place. Atmospheric, emotional, appropriate... we were getting good stuff.

The next few hours were rather tedious. We were backtracking to Moscow to catch the train west, covering the first part of the great Siberian route towards the Urals. We'd wanted a train ride regardless – it is integral to many key scenes in Russian books, and gives a little insight to the Russian psyche – but I'd argued for us to travel south, to lay a visit to those special snowdrops in Crimea, and to then travel along the coast in Ukraine to where Chekov, ill with tuberculosis, spent most of his final days. I also thought it might be warmer, and more pleasant. But no. Boris insisted despite the current settled Ukrainian position that we travel towards the freezing Arctic abyss to experience the true rail spirit, and he was right in that at Perm, our destination, we could have the unwelcome experience of a true gulag and a Dr Zhivago location. So west it was.

I'll give the Russians one thing – they know how to build impressive train stations. We got rid of the rental car and set off from Yaroslavkaya station, me focusing on keeping up with Viktor's back as we fought our way through travellers streaming into Moscow. We met up with Anton, who looked distinctly fresher than we did. We waited on the platform while Viktor disappeared off for a few minutes on a foraging expedition ('there are no berries on the train'

Grigory quipped) then we were on our way. The berths we were allocated slept four, but we had two between the four of us, which made the place feel quite spacious, with the little table at the window and all our bags and coats stacked up above us.

Viktor had brought tea bags and instant coffee. Apparently, there would be an urn of sorts at the end of the carriage, and he set out to get us drinks. Anton went for a look at who was on the train. I'd somehow got a Muscovite literary professor to agree to be interviewed on this journey – as I said, arterial train lines are the Russian blood, but we hadn't seen him on the platform. We'd already got to work on bread and cheese and chocolate – Viktor's well selected lunch – and were now settled into the journey. Grigory flipped open his laptop and flashed me a smile. I found myself smiling back.

'This okay? Russian trains are the best in the world.'

'Well, I can't comment on that, but I do like trains. The views. Haven't slept on one before though. Did you get to see who you wanted in Moscow?' Having shared a room with him, I sort of felt a little of a bond between us. I liked him, and away from the office I didn't mind chatting.

'Yes. My brother and my parents.' He considered something, then added, 'My brother's getting married soon.'

'Oh, that's nice.' I saw him considering that too. 'You don't like her?'

'No. I don't know her.' He clicked open a few things on his screen. I looked out the window across the multi-laned roads and dilapidated tower blocks. 'You don't know what someone is truly like when you have only met them one, or two times, but you can get a feeling about them.' He was thoughtful.

'Has he been with her for long?'

Grigory looked up from his screen and smiled. 'No.'

It begged another question, but his tone implied the conversation was over, and then he changed it.

'I think you're starting to understand a little Russian now, are you not?' I was about to say no, cover my tracks, but then he said 'I can see you understand little things. In the car, for example.'

'If you know something about me, then why ask?' For some reason it annoyed me, like he'd been spying on me.

'But what do I know? Maybe I don't know. Maybe I'm guessing.'

I gave a slight shrug and gazed out the window to avoid his gaze. Bedraggled foliage made its home around rusting sidings. Fields stretched for miles.

'I guess though that you can at least speak a little Russian.' Very diplomatic.

'And why do you guess that?'

He paused to consider his response, his eyes almost gleaming as he relished the challenge, his finger tracing the edge of his thumb nail.

'You pay a lot of attention to people speaking a language you don't understand. Most people, it goes above their head. You wait for them to finish speaking.'

'I'm just being polite.'

He twitched a smile. 'Yes of course.' He shifted, leaning forward, ready to flip his trump card. 'If you want to learn Russian, which is maybe what a smart person would do who works with a lot of Russians around them and a national situation that looked like learning Russian would be advantageous, then I understand there are good night courses at the university.'

I nodded. 'That's true. I learnt Spanish there. That would be a place to go if you wanted to learn.'

'Yes,' he leant back again, accepting I wasn't biting. 'It's what a smart person would do.'

We looked at each other, then both our gazes naturally drew towards the window, as the glorious Russian vista stretched out. We were journeying west, and in the back of my mind was the unconfirmed threat of being sent out here to travel even further west, to make more of this. Boris had been quite assertive that we would only cover this area, but there was so much more material and space to exploit. I knew I'd be journeying through this huge country again.

We got to work. Anton had found the professor, had enjoyed a chat, but had agreed to leave him to enjoy his lunch in the buffet car before returning to interview him. Anton himself was in the adjacent berth. Viktor returned and pulled out another laptop – his bag must have been so heavy – and we revved them up.

We cut down the audio. I was pleased with the material we'd built up, the interviews, the atmosphere from Moscow, the countryside, the canals and echoing floorboards in the dachas. I'd dredged the archives dry of relevant material back in Edinburgh, and hired actors to read the chosen literary excerpts in English, so as I scanned through my vault of sounds, it looked like I could have some fun with this.

Minutes turned into hours and Russia, like a new universe, just kept on expanding, and like the night sky as it darkens and your eyes accustom, birch trees began appearing, then filling the view. I listened over the material as I watched, and started to hit my stride, getting a sense of how of the programmes might be structured. By dinner time, having worked through a few instant coffees and one dubious toilet stop, we stopped for dinner and a chat. We'd been working opposite each other, Viktor and I, most of the afternoon, apart from the moment I went through to speak to the professor and held the mic while Anton chatted. Him and Viktor went in search of passengers to accost and talk literature and passions, discovering a star in our carriage attendant Natalia, and Anton created a script with the chatter, drinking and laughter of the third class in the background. It was good stuff.

I stood up. We were pulling in to another huge station building, massive windows and Russian turrets. The platform looked busy and from British trains I knew this might be the best time to grab a table in the dining car.

'Viktor is sorting us food,' said Grigory, 'it should be better than the train food.'

A few minutes later Viktor arrived with hot pies, potatoes and some other goodies. I realised the platform looked so busy because people were selling hot meals and snacks at the edge of it. People with some superior kind of internal central heating system. It was good. Genuinely homemade filling fare.

By the time I'd decided to give up editing I'd made two programmes in rough, over-long, form, with Anton adlibbing scripts that we'd polish after feedback from Boris. Viktor concentrated on dropping them into a file for Boris – slow on 3G reception – and then talk turned to sleeping arrangements.

'We can all sleep next door, if you'd prefer...' asked Viktor.

'I don't mind sharing a room, but no snorers.'

'Maybe you snore,' suggested Grigory.

'I don't snore.' I then flashed him a look just to check he wasn't going to disagree. They chatted in Russian with a lot of shrugging then Viktor told me Grigory would sleep here.

'It does give everyone more space.'

'I don't mind,' I said, which was sort of true, because I felt a touch of excitement at the idea of spending more private time with that man, even if it was asleep.

So I slept on the same surface I'd spent hours working on earlier. Grigory settled down across the table from me.

'You know, Viktor said he'd sleep here but he was afraid if he made a noise you might stab him.'

'A justifiable fear,' I replied.

There was silence, apart from the rhythm of the train. Then Grigory piped up again,

'Do you like Russia: what you see?'

'I've hardly seen any of it.' I sat up. 'That's not an invitation. I do not want to see more of Russia.'

Grigory was lying with his forearms across his forehead. 'Admit you enjoy some of this,' he insisted.

I considered the forests, the meals, the dachas, the train... and us getting lost and the creeping cold.

'I'm a bit of a home bird,' I admitted, 'but some of this has been fun. Tiring though. Can't wait to get home and relax.'

'You don't have to get up early tomorrow, you can relax on the train.'

'If we don't get up tomorrow to an email from Boris immediately demanding more edited material, I will be amazed.'

'We can tell him the reception was bad.'

'Are you not missing a lot of work? I thought you were a pretty crucial cog.'

'Maybe I'm missing a little, but who could give up the opportunity to spend time travelling with someone so special as Viktor?'

I laughed. 'He is pretty special. But he's pretty good in media, I have to say, if not organisation.'

'You like him, don't you?' His eyes narrowed. 'I find it funny that you seem to like him so much. I would have thought he would be too... soft for you.'

I thought about how to phrase it. 'I think, ultimately, Viktor is quite a sweet guy. He's a nice guy. He's not a creep. No offence, a lot of your colleagues aren't that nice. In Scotland being a nice guy is highly valued.'

He pulled himself up to rest on his elbows.

'But I'm a nice guy, right? I'm not, I haven't been, mean or rude. We joke sometimes, but we're joking?'

'I know when you're joking.'

'You know I only go on at you about your silly games at work because I think you can do better?'

This was getting pretty deep. 'Yes, thanks Grigory.'

'Boris thinks you are very smart too. That's why he pushes you. That's why he has you up on the top floor. He wants to help you get better.'

'Right.' Deep down I knew that, but I didn't want to admit it. Work had been more interesting, if intense, since I came to work more directly under Boris. I stared at the door as an attendant, I guess Natalia, passed, and heard Grigory shifting. 'Why did you come with us this week?' I'd wondered it a few times. Grigory wasn't directly in this team. He also wasn't one of the foot soldiers who would normally do this running around.

The atmosphere changed as we were sucked into a tunnel then shot out again. I wondered if he was asleep. 'I heard there was a vacancy.'

'But isn't babysitting me a bit below you?'

'No, if you don't view it as just babysitting. What would you be thinking just now if it were Viktor and Aleks here with you? Would you be liking Russia? Would you be making a sympathetic programme about Russia? Maybe, I don't know, it is the subtle differences. But yes,' he leant up onto his elbow, 'I wouldn't usually be going on little vacations like this. This is soft diplomacy.'

I looked across at his shadowed face with its subtle attempts to influence me. I relaxed and snuggled further into my blanket ready for sleep.

'You know, we don't have much time on this train together, and I think we have done enough gentle conversation.' I looked at him, startled at what he might suggest. 'Shall we practice some of your Russian pronunciation and vocabulary?'

'Shut up.' I said, and lay back, twisting myself towards the wall.

I could hear him chuckling to himself as we settled down to sleep.

Viktor did indeed greet me in the morning with an announcement that Boris wanted more material, but he was exceedingly cheery to report that Boris was impressed with what he had heard. I edited, we chatted, we ate. I finally did my proper walk up and down the train, somewhat stuffy in places, downright whiffy in others. Natalia gave me a broad smile and greeting, and I dropped my inhibitions to return the greeting and offer a little, very basic, Russian conversation.

We arrived at Perm at lunchtime. We did some recordings, talked of the city before Soviet times clambered in with its concrete dreams, and grabbed a McDonalds lunch, but all of that dims in my memory to a small footnote to the gulag, Perm-36.

We had a driver arranged to take us two hours into the light snow-covered landscape to this prison camp. There we saw the wooden buildings and barracks built by people, some of them the writers we were discussing in the programme. There was a reverential silence as we picked our way through frozen mud and recorded about how Russia has treated its literary stars.

That night we slept in Perm. We were almost at the end of our journey, and, over a very decent steak, chips and red wine, the four of us had a convivial evening.

We flew back to Moscow the following morning, exhausted but ready to pick up that final recording with the previously unavailable expert, then catch the plane home. I'd hoped for a clear day and an eagle's view of this patch of the country, but the weather had become even more wintry. We managed to take off in the snow from Perm and didn't see ground until we broke through the cloud to land in Moscow.

'I hope this doesn't get worse and we can fly home.'

'Don't worry,' said Grigory, who'd been my neighbour in the flight, 'we're used to snow.'

But it wasn't snow that was the problem, it was fog. Despite me wearing the five layers that made my companions laugh when I unpeeled them in the restaurant the previous evening, I was told it was the relative warmth that was casting this veil over the city. We arrived for our flights, but the airport was in a state of purgatory.

People thronged the restaurant, loitered around shops, languished on the floor slumped over their bags. We dared the departures board to blink first, and lost. Finally, the airport officially shut and huge queues formed to get rebooked on other flights. We waited, one hour, then two hours. Viktor was tasked to see what was happening, but we had to wait, and wait further. Anton wasn't with us any more – he'd gone back to his family on the outskirts of Moscow. Grigory was itching to leave and return to the flat he had in the city, to deal with the chaos later. We weren't on a commercial flight, it was a special military-linked one, but no one seemed to be available who knew what the new schedules would be. Finally, Viktor concluded we should just leave, and booked the last rooms in the last choice of local hotel that wasn't packed out with airline passengers. He needed to stay at the airport to get confirmation of the flights, so Grigory agreed to drop me off at the hotel, and then return to his flat.

It was awful. I don't know how long Viktor's list was, but I hope this place sat about 88th on the numbers he called. Even the approach was foreboding, as we turned into what seemed an industrial park. Inside it was dank and smelly. Men sat around drunkenly on the stairs waiting for the evening to begin. Grigory dealt with the harried receptionist and guided me up the stairs to what was my room. I couldn't see a window, which was what I first looked for when I smelt the place. Grigory stood beside me as the door swung shut, staring at the single bed and chipped bedside table. I remember thinking he smelt really good, I think it suddenly coming into relief against the disgusting backdrop.

'Alright,' I turned to him. I was a grown up. 'See you tomorrow. Are you picking us up?'

He looked at me. 'Is this ok?' As on cue, the screams from a neighbouring couple started reverberating through the wall. Some sort of thumping followed. We stood listening, me pretending it was normal but unable to give any sort of quip. Him studying my expression. Inwardly, I felt horrified at the prospect of a night here.

'Would you prefer to come and stay at my place?'

It was just what I wanted to hear, but I knew it was wrong. Being away from Scotland meant I'd forgotten just how far apart on opposing teams we sat. Now, as our flight home loomed, I needed to get back on side.

He saw me hesitating. 'Obviously, I have two rooms. My brother has a room, but he's not using it. You can stay there, unless you want to stay here.'

Who was I kidding? What would I be proving if I stayed in this shithole? I nodded. 'Thanks. I'd prefer that. But...'

He knew instantly. 'We'll pick up Viktor here at reception. He won't know you haven't stayed. You just go in and give your key back. He won't know.'

'But I'm just crashing at yours.'

'Yes of course.' There was the sound of a mob rampaging along the corridor. Someone lunged against my door with such a thump I thought it would cave in. Laughter. 'Let's get out of here.'

He put his hand on my back, and it felt comforting. I had thought I would be surviving in this place alone, and suddenly I had a saviour.

We negotiated the crowds – even this dump looked like it would be fully booked in this pea souper – and found a taxi outside with a driver keen to make a profit on his return trip.

'I'm sorry you had to go there.'

'That was awful. Moscow five stars?'

He scoffed. 'You can book it by the hour. I don't think it's your kind of place.'

CHAPTER 18

Grigory's was my kind of place. He was eight floors up, in a modern apartment on a wide road. The flat had an open plan kitchen, with stools along the near side of the island, and a giant L-shaped black leather sofa in front of a big TV sitting beside a broad window showing the lights of the city spreading out into the distance. It was all very bachelor pad, but high end. He showed me to my room – grey linen, mirrored wardrobes. He was across the open plan area, with an adjacent bathroom. I heard him carry his luggage through and I collapsed, face up, on the bed with my arms spread out. I closed my eyes. I could smell the clean bedding and the clearer air, and was so glad I decided to stay here. I was exhausted.

'Anna?'

I jolted and sat up. Grigory was standing in the doorway. 'You want to get some food? Or you can stay here and I'll go?'

'No, I'll go.'

'You look tired.'

'I am tired: tired of doing nothing and waiting, but having a stroll in a shop will help.'

We went to a local shop, embedded beneath lots more flats. Grigory perused the ready-made section, but I went for my staple – pasta – and suggested a quick and easy spaghetti carbonara with a salad. 'If you can cook anything, I'm impressed,' was his response.

Well it was red rag to a bull and I had the munchies, so I also threw in some other baking ingredients, we grabbed some ice cream, and retreated through the now freezing fog to the flat.

Of course, as he would say, Grigory had decent wine at the flat, so he uncorked a red and sat at the work top on one of the stools, both pristine white and looking rather expensive, sipping his Bordeaux as I fried the bacon and cooked the pasta. He didn't have scales, silly me, so I estimated the relative proportions for the cookies and chopped up chocolate to go in.

'That's for the carbonara?'

'No! Do you never cook?'

'No, it's alchemy, isn't it?'

'What do you eat in Edinburgh?'

He thought and cocked his head. 'I eat with friends, out. I eat a lot of takeaway – not Chinese or pizza, but there are places you can order good food off the menu and take home. I work late a lot, so I get it on the way home. I eat in the canteen we have on George Street. I buy ready-made meals. I eat fruit,' he said, sensing my disdain, 'I eat toast. I can poach an egg, I have that on toast a lot, and cereal.'

'If you can read a recipe you can cook.'

'I like to be cooked for. It's like tea: it tastes better when someone else makes it. I don't understand how you can come home from work and think, 'great, now I have to chop some vegetables'.'

'It's relaxing.'

He picked up his wine glass. 'This is relaxing, and watching someone else cook for me, that's relaxing.'

'Well, you can chop this.' I rinsed the lettuce and tomatoes and placed them on a chopping board and put them in front of him. He did as he was told without complaint.

'Shouldn't we invite Viktor?' I asked, the thought having niggled at me for hours.

'No, he's fine,' was the reply. It wasn't my flat, so not my place to argue.

We ate at the bar, Grigory admitting he was embarrassed

that he hadn't bought a table. He told me the flat was joint owned by his brother and he, but his brother had now moved in with his fiancée. His brother was planning to keep the place though. It sounded like an escape pad. Grigory didn't sound too pleased for his sibling.

'So you don't like her?'

'I've already answered that. I don't know her.' He pronged some tomato and avocado. 'It's been very quick. She's,' he looked at me, his chocolate eyes probing my motives, 'this is a private conversation.'

'Yes,' I said, 'you're talking about your family; obviously it's private.'

He nodded. 'She's pregnant. And she, we, are Russian Orthodox. So...'

'Oh. So were they dating?'

'Yes. Well, he was seeing her.' He waved his fork toward the room I was staying in. 'That's why he wants to keep this place, you can say he's a little nervous about his fate, and I like it too.'

He suggested a film. He had Netflix and let me choose. I went for a thriller. The oven had been baking the cookies, and I took them out, crispy on the outside and soft with molten chocolate in the middle. I placed one each on a plate and topped it with a dollop of ice cream, then sandwiched it with another cookie, the soft doughy middle forming a dome over the melting ice cream before hardening.

Grigory sat on the soft with the control and I passed him his bowl and a spoon.

'Wow,' he said, 'good dessert.'

We watched Matt Damon save his own skin, then the rest of mankind's and munched our pudding. I didn't mind staying over in Moscow if this was the result: it's what I would have been doing at home at that moment if I had the choice. Grigory's phone rang. It was Viktor. They chatted and he hung up.

'Early flight tomorrow. This should clear.'

'Did you tell him I was here?'

'No. I said you thought you were going to bed. He asked if your room was okay, I think his isn't too nice. I said it was. But,' his eyes twinkled, 'you probably already know that.'

I shook my head. I heard the times and hotel, but not much else.

We paused within the lull that fills the room once a film ends. I pushed the last drips of melted ice cream around my plate.

'Are you going to talk to me when we get back to Edinburgh?' he asked, filling the void.

'I always talk to you.'

'You say hello,' he conceded. 'You are very polite, in your British way. Although... You are quite hot-headed for a Scot.' I didn't think I was hot-headed. 'That's not a criticism,' he added, seeing me tense up.

There was another silence, then I asked in reply, 'Are we going to be at war with each other soon?'

Grigory stretched his legs out, and leant forward to put his wine on the coffee table. He held his palms up then dropped them, studying his fingers. 'I hope not. I think it's possible to win this without a war.' He looked up, crossed his arms. We'd never talked frankly about the situation. No one ever talked frankly about it: we all lived in freezing fog.

'Win it. Do you mean resolve it? Surely it can only be finished when one party decides that Rockall doesn't belong to them? And we're not. Europe isn't going to agree either.'

He thought for a moment, weighing up, I guess, the truth and what he was willing to tell me.

'Rockall was there, uninhabited, we laid claim to it.' He saw me ready to interrupt and declare my patriotic sentiment and he held up a finger, 'and you think we want it because of oil?' It didn't need to be a question. The biggest elephant in the room wasn't mentioned because it was so obvious. 'You know why St Petersburg exists?' I thought of that classically European style of city, its canals and designed beauty, so contained compared to the relentless expanse of Russia.

'It's a trading post, with access to Europe by water?'

I guessed the last bit, but weren't all cities built on water built for the water? Grigory tilted his finger, still pointing at me. 'To build a navy. The water gave us the Russian navy.'

I shrugged. He continued. 'We needed a port. A country has a port; it can have a navy. As Peter the First said: a ruler with an army has one hand; with a navy he has two.'

'But you still have your port.' It was dawning on me what he was saying, and with it a creeping horror was coming over me.

'Yes we have ports. We have St Petersburg, we have Vladivostok. Can you imagine if we had Scotland?'

'Orkney.'

'Yes, Orkney.'

'You have Orkney already.'

'Yes. It will get bigger.'

'You want Scotland to be a giant Russian military base?'

'No,' he sighed and scratched his arm. 'I'm a diplomat, Anna. Can you imagine...can you imagine if someone managed to go to a free, democratic, wealthy country and take control of the main infrastructure to enhance your own country's dominance in the world, without firing a single bullet? That person... that team... it's never been done before.'

'You don't... is this just a challenge to you?'

He threw his hands out. 'It's the biggest challenge. It's never been done before.'

'This isn't about the rock.'

He shrugged and stood to gather up the plates. The conversation was ending. 'The rock. The oil. All the ministers in Scotland thought it was about the oil. God. Do you have any idea how small the resources are in Scotland compared to Russia? The oil.' He snorted. 'It's a dribble.'

I followed him to the kitchen.

'But the leak, about the oil...' I saw him smiling. 'Was that you?'

'It was a good move, huh?'

I had this bizarre clashing of emotions, at loathing his arrogance but admiring his intelligence. I really love an intelligent man, but the whole thing stank. 'You came to invade my country just to prove how good you are?'

'No. Look,' he put the plates into the sink, 'I love my country. I want to represent my country well. I want my country to be powerful. You sit on the edge of a Europe which doesn't like us, for some reasons I understand, and some I don't. The Ukrainian problem: that's interfered with our navy power there. That's our land. They are Russians. Europe should mind its own business. I want Russia to have a powerful navy, the most powerful navy in the world. America isn't just full of superheroes. It too wants control, despite its protestations. It pretends to be cool when it's provoking us. And we're one of a few willing to defend the weak in the Middle East.' He put his hand up to silence me. 'We aren't coming in to neutralise the Scots, but you do sit in a very useful position. We just want to control a little more of the water going west, to protect our best interests. Scotland did it, Scotland had an empire too. Your ships you built have sailed everywhere, but then you were part of an empire that thought it was doing the world good. Well, a navy in Scotland would be good for us. I love Scotland. Everyone loves Shotlandiya. We don't want to change it, but we want its water. Don't pretend you don't understand. It's not emotional. You're smarter than that.'

My brain was whirring to reconcile emotion with fact.

'But you've no right! How can you think it's reasonable to make a grab for water like that? What if it isn't agreed? Are we going to war?'

He sighed again, and stretched his back. 'You know there are many of us with views over what goes on in Scotland. Some people like me want to negotiate. Some people don't.' He shrugged. 'I think if it came to war it wouldn't last very long. We have our bases already there. Look, it's like its

143

business. It's nothing personal. Come on.' He nudged my shoulder in a friendly cajole.

I looked at him warily. We could never be friends. 'I'm tired.' I went to the bathroom and washed my face, staring into the mirror to make my head stop throbbing. I didn't know what to do, but I don't think there was anything I could do. Maybe I could spread the word, but surely everyone knew now this wasn't just going to blow over.

Despite my tiredness I slept badly that night, and the next morning I went with Grigory to check out of the hotel and met Viktor while he waited outside in the taxi.

'Looks like you slept as badly as I did,' quipped Viktor.

'Yeah,' I said, 'let's get out of this dump.'

Grigory bought me coffee and kept on trying to catch my eye. I knew he wanted me to confirm that I wasn't upset. But I was, and I held him completely responsible, just as we were getting on so well.

We sat at the gate finishing off our drinks before we boarded. Viktor had gone for a brief wander. Grigory leant forward. 'Are you alright?'

I gave him a stony stare. 'No.'

'Because of our chat last night?'

I sighed, trying to control myself. 'Yes. I suppose you think it's juvenile of me to be annoyed.' I looked away, unable to hold his gaze.

'Not juvenile.' I heard him say. 'But I think if you think about it with a composed mind you will see that it's just politics. I don't want you to hate me. I'm trying my best for Scotland.'

'You're trying to take over Shotlandiya.' I drew out the syllables mockingly.

'I'm trying to control Scotland without anyone getting hurt. There is a growing momentum in Moscow for that to come to an end. In many ways I'm on your side.' He leant forward and touched my knee. 'I mean that, Anna. I'm not spinning you a line. Don't hate me. Please.'

144

God, I hated him. But I also found myself being drawn to him. And his forked tongue.

CHAPTER 19

I f I was feeling a sense of foreboding about the future of Scotland, I wasn't the only one. There was a heaviness to public life now. I might have been over sensitive, but it seemed that a hushed tone took over exchanges at shop tills, a sobriety during nights out and a heightened awareness of being monitored in the office.

Back after only a handful of days away, I noticed over the next weeks a presence that I hadn't before of Scottish military uniforms on the streets of the city. More flags flew – both the Saltire and a few Union Jacks for those who pined for the past and who perhaps wanted to remind our visitors of our closest ally.

Day one back, though, and the Russian greeting was jovial. Boris tapped away on his glass and I attended his desk. He pulled his half-moon glasses off and gestured towards Aleks's empty chair. 'The interviews are good I think. Some nice stuff there.' He queried a few things about the content, then leant back, crossing his arms as Aleks entered, and scowled at me sitting in his seat. Boris asked in Russian whether Grigory was in the building, although I pretended I didn't know that. I felt my cheeks redden as Aleks answered in the affirmative and turned to fetch him.

He arrived a few minutes later, clutching his normal bulging leather case, impeccably groomed in his shirt and tie. They exchanged greetings and Grigory said hello to me with a smile and a meaningful look. I nodded at him. Aleks acted as gopher and wheeled a chair in which Grigory took, before Aleks pretended he had something important to do elsewhere.

Boris started talking in Russian. Something about me, and the programmes, and I guessed about what Grigory thought of them. I saw Grigory's eyes flitting from Boris to me, monitoring my reaction to the speech. I think Boris called me something derogatory from the way he phrased something.

Grigory gave his response. Boris laughed.

'Very good, very good. You've been a good girl, I hear. Maybe we have tamed you.'

I got up to leave. Grigory gave me a tight smile. They exchanged pleasantries and Grigory gave me a nod and said goodbye.

'Right, bye,' I said, my tone cool but feeling my heart beat a little faster. I'm sure he brushed past me intentionally.

I spent quite a lot of time despising myself over the next few weeks as I worked on this series that explored an enlightened Russia. For finding myself attracted to a man who wanted to take control of my country, and then for being too frightened to defy the unspoken censorship and join the few protestors who tolerated the Russians' hounding of them. It was the first time I felt like a traitor. A proper, collaborating traitor. If we had been fully at war I would have been pumping out propaganda material for the occupying force for the previous year. I disgusted myself.

Day to day however nothing much changed in what I actually saw and interacted with in my life. My new bosses had decided to create an online Russian portal for the positive content the SBC was pumping out, letting their own countrymen be dazzled by our programming too. It meant a lot of my programmes were to be made available in Russia, and more importantly, in Russian. I had to work closely with Viktor to see what material we could use when, and with Julian who was good with online material.

I heard Grigory got promoted, so no more Russian recording trips for him, I thought. For all his mentions of it, he wasn't a Russian bear. Quiet, hidden but deadly: I decided he was a snow leopard.

Although I sighed at the extra workload, it was all the sort of thing I thrived at. Seeking out stories, new media, fertile ground, and my brain whirred at the extra mental stimulation of the language. It was my dream job; but for the wrong people. In a way, the team, without Aleks, was fun.

Viktor had found his stride with the humour and language, so we'd rub along quite nicely with a bit of teasing here and there. He too didn't seem to fit the mould of the typical Russian soldier, and I often wondered whether my department was some outpost for experimental foreign diplomacy.

There was a silent understanding that Viktor was enslaved to the Russian military, but his heart belonged in media. He was, at times, outgoing, verging on camp, and I wondered whether he was migrating towards where he naturally felt most comfortable in his personality, away from the severe life amongst his colleagues.

He would ask me about my tri training, I would tease him about his weekends, which he liked to keep a veil of secrecy over, but we disliked and admired the same people, which meant we could gossip easily together. And he was very indiscreet about gossip.

One morning I arrived in work as usual and had a little of my own. I'd been running early that morning, looping back up the hill to my road, when I had to step out into the gutter to overtake someone coming out from a gate. Grigory's gate, and it was a well-dressed, attractive woman.

'There was a bit of a walk of shame going on there,' I confided in Viktor, a smile on my lips but a weight on my heart.

I said it almost without thinking and got on with my day, Viktor receiving the intel with a grateful raise of the eyebrows and a giggle.

I had editing to do, and managed to book myself into the little studio for most of the week without Boris catching on. A couple of days later there was a knock on my door as I polished some audio. It was Grigory.

'Hello,' he still had his outdoor coat on, the glorious crisp days of late Autumn in full swing, his thick hair neatly swept to the side, 'do you have a moment?' he asked, standing over me in the small padded room.

I nodded, thinking of him being won over by someone else and being a little jealous, despite myself. He sat down in the contributor chair and pushed the mic away from his face.

'I heard you saw someone coming out of my house the other morning.'

The flush raced up my neck, engulfing my face. 'Oh, right. Sorry. I just saw it before I came into work and mentioned it to... sorry. Is that bad?'

'No. No, you can say what you want. But I don't live there anymore. That's not my house. That woman, I don't know, she must be the new tenant.'

I felt a euphoric sense of relief that I pushed aside to dissect later. I nodded. 'Alright, really sorry, shouldn't have said anything. You weren't embarrassed, were you?'

He gave a little snort. 'No. It seems that sort of news impressed people.' He stretched one leg out and rubbed his knee, then he returned to his habit of inspecting his nails, 'I just wanted you to know that I didn't do that.'

'It's none of my business, sorry. I shouldn't have said.'

'No. It doesn't matter. I mean, I wouldn't want you to think I had done that.' He looked me firmly in the eyes, then lowered his gaze, 'I just...' There was a sharp knock and the door wrenched open. A Russian voice told him they were ready. 'I'm sorry, I have to go.' And he was gone.

I stared at the space he'd vacated and wondered at the conversation. Maybe it was because he'd told me about his family being fairly religious, or maybe not. I hoped not.

Christmas was approaching with the river of lights cheering up George Street and gorgeous trees filling the Georgian terraces of the New Town, but the Grinch had his own present to spoil Christmas for us.

'Anna!' ordered Boris, 'meeting upstairs now. Julian! Now!' We stood up looking at each other in a bewildered manner. Downstairs the rest of my colleagues were being herded up, Jennifer and Craig filing up the stairs with expressions as questioning as the rest of us. We were shown into our kitchen area and it was noted by most of us with little elbowing motions, the two Russians in uniform who stood in front of the door blocking our way out. Then we waited.

Boris stood in front of the TV, Aleks standing a little aside. The door opened and Grigory came in, and joined him at the front. The scattering of seats around the little bistro-style tables had been taken up early, and some donated to a few older or pregnant colleagues, so I stood at the side, leaning against a cupboard. After a while I pulled myself up to sit on it, then Viktor came and joined me, and Andrew perched to my left. The room became busier as more news colleagues came in, identifiable by their suits. It became hot and stuffy, someone fiddled with the window, but it still felt over full. We were fish stuffed in a barrel.

Finally, the last person was admitted, and the man who I might forever regret recording in secret that day in Islay entered. Mikhail Burkov. He was often in the news room and I chose to stay well clear of him, yet he worked his way to the front, turned and cleared his throat.

'We wanted to announce to you a change in the relationship between your employer and the Russian state. Of course we have been present and helping you for the past six months, but now, to be clear, the SBC is under the control of Moscow. Accordingly, any disciplining issues will be resolved by us, and you will officially answer to us. This may not change some aspects of your work, but to be clear, there will be little tolerance of dissent. Do people understand?'

Carole from news lifted her arm.

'Yes Carole,' Mikhail said while sighing. I saw Grigory beside him flick a look in my direction and look away.

'Does this affect our pensions?'

'No,' he said.

'Do the unions know about this?' On first appearances Carole always looked like a mouse, but she knew what mattered about work for her, and she wouldn't give it up easily.

'They do now.'

'Well, there might be a consultation.'

'The unions can consult all they want. In the mean time you answer to us. All of you.'

He scanned the room. There was a hush. Then he left.

'What does this actually mean?' I asked Viktor in a low voice.

'It means you must behave yourself.' He patted me on the leg and jumped down. I sat for a minute as people crowded around each other despairing at the ambiguous threat of it. Then I saw Grigory, looking concerned as someone asked him something. He gave a short answer then walked past. He looked at me, and mouthed 'it's okay' before he too left.

CHAPTER 20

So it was a depressing approach to Christmas. The weather was mild, wet and windy, with a scattering of Russian fighter jets swooping by the castle and off towards Fife, causing heads to duck in Princes Street then look around at each other in bewildered terror before carrying on into Jenners to buy some Argyle socks and Hermes scarves for Christmas presents we suspected would do little to give festive cheer. Perhaps unsurprisingly the main event didn't brighten me up either. At my sister's, who did a great job canapé-ing, sparkling and pretending my chocolate log didn't look like an extended cow pat before rescuing it with some holly, I sat feeling like the spinster third wheel as my parents crooned over their grandchildren, my sister joshed with her husband and his brother and new fiancée lost themselves in a vomit-worthy display of love. As everyone tried to guess what film my brother-in-law was demonstrating with his flailing arms and sunken party hat, I wondered if the whole world was living in an entirely different paradigm.

I returned to a cold flat and a tough writing deadline from Boris, who'd decided no war was going to stand in his way of a Russia media conquest. I'd gone for the comfort food route, with lasagna browning itself in the oven and a chocolate cake oozing icing on the side. The dark windows were steaming up to a backdrop of Nina Simone and I'd a glass of red in my hand and thick socks on my feet.

The doorbell rang.

I crossed the hall to pick up the intercom, hoping it was a delivery because anything else would be embarrassing to receive in my shabby loungewear. 'Hello?'

'Hello. It's Grigory.' I waited for him to tell me he was trying to get upstairs. He paused, waiting for the buzz in that didn't come. 'I have something for you,' his tinny voice said.

My imagination flashed through several possibilities – equipment... wine... bomb... then I felt that flush appear again, and I pressed the buzzer before I said anything stupid. He came through into the hallway holding a package he'd been shielding from the rain that had swept in, his face red and wet above his coat, his glasses steaming up in the hall. He held it out to show me. 'I have a Christmas present for you.'

I stared at the wrapping. 'Oh. I don't have one for you,' is all I could manage.

He laughed. 'That's okay.' His coat dripped onto the wooden floors.

I paused, wondering what to do, and then snapped into action. 'You want to come in?'

He followed me, taking off his coat, and shoes too, I noticed, before coming into the kitchen and rubbing down his glasses. I had that familiar sensation of whirring excitement at being in his company, mixed with comfort and familiarity. He took a seat at the table, sitting at an angle to face me.

'You like a glass?' I gestured towards my red.

'Yes please. That would be very nice.' He plonked the package onto the surface of the table and ran his hand through his hair, dredging the water away from his face. I poured out a glass, glad I'd decided to treat myself to one of my better ones, while watching him make himself comfortable. 'How was your Christmas?' he asked.

I handed him the glass. 'A bit rubbish, to be honest. No, it was good.' I leant back against the counter, still a little wary, or maybe just on my toes. 'It's different, now I'm single and my parents are mostly away and my sister has her own family. I'm a bit of a third wheel. But it was nice. It was,' I waved my hand around, looking for the best word, 'Christmassy. Were you at home?'

'No. I was here.'

He gave me a look as if to say 'we were both in the same boat'.

'Did you have a dinner?' I asked, imagining a ready-made meal on his own and feeling sorry for him.

'Yes, with a few friends. We had a turkey. It was good. Vladimir can cook, actually. But, like you, it doesn't feel like the right Christmas.'

We both looked at the package, some of the green holly paper thinning where it got wet.

'Open it,' he instructed.

'Okay.' I felt awkward, and embarrassed, and hopeful as I put my glass on the counter and approached the table. I tore off the paper to reveal a large box, perhaps for boots, whose lid I lifted. Inside were three bowls. Three aquamarine blue ceramic bowls with white rims, sitting neatly inside each other. I stared at them. They were ones I'd commented on in the artists' studios in St Petersburg. That was months earlier, and I'd just fleetingly commented on them within the context of a busy day.

'Oh my God. Thanks.'

Grigory took a sip of wine. 'No problem. It was an easy gift. I knew you'd like them. I was going to give them to you before Christmas, but I know it's been a hard time for everyone.'

I reflected on the siege mentality in the office, remembered his role in it, but then I looked at the gift. The embarrassment filtered away to be replaced by happiness. They were beautiful. I put the lid down on the table and picked a bowl up, admiring it as I spoke. 'So did you get what you wanted for Christmas?'

'Unfortunately, no. I was quite disappointed.'

'Oh really?' I put the bowl carefully back and looked at him. 'What were you hoping for?'

'Well,' he shifted in his seat, 'I really wanted some lasagna.

But no one made me any.'

'Huh!' I started in disbelief, swiping my arm in a reflex mock slap in the air, but then I laughed. His face exploded in a grin, so uninhibited he looked like a delighted puppy. 'Well Grigory,' it was a good line, 'would you like some lasagna?'

'You have lasagna? That's amazing. I'd love some.' Then he hesitated. 'Is that all for you, or someone else...?'

I shrugged. 'All for lonely old me, and for tomorrow, and maybe the next day too, so there's plenty.'

I made an attempt to set the table: pulling out placemats that needed a wipe and lying out the cutlery, before dishing up, adding salad and topping up the wine. We ate, not chatting much, and when we did it was easy.

'You know the other thing I really wanted for Christmas but didn't get?'

'Was it chocolate cake, Grigory?'

'Yes!' He leant forward, knowing he was pushing his luck, but that he'd get his way. 'How did you guess?'

'Well, I'm not totally daft. Would you like some chocolate cake?'

He laughed again. 'I would love some chocolate cake.'

'I don't suppose ice cream was on that ignored list too?'

He leant back, resting his hands on his head. 'Why, actually, yes. It was. I was very deprived.'

'Well, you must have been a right shit of a boy this year for Santa to have been so mean to you. Did you try to invade another country, perhaps?'

'Oh Anna,' he flapped a hand at me, 'I thought we could avoid all that.'

'Sorry, it's pretty unavoidable. I'll give you cake, and ice cream; but it doesn't deter from the point that I'm really pissed off with this situation.'

'Well, you know my position on that. I'm sorry.' He twisted in his chair to watch me slice the cake, 'and you know that's just politics. It's just...' I turned and gave him his cake, then dumped the tub of ice cream in the middle of the table before sitting down with mine.

'It's just your ambition,' I finished for him.

'No.'

'Oh come on, it is. You're making your mark, aren't you?'

He sighed, conceding the point, but then, pointing his spoon at me, 'but you aren't doing so badly out of the situation yourself.'

'I can only do my best in whatever situation presents itself to me.' I popped some cake in my mouth. Really good.

'Well, that's what we all do. This is delicious. Thank you.'

'Thanks. Your turn next. Take away I assume.'

We devoured the food then Grigory swept up the last of his crumbs and put his spoon down.

'I actually wanted to ask you something.' He tapped his fingers against the table, studying his hands. 'I want to ask you something and have your honest opinion, because I know you are a very honest person. Sometimes a little too honest.' He looked up at me, now also finished and resting my arms on the table, awaiting the question. 'And once I ask you the question, if you don't like the question then we put it into history and it's not mentioned again.'

I was curious now. 'Alright.'

'Okay. I...' looking at those bloody nails again, 'I find myself wanting to spend more time with you.' Then he got me directly in the eyes. 'I wondered if you would like to see some more of me. Go out with me.' He smiled at the awkwardness of it, and me staring at him in surprise.

Honestly, it was what I'd been hoping for. Someone who thought like me, someone smart, someone I found attractive... someone paired for me unlike everyone else who swam around me like shoals of fish. But he was also him. It couldn't be.

'I'm sorry.' There'd been a silence as my hopes rose and my reason dashed them. 'I couldn't. I do like you, but I couldn't. Can you imagine... I couldn't do my job. My judgment. Even if I knew it was fine it couldn't be trusted in the department. How could it? I couldn't keep my editorial integrity. If people knew...' I was convincing myself, realising how much I wanted to say yes.

'People don't have to know. I won't tell anyone.'

'But then what would we do? We can't go out.'

'We can do this.' He held his hands out. 'You don't enjoy this?' He had pleading eyes. 'We can do this,' he repeated.

'No. No, I'm sorry. I'm really sorry.' I stood up, picking up the plates and putting them in the sink, replacing the ice cream into the freezer, forcing my shaking fingers to obey, clearing up, closing the meeting, trying to show that it was time to go as my insides clawed at me to change my mind. I heard his chair scrape backwards.

'Do you want some time to think about it?' I pressed my hands against the counter top, leaning backwards, steadying myself.

'No, I don't think so. I'm sorry. I'm really sorry.'

'You don't like me? I really like you. I do. I think we are good together. I think we are good for each other.'

I stood shaking my head. Pushing away everything I wanted. 'No.'

'Anna.' He took a step towards me. I thought I was going to cry.

'Grigory,' I couldn't say any more, felt a sob rising and I covered my face.

'Okay, okay,' he made for the hallway and started to pull on his shoes, 'I didn't want to upset you. I'm sorry.' I managed to look at him, and saw his face was full of pain too. He stood up. 'It's just politics, Anna. Please.' He pulled his coat on and held onto the handle. 'If you change your mind...'

I pulled my mouth tight and took a deep breath, studying the floor. 'I know where you are.'

'Yes.' He pulled the door open. 'Whenever that is. Whenever.'

He left. I closed the door behind him and heard the security door shut. I stood in my hallway and burst into tears.

CHAPTER 21

I didn't see Grigory for a few days after that. He featured in the background of a Guardian article about the betrayal of our seas, but I managed to flick straight past that quickly. I knew I'd made the right decision. I couldn't make any other decision. I started fantasising about a sudden political love-in that resulted in instant friendship between our two nations, and Grigory would stride into the office and proffer his hand, which I would be proud to accept and we'd walk off to dinner....

'Anna!' Boris was standing over me. 'There is a man here to speak to about your next Russia trip.'

I stood up and sighed. 'What Russia trip?'

'To continue the series. Don't pretend you didn't know.' He walked off towards the news room, I followed as I was now accustomed. He waited by the open security door for me. 'What's wrong with you? You look like shit.'

'Thanks Boris. I think someone just told me I was going back to Russia.'

He thought that was funny.

After the meeting I saw Grigory. I'd gone to grab some lunch in the drizzle. He was loitering, staring at his phone with a confused expression. Then he saw me.

'Hello.'

I'd seen him and was trying to do a subtle curve around him, but since that failed I stopped. 'Hello.'

He cocked his head towards the cafe, his lenses speckled with rain. 'You want to get lunch?'

'Eh, no. Well, yes. I am getting lunch. But I'm in a hurry so not sticking around. Sorry.' I remained a safe eight metres away from him.

'You want to get a coffee?'

'No, I don't think so.'

'Nothing.' He was just confirming the obvious.

'Yeah, nothing,' I stated, my voice fading.

He dropped his head and turned to walk up towards the high street. I made my way to the cafe. It was going to be a long, boring afternoon, and I'd just made it so much worse.

I'd gone down to grab some more CDs. The office was half empty.

'Where is everyone?' I asked Sarah, whose head was buried in her computer.

It took her a while to drag herself out of her research, but then she leant back, counting on her fingers. 'Andrew away, Chris on his Salford placement, Greta on her World Service jaunt in Malawi.'

I looked around at the empty seats. 'It's deserted.'

She nodded. 'Well everyone's abandoning ship. Don't think Andrew's coming back.'

'Since when?'

'What do you mean?'

'Since when...' I waved my hands around at the ghosts of my old colleagues, 'since when did people start leaving?'

She looked behind her at the other empty seats and looked back at me. 'It's been months since this place has been full. Everyone's been sneaking away on one pretext or another. Gwen got her new job and left – think you were away then – Craig's in London.'

Beverley came out of a DAW and sat at her seat, eyeing me warily. I felt like it was another life since I would come in here to a full room and lots of chatter.

'Don't stay too long down here,' she said, wiggling her mouse to reactivate the screen, 'you'll get the bends being away from your natural environment.'

I felt my pulse quicken. 'I didn't have a choice, Bev. Jennifer told me to go too.'

'Hmmm,' she said, avoiding my eye by staring at the screen. 'Well, I hear you're very happy there, so at least it's all worked out for you.'

'How have you heard that?' I said. I saw Sarah form a word with her mouth as if she was going to advise me to stop, then decided against it as I walked around the nest of desks to stand beside Beverley. The remaining members of the Arts team filtered out of the meeting room, gathering beside us.

'Well, I heard you've been thriving with your productions, getting real help with your recordings, and that you're very much throwing yourself, in all senses of the word, into your relationship with some particular people in a way that other people might view as being blatantly opportunist and inappropriate, with other words to describe it.'

What the fuck was she talking about?

'What the fuck are you talking about?' I leant my hands on her desk, partly to hold her attention which she was trying to pull away, partly to support myself because I felt like collapsing on the floor, and partly to stop myself from doing something else with my fists at that moment. I'd done everything I could to avoid this. Had he said something, paved the way to put me in a position where I'd have nothing to lose? He wouldn't be so awful, surely?

She pretended to scan emails. I could sense the silent tension in the room as everyone waited to hear what was being said. 'Well, I hear you and Boris work,' she looked at me, 'very effectively together.'

The venom had struck. I was furious. The blood rushed to my head and I had to stop myself from grabbing her frizzy mousey hair and ripping it off her head as I threw her over the desk.

'I'm not doing anything with Boris. Are you fucking joking? Or are you just pathetic because you can't come up with a semi-decent programme idea any more, any more than you are capable of putting together a programme even if someone lays it out for you like a join-the-dots.'

I'd hit a nerve, but she just stared at the screen. 'Anna,' Stephanie, from the Arts team, approached me, 'let's not have this escalate.'

I stood up and stared at them, all watching me. 'Is this what people think? That I play trade with myself like this, to get to make programmes I don't want to make for people I don't want to work for? It's so,' I flailed the arms around my head in my fight to wrestle words out of the chaos erupting there, 'it's so retarded.' Awful word. I couldn't think. The ceiling started swirling as I struggled to control myself. Then Boris walked in. 'Boris!' I screeched, having completely lost control of my voice, 'they're saying we're sleeping together! This bitch is saying I'm sleeping with you so I can edit better. Or,' I held my hands up to the strip lighting, trying to articulate it.

Boris stood by Jennifer, who he'd been accompanying, and took stock of me standing there trembling and beetroot, the crowd around me. He looked unimpressed.

'Stop behaving like schoolchildren with your stupid playground name calling.' He stabbed a finger at me, 'you, go upstairs and finish your writing. You,' he stabbed a finger at Beverley, 'if you want to be a witch go and take your broomstick and jump out the window. Now everyone, you think it is recess time? Get to work.'

I wanted more. A proper denial, but he wafted me away with his hand, and I broke through the crowd and left the office. Half way up the stairs I felt myself wobble. I sat on the stairs and put my head in my hands. I'd rejected someone I really liked to remain loyal, but was called a whore anyway. And all the people I liked most in the office had left. How had I been so stupid to let myself be blind to the exodus and not save myself? I'd have to go, get away from it all.

I realised I'd forgotten the CDs. I'd get Viktor to go and get them. No way was I going back down there for a while.

Transmission dates ignored my emotional trauma. I wrote and edited numbly, waiting for the minute to log off for the day. Boris continued berating as normal. The space idea I touted a year earlier finally looked like it might be possible. Boris had ordered me into another meeting to discuss with someone called Dmetri who could talk about access. The idea had morphed into a bigger one, encompassing a high online content. Julian was late coming from Glasgow and Dmetri was arriving shortly.

The situation was fraught since the UN had decided to place sanctions on Russia, although as far as supplies were going we were fully stocked, with so much filtering through our country then straight onto planes to Moscow. It was obvious the outcome now was either capitulation to Russia, or war with Russia. Our waters were filled with shoals of Russian subs, our skies with Russian planes and I was sick of being a pawn in it.

I entered the meeting room to Boris and unfortunately Aleks too, who I thought was outdoing himself in performing his usual atmosphere freezing effect, before I realised the window was open. Great, it was going to be worse – they were going to make this take place in a fug of Russian cigarette smoke.

'Dmetri will be here shortly and we can talk a little about the plans. You might be able to go to Korolev to learn a little more about the work there.'

'I'd really rather not go to Korolev.' What kind of frozen desert could they send me to now?

He handed me some papers. 'Well, you have no choice. Here are my edited outlines.'

'Well, I do have a choice, Boris.' The table phone rang

and he answered it, then hung up and stood up.

'That's him.'

I was left in the Arctic room with Aleks puffing away with his viper's gleam in his eye.

'You think you don't have to do this?'

'I don't have to be here. I could quit.'

He exhaled, deliberately blowing the smoke he knew I hated in my direction and not towards the window. 'It is better to be paid for a job than be forced to do a job unpaid, I would think.'

'I could leave.'

'And where would you go?' He was mocking me: eyeing me as a cat does a mouse hemmed in by his paws.

'I'd go to the airport, Aleks.'

He leant forward, tapping his ash out in a coffee cup. 'And what would you do at the airport?'

Was this a trick question? 'I'd buy a ticket.'

'And then what?'

I didn't want to walk into whatever trap he was laying so enjoyably, but there was no option. 'I'd go to the check in.'

'Yes, and they would say you couldn't go.'

I could feel my neck heating up, my breathing getting heavy as I resisted slapping him. Could they do that?

He leant back in his chair. 'So now you think, I'll drive. I'll drive to the border. But you know we check the border. Maybe you could run,' he started swinging his arms back and forward, his elbows bent in what I assumed was a mocking impression of me, 'you can run away from the road and over the hills and the fields. Run, run, run, until you collapse and some nice little English farmer finds you and takes you into his house for tea.'

He glanced up and stubbed his cigarette out, standing up as Boris and Dmetri entered. Dmetri had a carry-out of Russian cigarette stench on him to bring to the party, and a Pictionary definition of grizzled. Boris introduced us both, he shook my hand and sat down. Speaking in Russian he talked about the set up, and the hopes for access. He invited me to explain a little about the recordings and images we'd like.

I was still seething at my conversation with Aleks, but I sighed and said 'so Dmetri, we were hoping...'

'No Anna. Dmetri doesn't speak much English, it's been a courtesy so far. And I have had a report from your teacher who tells me this conversation is entirely within your strong capabilities in Russian.'

Bastards. I'd been studying now for months, and finding it easy after the initial hurdle to pick up words with my constant exposure to the language. However much I didn't want to play the game their way, I had no choice. I ignored Aleks staring at me, and rephrased in my mind, and asked in Russian.

Dmetri started answering then I saw Boris gesturing over my head for someone to come in. It was Grigory. He looked around the room and gave a hesitant greeting before looking at Boris.

'Well guess what?' Boris said in Russian, very proud of himself. 'I said to Anna I had spoken to her teacher and that she could speak the language, and she believed me!' He bellowed with laughter, Aleks too. 'She can do it though! She can!'

I was furious, staring at the open window and wanting to jump straight out.

'That's good to hear,' is all he said. I looked at him and he gave me a nod. 'I have to go. Speak soon.'

'I'm sorry for the disturbance,' Boris said, patting me on the arm, 'now continue, that's very good.'

I felt like a child being dragged up to play the piano for obnoxious guests, but I got through it, eventually, with not just a few terse corrections from Aleks, before Boris told him to take it easy.

Finally it was over. I pushed back my chair, said thanks to Dmetri, and hid in a cubicle in the ladies room, sitting on the loo with my head in my hands. Then I stood up, splashed some water in my face and told myself in the mirror to pull myself together and get on with it.

I stepped out and saw Grigory by the lifts. I was still angry and when he saw me he instantly registered it. 'Are you alright?'

'So I can't leave now?'

'Leave where?'

'The country. I can't get out.' He looked like he was going to deny it. 'Aleks says I can't. I can't go.'

He threw an angry glance towards my office then looked at me. 'You want to leave?'

'Can I leave?'

'If you really want to leave...' he leant towards me and lowered his voice, 'If you really want to leave then I could maybe get you out. Maybe to Moscow and then...' He sighed. He looked really tired, frown lines across his forehead.

The lift opened and some of his lot came stepping out, a mixture of uniforms and suits. He greeted them and turned to talk to me, but I'd marched back into the office, still furious.

CHAPTER 22

We'd been working towards the space progamme deadline for weeks. A rocket launch that we had access to was drawing closer. By now, Scotland was properly in lock down. People I knew, or knew friends of, who had alternative lives they could lead elsewhere seized those opportunities and left. Some were stopped. I heard stories of people being accompanied back to their homes from the airport and told they had to stay. Engineers, business owners, a beauty therapist, but then her father was a prominent businessman, so I think it was political leverage. Others managed to leave. My parents told me to leave, that they'd heard war was inevitable. I told them I didn't think I could. I even drove to the airport one day, passport in hand and asked for a flight to Stockholm, but they scanned my passport and directed me to the Russian-manned enquiries queue. Then my sister left with her family, and I felt quite alone.

So then I returned to work, tapping away sullenly and trying to escape the office as much as I could. I found myself taking longer and longer runs, trying to run away from the city. I started driving out to the Pentland Hills and running up and along, up and along, higher and higher, looking out south over the land towards the border and wonder if I could, indeed, run through it.

The Russians had their main office on Queen Street, with views over the New Town and down over the Firth of Forth to Fife. There was always a queue on the main road out there as the Russians completely ignored the parking restrictions and dealt with any brave parking attendant by going out and threatening them with physical violence, all show of politeness now evaporated.

Viktor stood up from his desk in front of me and turned around. 'Boris says I've to bring you to Queen Street. You need to fix some part of the proposal. He's written notes and you must finish it.'

'Right now?'

'Yes.'

'At quarter to five?'

'Yes.'

'And you have to accompany me?'

He nodded. I knew why. Boris thought I'd just wander home if Viktor told me to get out the office. I packed up and we walked up the High Street, passing tourist shops and pubs now accepting the ruble, over all the train lines and down to the entrance of the Russian hive.

He spoke to security and another man in uniform took the baton from Viktor and told me to follow him.

'You're not coming?' I asked him.

'No. I did my job,' and he sauntered off to whatever he wanted to do, as I was scanned through into a warren of uniforms, desks and flimsy grey partitions. All men, I thought, until I thought I heard the shriek of Marina and I hurried closer to my guide. We existed in different orbits now, but best to avoid a collision.

Boris was in a floor full of glass offices so packed with filing cabinets that they formed their own walled enclosures. He was with another man I didn't recognise. I was ushered in. 'Sit there,' he said, and I sat in the corner on a chair by some filing cabinets. He started to talk to his companion again then stopped. He stood up and opened the door.

'Stand up,' he said to me, and he picked up my chair, carried it out to the corridor directly outside the door, and placed it by the wall. 'Sit here. Don't move. I'll be quick.'

I put my bag down and sat, pretending to be unaware of the looks from either end of the corridor. I then picked up my handbag and rummaged in it for a while, pretending I was busy doing that. Someone passed, I felt the warm stagnant air move over me and I was aware of them looking down at me, curious, but I pretended I didn't care.

Thankfully Boris opened the door finally and his colleague left. 'Come in. Sit here.' He pulled the chair back in. 'Here, read this.' He was still preoccupied with something. I looked through the notes. There were a lot of changes. 'I need to finish the main section.' He started tapping at a computer and then his mobile rang. He answered and swore and hung up.

'You must stay here. I have another meeting. This is very annoying.' He stood in the doorway. 'You must stay here. We must complete tonight.' He took a step out into the corridor, then stepped back in. 'No. Come with me.'

Like a dutiful dog I followed him as he walked along the narrow corridor, passing office after office then more open sections filled with rows of desks, loads of filing cabinets and computers and paper and maps. He stopped every now and again, tutting and sighing. Then he came to another office and stuck his head in. I stood behind and waited, tiredly looking around.

'Anna. You stay here. I'll be back at some point.'

He opened the door for me and I walked in. Grigory sat at a desk in front of shelving with rows of books and piles of paper. He smiled at me. The door swung shut behind me.

'Boris is keen that you don't run away. You want to sit down?'

He pointed at a soft chair behind me, which I took, thankful it wasn't another one of the stiff metal ones.

'Are you alright?' he asked me.

'I'm really tired. Is he going to be ages? I can't believe he's going to make me wait.'

'I don't know. I don't know what he's doing. He's very keen for you to stay here though.'

I rubbed my eyes and slumped back in the chair.

'Would you like some water?'

'Oh, yes please.' I was so tired, or so weary being in that hot, stuffy office and being made to wait, that I'd forgotten I was angry with him. He got up and went round his desk before kneeling down to open a little fridge.

'You all have your own fridge?'

He turned. '*I* have a fridge. I got it myself. I like to keep my food and drink in it. It's very handy.'

He passed me a bottle of water. Scottish water, obviously. 'With all your home cooked meals?' I asked.

'Of course. I print nice pictures on the front of them so I remember what they are.'

He returned to his desk and leant back, mirroring my pose. 'You asked me before about leaving. Have you tried to leave?'

'Sort of. I just sort of tested it to see if I could.'

'And you can't.'

'No. Well, I bet I could if I really wanted to.'

'Yes. I think if you put your mind to it you could.' He leant forward onto his desk, and looked at his fingers so I knew he was going to explain. 'There is a list, which different people can contribute to, and it contains names of people that we think, at the moment or in the event that circumstances become more... testing, in Scotland, that we think we should retain in this country.'

'To make use of them?'

'Yes. In a variety of ways. As leverage, that works very well, whether you agree with the principle or not, for their knowledge or for the work they do.'

'I'm on that list.'

'Yes.'

'Who put me on that list?'

'Surely you can guess that?'

I almost said it was him, then I went for Boris. He nodded.

'I'm sorry. Do you want to leave, or is it just that you can't? I thought you might like the work you are doing.'

'I just quite like the principle of being free, Grigory.'

'Yes, but how many of us are truly free?' He looked serious, 'I meant it. I could probably get you to Russia if you felt trapped here. You would have to come back.'

'I don't want a holiday in Russia.'

'Okay.'

His phone rang and held his finger up to ask me to wait, then he chatted for a few minutes. I picked up a piece of paper on the top of a pile, then put it back. Even with my level of Russian I could tell it was too boring to bother with. He finished with the call and hung up.

'You want to get some food?'

'I'm not allowed to leave the building, I believe, but yes I would.'

'I have some wonderful homemade cuisine in my special fridge, which I have cleverly put into sealed microwaveable containers to be eaten in the building.'

I chuckled. 'Oh do you? Alright, and do you have a clever little dining table you fold out here too?'

'No. I'll show you.'

He knelt down and picked out different packages. I came over and looked. 'Oh, lasagna.'

'We won't have that. I'd be embarrassed. Look, a Chinese meal with rice and a chilli. Okay?'

'Sure. Is this what you do every night?'

He flicked the fridge shut with back of his foot and looked at his sad meals. 'Unfortunately, recently, yes. Let's go.'

'Will you tell Boris?'

'He can call me.'

He directed me along a passage then round more offices and past more desks, then we were at a fire door. He pushed it open with his back and held it for me to pass. The air was cooler in the stairwell and I instantly felt more alert.

We walked up the steps for two more levels then went in another door. It was a common room of sorts, under the eaves, with some small tables and a microwave, toaster and sink. Cups lay neatly upturned at the side. A few newspapers lay scattered about. By the door a Russian sat eating soup and reading the back pages about Manchester United. The men nodded at each other.

I stood at the window and looked across at the rooftops and the chimney stacks. Grigory sorted dinner. The other chap washed up and left.

'Do you want half and half, or which one?'

'Can I not have the chilli?'

'Okay.'

The microwave pinged and he sorted the plates. I got us water from the dispenser. We sat down.

'This isn't, like, the canteen?'

'No. There is a nice, rowdy, noisy, stuffy place in the basement that I thought you would particularly hate.'

'Yes, think you got that right.' I started eating.

'It's okay?'

'Yeah. Yours okay?' I motioned we could swap if he wanted, but he shook his head.

We tucked in. I realised now I'd woken up that I didn't know what to talk about. I didn't want to get angry and talk about work with him, or politics, but I didn't want to get too personal. I don't know if he felt the same, but we ate in silence.

'Have you been west again?'

'No. I will soon though. I've been busy with work, but I'm the only one with the key in Scotland now so I have to check on it.'

'Your family has all gone?'

'Yeah. You know my parents live abroad, and my sister has moved back south with her husband. He's from Warrington anyway.'

He digested this and didn't pass comment. 'My brother's wedding is soon. I need to go back, but not for long, I have such a commitment here.'

'Well, it's good you can get back.'

'Yes. I'm best man. Make a speech.'

171

And then, I can't remember whether I heard it or felt it first, but it was like we were being swallowed up, and a crash, and a vacuum of power that went to suck us in and spit us out then BANG, and the door blew in, and dust exploded out, and the tables thought they were in a storm at sea and shunted about, and I fell off my chair and got knocked sideways by another, and then silence, and the air was thick with paint, or dust or ash and I didn't quite know what had happened.

I breathed, but I was breathing in plaster dust, which made me cough. Alarms were going off, I could hear shouting, my ears were ringing. I leant over to spit out and felt an arm touch me. 'Are you okay?' he asked.

Grigory's glasses were all dusted up and his whole body shabby, on all fours on the floor. 'Yeah,' I croaked.

We sat up, my head sore from where something had hit it. I thought I could smell burning and smoke now drifted up through the open door and wafted into the room, consuming us. Grigory crawled over to the stair well and looked down. I could hear more people shouting now, and sirens in the distance. 'Was that a bomb?' I asked, inspecting my dust-coated body. Nothing broken but a few grazes.

'I think so.' He stood up slowly. I saw him wince. He spat out some dust.

'Will there be more?'

'I hope not.' He moved slowly towards the window and started tugging at it. He turned and picked up a chair and crashed it against the frame, smashing the glass. I picked my way across the floor towards him.

'Who would set a bomb off?' My mind felt foggy.

He put the chair down on top of a mound of debris and looked at me. 'A lot of people. Your head is bleeding. Are you alright? We'll go out here.' He pointed out through the jagged fragments.

I staggered to the window and looked out. 'And down?'

'No, we can go along and then over. There must be a fire exit. Look, get up here.'

It was now raining outside, and the rain was blowing in the window, helping me focus. I concentrated on the window sill and lifted my foot up, letting Grigory take my weight and push me out. I tried to not look down and swung my leg round onto the gutter, wincing as I caught a finger on broken glass, before climbing up onto the slates and then the roof. There was a flat middle section that I scrambled onto, and sat down. He followed me. 'You alright? We have to move. We don't know how stable this is.'

I took a few deep breaths to steady my trembling legs then stood up.

'Yeah, I'm okay. Let's go.'

The wind was cold up at this height and it slapped the rain against us. Grigory wrapped his arms around me and we staggered to the edge, where, as he suggested, there was a ladder taking us onto the next building. As I turned to climb down I looked back and could see smoke rising out from the building we were leaving. 'Should we be helping people?'

'No,' Grigory said from the top of the ladder, 'we should get to safety first.'

The sirens were all around us now, almost drowning out the shouting and traffic and horns. We climbed down and traversed the next roof, climbing over a ridge and stepping through puddles before we found another ladder, making what seemed like an endless descent on shaking legs to the ground.

I was trembling with cold, with adrenaline, with shock: I don't know. Grigory put his arm around me again, more in support than comfort, and we staggered together along the lane and then round and down onto Queen Street. Someone shouted at us to move the other way but we walked on, in the dark and in the rain, through the grandeur of Charlotte Square and onto Dean Bridge.

I stopped as I saw the road home. 'I haven't got my keys!'

They were in my bag in Grigory's office. The wind swirled as I held my head in my hands. 'I don't have my wallet or my phone!'

Grigory grabbed my arm. 'Just come to mine. It will be alright.'

His was nearby: his new place. He cajoled me forward, pulled out his keys at the main door, and we climbed up more stairs until we came to his flat. I walked in and slowly lay down onto the floor, facing the ceiling, hands on my face, trying to stop the world spinning. I think Grigory just sat down, and we both paused to let sink in what had happened.

'How many people do you think were in there?' I asked over the ringing in my ears, more apparent now in the quiet lounge.

'I don't know. About thirty, maybe, still? There would be a handful of people at least downstairs. That man who we saw eating, he'd be there.'

'I wonder if Boris had come back.'

'I don't know.'

I lay there a little longer, then started shaking with the cold again. I realised my mouth was all gritty and dry. I got up.

'Can I get a drink?'

'Yes, of course.' He started to get up, but I'd already found glasses and was filling them. I passed him one, and in the light saw how his face was covered in the dust.

'Oh God, do I look like you?'

He looked at me. 'You have blood on your face.'

I took a swig then went through to the bathroom. I looked awful. Soaked from the rain with dust and blood coating my skin and hair. I leant over the sink and rinsed my face, then I looked down at my clothes. I was covered in dirt and dust from head to foot. A feeling of revulsion filled me. 'I'm having a shower,' I called, turning to switch it on, desperate to cleanse myself.

I tore off my tops with shaking hands, wrenched off

my shoes, grappled with my wet jeans and underwear then climbed in the shower. It dredged through my hair, warming me up and purifying me. I pressed my forehead against the wall and watched the filth go down the drain.

'Can I have a shower?' He was standing in the bathroom now, all disheveled and exhausted.

'Yes,' I said, and I didn't move.

I heard him get undressed, tugging off his own shoes and the clink of his belt on the floor. Then the shower door swung open and he climbed in. I stepped aside and leant with my back against the wall, giving him most of the water flow, closing my eyes against the spray. I felt the deflection of the water off his head and body, heard him wiping his face and hair. Then he stood and I leant away from the wall and stepped close to him.

I put my arms around his torso and he wrapped his arms around my back. We stood there, in the shower, resting against each other and comforting each other, knowing it had been so close to the end that night.

I tilted my head up and he leant down to kiss me, and we held that pose, him gently kissing me and me holding him. Then it was like something switched on in us, and we kissed properly, wanting each other. He kissed my neck, my chest, pushing me back against the wall, moving his hands around my body. Then he went lower, holding my waist, then he went inside me, taking me by surprise with his mouth. I held his hair and caressed his head until I came. He stood up, water pouring over his faced. He kissed me on the forehead and held me close. I felt his member press up against me and put it into my hand.

'Where would you like me to put this?' I asked.

He looked into my eyes, pushing wet hair off my face. 'In your mouth.'

So I did.

CHAPTER 23

Afterwards we held each other for a while, before sitting down, legs entwined on the shower floor, then Grigory told me I was his now.

'I don't belong to anyone,' I told him.

'Well, you're not running away from me now.'

I untangled myself and opened the shower door, drying myself off with a towel. Any scratches I'd received were no longer bleeding. Grigory followed shortly afterwards, pulling on a dressing gown and his glasses. 'Would you like something to wear?'

'Oh, yeah, thanks.' I picked up my pile of dirty clothes. 'I take it you have a washing machine?'

He nodded and we went through to the kitchen and stuck on a wash then dry load, before Grigory brought me through a neutral t-shirt for me to put on.

'I don't suppose you have a hair brush?'

'No, I'm sorry.'

'To follow that, I take it a hairdryer isn't available?'

He shook his head. 'I'll need to get supplies.'

'Well, we'll see.' He passed me another glass of water.

'Would you like something stronger?'

'No, but I am pretty hungry now. Is all your food in the office?' I felt a little normality return to my reasoning.

He started opening cupboard and fridge doors. 'I'm afraid I might only have toast to offer you. We can get a delivery?'

'No, toast is fine.'

We ate a little, he made a few phone calls, I guess confirming his live and uninjured status, then he went over and clicked on the TV and perched on the armrest. I stood behind him, watching a familiar road filled with water plumes, flashing lights and pissed-off Russians. Eight dead. So far.

'Have you heard of anyone you know being in there?'

'I know of someone.' He flicked it off. 'I don't want to watch that.'

'Do you not need to go and deal with this?'

He leant over to me, and pulled me close, the towel holding my hair up flopping onto the ground.

'I'm not working tonight.' I looked out through the rain to the lights from The Shore, the old port of Leith now dotted with towering flats. His hands were holding my waist, running up and down, feeling my torso. 'We are together now, you accept this?'

I looked him in the eyes, and took a deep breath, trying to gently pull myself away, but he held me close. 'Grigory, I can't see how this will work. I just can't. It would look so bad.'

I reached my hands round to my back and took hold of his fingers in my own, and tried to prise them off me while secretly enjoying the intimacy.

'Nobody will know.'

'That's not possible.' He pulled me close now, so I was off balance, half resting on his lap.

'Nobody will know.' He pulled me further so I fell against him, and I let myself sit on his thigh and lean against his chest. He kissed my cheek and I felt his emerging arousal. 'I promise.'

I didn't say anything but turned my head, studying his stubby eyebrows, then I pulled his glasses up to sit on the top of his head. We kissed again.

'You want to go to bed?' he asked.

'Since I already happen to be here, alright.'

'A little more enthusiasm would be appropriate.'

'Look, I'm British: you can't expect too much overt enthusiasm.'

He carried me through to the bedroom, which, like his

Moscow apartment, was very muted and grey, with white sheets. He leaned over me on the bed and stroked my face. I ran my fingers down his arm, and he leant in to kiss me.

He swung his leg over and sat up a little before leaning down to kiss me again.

'What's that?' I asked.

He lifted my hand away from his torso where I'd felt the scar tissue decorating his lower ribs. I hadn't noticed it in the shower.

'Nothing. An injury. Just ignore it.'

He kissed me again. He had a tattoo I had noticed in the shower, sitting below his collar bone down over his right chest.

'What's this?' I asked, tracing the dark lines with my free hand. He took hold of that hand and placed it over my head to join my right.

'A memento,' he said.

'Mr Rankovic, are you a bit rough?'

'I can be,' and he smiled, and kissed my mouth to smother by laughing protestations, before releasing my hands and wrapping me in his arms. I couldn't deny myself. I loved him.

I woke about six and went through to check my clothes were dry. I gave them an extra blast of heat then had a drink and borrowed a toothbrush before tugging on the slightly damp denim.

'Anna?' There was a tone of urgency in it. I stepped into the doorway. Grigory sat up in bed, his hand pulling back from where he'd just placed his glasses. 'Where are you going so early?'

'I've got to go.' I said, 'Friends of my parents have a spare key to my flat, and they've got work so I don't know when they leave.' He nodded and rotated himself out of bed. 'You don't need to get up,' I added.

'I'll come with you.'

'You can't come. People will see!'

He sat, rubbing his face, his glasses popping up and down under his hands. 'Anna, what are you going to tell people about where you stayed? You will likely get your bag back, with your keys, so it will be known you didn't have them.'

'Well, I won't say I stayed here.'

'Of course you stayed here. Well, not here...' he said, sweeping his hand over the bed, 'or maybe you slept here, and I slept through there, I don't know. But you had to sleep somewhere. And so, I slept on the floor, or wherever, and now I'm going with you to check you get into your flat okay, because if you don't I'll have to see about getting you help. You have no phone. Of course I'm coming with you.' He stood up and saw me about to hurry him. 'I'll be quick.'

'Okay.' He started opening drawers. 'You know, I could go see if they're in, and then come back here if they're not.'

'I'm coming. Look, I'm ready.'

We walked back into town a little, then crossed west and made our way towards the bigger houses that edged into the West End. It was a nice morning, but I should have remembered that my coat was festering in a bombed out building and asked for the loan of another layer. Grigory didn't grumble when I made him wait outside the gate as I went up to ring the doorbell. Luckily Eric answered the door quickly, fully suited and booted, and handed over the keys after a fairly truthful explanation.

'You want to call your mum here?' he asked, his eyes wide. His wife, Jasmine, hovered with a gaping mouth, offering coffee and toast and clothing, but I assured her I had all that at home.

'So where did you stay last night, for goodness sakes? You could have stayed here. Anytime you have a problem: you know that.'

I thanked her, but told her it was fine: I stayed at a friend's place. Which was also sort of true. No, I didn't want a lift back: it was a lovely morning for a walk. I knew, also, they walked into town, so it would be an inconvenience. I promised them I would call if I had any more travails, and that I would also be calling my parents that morning.

Grigory paired up with me as I turned onto the road. 'Nice people.'

'Yes. Old university friends of Dad's.'

'So you're not all alone.'

I nudged him. 'Whatever.'

He accompanied me home, and hovered some more while I called Mum and told her I was fine but had been in the vicinity of a bomb, which she knew nothing about, yet, so I thought I should call to put any potential worried minds at rest.

'Okay darling, thanks. We're off golfing shortly so I'll speak to you soon.'

I hung up and Grigory came over to me, wrapping his arms around me.

'Okay, I'll see you soon,' he said, giving me a kiss on the forehead.

'Well, you know where I am.'

'Yes.' He left.

I showered, ate... the usual, and walked into work. Half way there I realised that Boris might be furious I hadn't picked up the proposal edits from him when I escaped the previous night, then I reasoned that Boris could well have returned to the building just as the bomb went off.

I entered the SBC with some trepidation, managed to get a temporary pass from Sam who entertained my excuse of being blown up with the same eye roll as he would if I'd just forgotten it, and walked up to the office. I saw Aleks stare at me from his desk and his lips move as I passed. Boris spun around and saw me.

'Hey! You're alive!' He jumped out of his glass den. He actually looked pleased, his arms held out almost as if he might hug me. I took a sidestep.

'You too, I see.'

'Yes, you don't look as happy to see me.'

I looked past him to Aleks sitting glowering at his desk. 'Obviously I'm delighted to see you're fine Boris,' I said.

'Where were you when it happened?' he leant against a desk and crossed his arms.

'Upstairs. Grigory wanted to eat dinner in that upper common room area.'

'Ah. Lucky. You'd be dead now, otherwise.'

'Yeah. By the way, I don't have anything. My bag is still in the building. So I don't have my notes or phone or anything.'

'That is stupid. You should always keep your essential documentations with you at all times.'

'Thanks, Boris.'

I went to my desk and switched on my computer, looking out the window and reflecting that it was like nothing had changed, but it all had. Viktor sat down in front, spinning his chair around, a smile across his face.

'Are you all right? I thought you might be dead.'

'Yeah. Although do you think Boris would believe me if I said I needed a holiday to recover from the shock?'

His incredulous expression told me the answer. 'A holiday?'

Just then Grigory walked passed me with a swift greeting, now fully dressed for work. He put his papers down on the desk two down and turned the computer on. I couldn't help but stare. Boris came out to say hello, and they had a brief chat. I tried to pretend I didn't notice him as I logged in, but it was kind of strange he was suddenly behind me. Maybe a bit creepy. Then I couldn't resist. I turned around. He was studying his phone and he lifted his eyes to meet mine.

'What are you doing here? Are you working here?'

'Yes, today. Some idiots blew up my office. Don't worry, I won't be bothering you for long. Aleks has kindly agreed to move into the news area while I wait for my new office to

181

be ready.'

He gave me a smile, knowing this would be music to my ears. I looked over towards Aleks, who was now standing over his desk assembling piles of paper to take away.

It was like I was being rewarded for my choice last night. I felt a grin spread across my face and I had to force myself to look at my computer screen. My smile faded as I saw the news updates about the explosion. Ten dead. No Scots.

'You'll be pleased about that,' I jumped at Viktor's intrusion and frowned at his meaning. He reached behind him to grab some paper off his desk. 'So now you are alive and in a happy mood, I think it's a good time to talk about our next recording trip.'

I took a deep breath and leant back in my chair. 'And when's our next recording trip, Viktor?'

'In a couple of weeks.' He tried to give me an encouraging smile.

I flopped my head onto my desk and tried to cover my ears with my hands. Viktor tapped me on the back of my head with his notes.

'Okay, we'll do a meeting after lunch then.'

As predicted it was a journey further into deepest darkest Russia, this time Siberia, and I noted that we weren't yet going the full hog to furthest away Vladivostok, so it was to be continued. Mammoths, ice fishing and some adventuring Scottish missionaries were on the menu. Not literacy this time, but a mixture of stories and flavours from the cold wastes. And we were going in March, so it would be cold.

'It's just you, me and Anton this time,' Viktor said, after he'd given me the details.

'Oh, have I passed a test?'

'Yes, you are a good girl now. And there's really no place to hide where we're going.'

I looked at the map. It didn't look too bad until I realised the small section of the country I was looking at was about four times the size of Britain. 'Sounds great. Have you booked us somewhere to eat?'

'I'm bringing lots of chocolate this time, just in case.'

...

'Do you actually wholeheartedly believe the rhetoric?'

We were in Grigory's kitchen, with him behind the counter chopping some onion.

'Yes, mostly. The bomb could easily be interpreted as an act of war, we have an official base here...'

'...don't bait a bear...?' His soundbite.

'Yes.' He paused and gave me a smile. 'You don't bait a bear. We have to be strong on this.' Vehement anti-Russian, or anti-appeaser as he would put it, Willie Grierson, had recently formed the Scottish Democratic Party from the more strident splinters of the SNP and I knew Moscow were watching this with worry. 'The SDP looks like it could contest in the Scottish Election. We have to be clear we won't tolerate any disruption from them or others. Bombing a military base is an act of war.'

'But making Russian soldiers visible on every street corner is pretty good for your overall campaign regardless, isn't it?'

He sighed. 'We have to protect ourselves. And others – bombs don't just kill their intended targets.' A note of irritation was in his voice.

'Are you sure it wasn't a Russian bomb?'

'It wasn't a Russian bomb.' He gave me an assertive glare. Discussion over.

We sat in silence, as we tended to do when we knew there was some political spark between us that neither of us wanted to ignite.

'Do you know who Free Caledonia is?' Social media savvy, capable of infiltrating Russian Head Office, but nobody knew who they were. Some of us thought they might be a secret

Russian group masquerading as Scottish terrorists to increase fear in the population. Grigory didn't reveal any substance to that in his reaction.

'Not exactly, but we have our ideas.'

'But Willie Grierson isn't one of them?'

'I don't know for sure. He's not stupid, but it doesn't mean he doesn't condone them. Now, I was trying to impress you by cooking this, but I've forgotten what I'm supposed to do with this.' He held up an aubergine.

'Are you sure that's for the recipe?' I said with a cheeky grin.

He looked at it. 'I hope so – it's quite large at one end, and uncomfortably spiky at the other. Ah, yes,' he put down the aubergine and held up a finger, 'that reminds me.' He crossed the room to his bedroom and returned holding something, then put the keys in front of me.

I just looked at them.

'That doesn't look like anything like an aubergine.'

'That's correct. You can't open a locked door with an aubergine. Now you can let yourself in, as agreed, and when you manage to find your spare pair that should be hanging up in the cupboard that you can't seem to locate, you can give them to me.'

I'd tried to keep it fairly low key, trying to see him only one night a week, making excuses of work and training, but within weeks we were at each other's most nights. In for a penny...

'Right. I'll get them for you. Although, of course, there's no need in the short term, unless you're planning on squatting by my warm radiators, in my warm kitchen, enjoying some piping hot tea, while I freeze my ass off in Siberia.'

He gave himself a wry smile as he considered something. Then he looked at me. 'I think you might finally learn what that really means.'

CHAPTER 24

We flew to Moscow then hopped on a plane to Irkutsk, the capital of Siberia. It was March now, the crocuses and daffodils decorating the parks of Edinburgh, but in this ice dominion it was winter. The air slapped the inside of my nostrils as we exited the plane, and I prepared myself for the days ahead. I was looking forward to a little time to reflect on my relationship with Grigory away from the intense Scottish scene, and this environment would give me plenty of travel time to think.

The plan was missionaries, mammoths and monologues, as Anton espoused the Siberian ways of chilling out, both physically and mentally. Sitting just north of Irkutsk is the world's largest freshwater lake, putting 'my' Loch Ness to shame, so I was told, and we were to tour round the great water with two deviations to pick over some mammoth bones and then explore the lives of some people who held the rather fanciful notion they could convert the Buddhists to Christianity.

We spent the night in Irkutsk, Viktor scoring highly for his choice of hotel this time, and set out in a jeep with our driver, Max, for the lake and to meet our fisherman Sergey.

This trip had a slightly different feel to it. Maybe I'd resigned myself to being ordered about on these things. Maybe I'd been exposed to too much of Russia to not feel intrigued. Maybe Viktor and I were now friends. I felt it was going to be fun. I won't detail the miles after miles we covered, the endless snow and limitless flat earth, but there a few episodes of note.

Max drove easily in road conditions that would easily grind Scotland to a halt, and it took a few hours to the edge of Lake Baikal, with me insisting on Anton stopping and giving a little spiel at the sight of the scored ice and little tents. Several hours more we met up with Sergey, who I knew within minutes would be a useful man to know if you wanted to survive the apocalypse. He'd been in the army, he'd worked as an engineer, and now he lived a self-sufficient life in one of the toughest environments on Earth.

The cold chipped away at any gap in my clothing, tiny ice picks freeze-drying exposed skin.

'Do you get used to the cold?' I asked in Russian.

'This isn't cold,' he replied, patting me on the head.

We hunched over a hole in the ice on the lake, in a tent that took the edge off the relentless wind, but remained far below freezing. A bottle was handed out. I shook my head.

'It helps with the cold,' and he passed it to me. I took a little swig. I wasn't sure if it helped, or whether the astringent sting that preceded the glow in my throat distracted me temporarily.

We sat by his little hole waiting for his line to tug and to pull out another slender silver omul. He would dispatch it then toss it into a bucket. He spoke of lost family, of the passing of seasons, of endurance. Finally, as my peripheries ached with cold, we emerged. Other jeeps lay scattered across the vast ice, looking like a large scale version of the stones school children might throw across a frozen pond. People ate at tables set up on the ice. People stood drinking on the ice. I tried not to think of the fathoms below us. We followed in the jeep afterwards to his timber-built house, me with teeth chattering in the back, Max seeming a little too relaxed and red eyed for my liking. He drove off to continue his celebrations, and we toured the plot, the garden lined in one side by a long greenhouse, a homemade well and a little timber building in the corner of the plot that I assumed was a shed, and another which was the outhouse.

He showed us where he smoked the fish, where he grew his vegetables in the short season available, where he drew water from the well he dug out. And then he showed us the little hut, which turned out to be a bathhouse. Anton and Viktor were invited to join him later. I, discretely, was not. After sampling some of the smoked fish, he invited Anton and Viktor into his smoky man cave and I sat by the fire inside, enjoying the peace and offered tea.

They returned and he dished out some tasty fish broth and we chatted without mics. He was a lovely, quiet, guy, whose face told stories of journeys, and education through tough life experience. I asked him why he chose here.

'Because there is always the lake. There's always water and there's always fish.' I was helping tidy away plates in the kitchen alcove as he pulled out another vodka bottle. 'But I don't always stay here. I have another place.'

'In Siberia?'

'No.' He reached over and pulled out my map, the edges frayed from over use, folding it out to the fresh sheets. His fingers traced over the creases, until he pointed out the spot, further north from St Petersburg, but sitting more in line with Moscow.

'By another lake.' Nero, it said. It made me think of the comforting high street at home.

'Yes. Where meat is to be fished. There is a convent there, if you are ever inspired by Russia to take the vows.' He gave me a smile, and a glass for the drink. 'It was my grandfather's dacha. Further on from the convent town, where there is peace. A good place to reflect on life.'

He pointed at a photo on the wall, him flanked by two elderly people, a blue house with a little red shed in the corner. Viktor stood to the right of the photo, by the arch, and took some of the glasses. I felt a little superfluous at times. When a recording is going well between your presenter and subject, the trick is to make yourself seem obscure to let the stories flow. At times I felt invisible. But it was nice seeing this amazing landscape, being told stories and just letting it all seep in.

We all sat around the vodka, the men swapping stories of Scotland and adventures in Russia.

'You will come again?' Sergey instructed me, as he extolled the beauty of the epic woods of the Taiga.

'Yes,' I declared, having warmed to this man, my head starting to swim with the drink, 'but in summer, when it's warm.'

'But then there are mosquitos,' Anton said, then with a gesture of his head towards me, he told Sergey how the Scots all complain about the midges. 'Midges, the midges!' He squeaked, mocking my compatriots. Viktor, too loosened by vodka, joined in, explaining to Sergey about this baby mosquito. Sergey laughed and looked at me with pity. Me and my tiny little temperate country; what did I know?

We travelled north the next day, having enjoyed a patchy night's sleep on the sofa as the men snored on the floor. Anton's job was to explain the defrosted Russian soul as he journeyed through the spa towns that lay to the north. Max had turned up an hour after we'd stated, but he didn't apologise and Viktor shook his head at me as I went to ask him what the holdup had been.

'Haven't we a schedule?' I asked him under my breath.

'Anna, we're in Russia,' is all he said. Out here, in the wilderness, and without Grigory I suspected, Viktor was taking on a man-of-the-wood persona.

We bounced over potholes and made our way north.

'I have a story for you!' Max shouted, a little loudly for sobriety, towards me in the back.

'Oh really?' I replied, without expectation.

'Yes. A new Old Believer settlement, up here. Very funny.

Silly people, heads full of clouds.'

I waited for the story, but that was it. I looked at Anton. 'Like the lady in the Taiga?'

He shrugged. 'I guess so.' He leant forward and gathered some more information. I found Max difficult to understand. We lurched over the edge of the road. I wished for a safe resolution to the trip. Anton leant back.

'Not New Believers. A sort of cult, a Christian cult, with that false Christ we talked about who lives in the South. But Max says, which might be good, that there are Americans. If you're interested.'

I knew of the Old Believers, communities who had refused reforms in the Orthodox Church centuries earlier, and who had retreated into various far-flung areas to avoid communist persecutions. I knew of the family who had remained without communication with the outside world for decades before being found in the Taiga by geologists. I knew there was a former traffic policeman who had declared himself the son of God, forming another community who were building their own towns out of worship for him. With the amount of space there was in Russia, I guessed there was plenty of room for all sorts. So what was this?

Max had heard the American couple were staying nearby on a temporary visit to secure some food. Anton had a date with some spa treatments of the masculine sort, so we separated. He was a pro at the recording now, and I was starting to think I was hindering the honest talk amongst these Siberian men.

Greg and Rhona, wrapped in white coats that looked like dressing gowns, and wearing rather muddy boots, were earnestly listening to their hostess when we arrived. They had wondrous expressions, as if they had just had lifelong cataracts removed. They were delighted to see us. Delighted with the day. Delighted to have a new friendship. Delighted with their fish. Only a little less delighted that their car was broken.

'But the Lord will be sending us on a new journey, today we think.'

'We could take you back,' I piped in.

Their eyes opened even wider. 'Would you?' breathed Greg.

'Yeah, no problem. Would your friends mind us coming and seeing your new home?'

'You would be our honoured guests,' Rhona said, clasping my hand in both of hers.

We clambered in the jeep. The journey was three hours, a mere stone's throw by current standards.

'Would you mind if I did a little recording? I'm a radio feature maker, like on NPR.'

The first flash I'd seen of hesitation swept across Rhona's face. 'Oh, I don't know.' Her brow furrowed. She was trying really hard to think about this.

'Sure, why not?' said Greg, shrugging. 'If that's their mission. Is that your reason for being here?' I nodded emphatically, sensing where this was going. 'Well,' he said, turning to his girlfriend, 'if that's their reason for being here, and they met us, and offered to help us when we needed help, doesn't that mean that God has sent them to record us?'

It convinced Rhona. I could sense Viktor's stiff neck, as he kept his eyes on the road and his mouth shut.

We arrived, and it was indeed radio heaven. Rhona and Greg proudly showed us their new village, from the timber living areas, to the communal sites where they ate and prayed together linked together by paths cleared of snow. The new church, beautifully hand-crafted with intricate carvings throughout the wooden design, was described in detail by another worshipper, whose English was impeccable. We were invited to dinner, to stay the night, to experience the beauty of a life surrendered to nature and the church. We jumped at the chance, although Max stood by the jeep with his arms crossed, then roared away to find somewhere else to stay that served vodka.

I cannot fault their hospitality. Rhona and Greg were proud to show us the life they'd chosen to lead, leaving behind Michigan and a disastrous trip around Europe where they were less enlightened by foreign lands and more disgusted by their own consumption of other cultures.

'We realised we were missing serving our own soul, we were feeding off the creation of others.' On a theoretical level it made sense. You could hear they were convinced. On a practical level it seemed completely barmy. To travel to one of the most obscure places on earth to build something for yourself.

'Is there not enough space in America?' I asked them.

'We found it here,' Rhona said, placing an arm around Greg and smiling at me. He nodded, curtly. I was starting to realise who drove this relationship.

Viktor started giving me goggle eyes. I stopped recording and went over to him.

'I have no reception. I should check in every day.'

'So?'

'We have changed schedule.'

'So?'

'I have to confirm that we are on track.'

'So what? Boris will salivate over this.'

He didn't seem convinced, his uneasy connection to the hierarchy sweeping away his relaxed manner of the past few days.

We stayed two nights with the Americans, sleeping on the floor on a rug in front of a stove in our own sleeping bags. It was enough.

The final morning something had changed. Rhona had said she wanted to go on a pilgrimage of sorts. A private one. Greg seemed annoyed at her choice, holding her arms and remonstrating in the doorway.

'We're supposed to be here together,' he murmured at her.

'You know where my place is,' she said, pulling her arm away and walking out into the cold.

His shoulders slumped and he stared at the floor.

'Are you alright, Greg?' I asked from my place sitting up in my bag. Viktor slept at my feet.

'Yeah. No.' His eyes slowly roamed over the timber frames and he sighed.

'I was going to ask you a few more questions, would you rather I didn't?' I had the recorder on. I'd delete it if he said no.

'No. Shoot. I don't care.' He ran his hand through his uneven tufts of hair. He'd told me Rhona had cut it. He sat down on the bed they'd offered us last night.

'Can you tell me what you think the future holds for you here?'

He smiled, and flicked something off his knee.

'You know. It was Rhona.' He looked at me. 'I, like, believe in God and all. You know, I'd go to church with my parents back home. But this, this is crazy.' He threw an arm out towards the groupings of small houses that existed beyond the wooden door. 'I, I don't want to live here. Like, who in their right mind would want to live here? When you could live in, in, America? Or anywhere?'

'So why are you here, Greg?'

He rubbed his neck, then wrapped his arms around it before sitting up. Viktor's eyes were now open, but he stayed still.

'Well, obviously. It's Rhona. I love her. Well, I loved her. She's always been passionate about stuff, which I liked. But this is nuts.'

'What are you going to do?'

He stood up, walked over to the door and pushed it ajar. 'I don't know. Stay, maybe, for a while. For the summer. But no way am I living here.'

He looked at me. 'Do you have any idea how cold it gets? And they have no TV.'

....

We left later that day. Greg was emotionally exhausted, his conversation with me apparently was some epiphany to himself that he had to deal with. He'd gone further, telling us how he suffered bronchitis that summer and the lack of medical care that was available; he showed us the failed latrines which he'd dug, which then flooded, then iced over in a mushy clump of stinking refuse, and he pointed out the hypocrites he felt who lived among the community, one of whom, he was sure, was accompanying the love of his life on her sudden retreat, peppering the journey with gifts of a more intimate nature than he would like.

He refused our offers of a lift to a bigger civilisation: he said he had to speak to Rhona 'when she decided to turn up'. We had a few hours of wandering and catching some atmosphere until Max decided to make an appearance, then we picked up Anton and journeyed on, and northwards, to embark on our mammoth hunt.

We'd met our experts and talked of the bones and lives of the mammoths they pick out of the ice each year, then returned south to drive back round the bottom of the huge lake, before spending another night together, bantering about the Americans on their Siberian pilgrimage and Viktor teasing me about my inability to cope with the cold, before heading north again up the east side of the lake.

We got out, legs forced to unravel from the jeep, to a place that wouldn't look out of place in a Western. A proper frontier town, which if it had tumbleweed rolling through it, could host the eeriest of Hollywood films.

We were here to record a piece in situ about the missionaries who came from Britain to tame the local Buddhist non-believers to the faith. One Scotswoman, Martha Cowie, a wife of a minister, spent twenty-two years translating the bible from Greek and Hebrew into Mongolian. How the locals must have viewed this lot I could only imagine. We stood at the obelisk erected for her, and wandered down to look at the ruins of the old Spassky Church, the sole remains of the village that flooded. I turned my head, at the massive Selenga River, at the distant lands that stretched out into Mongolia, and contemplated how a woman from my tiny country could journey across the unforgiving vast landscape to a place like this, over a century before, and not be swallowed up by the landscape.

We flew home a few days later. Our days journeying had been broken by stays in small hotels, with lingering dinners and funny stories, but I still stepped out into Edinburgh's clear night air exhausted. I'd started missing Grigory, and from the prospect of the enormous Russian world, my romantic drama in Edinburgh seemed such a tiny issue. I finally felt comfortable with it. I looked forward to seeing him again.

CHAPTER 25

I walked into work the next day. Outside my office building a police officer was facing several Russian soldiers who were standing by a jeep.

'You'll have to move that, Sir.'

His colleague stood by the police car reporting into the radio. The soldiers laughed, and shook their heads, pretending to not understand.

'Sir, there is no parking here. No parking at all. You'll have to move.'

One solder leant against the bonnet, smoking and ignoring the officer. The other laughed again and simply said, 'No.'

I walked up to my floor and passed the glass where Boris sat inside on the phone. He'd been sent a very rough version of everything. The programmes on the whole I was happy with, but the Siberian story, now I was back, seemed inappropriate. I'd taken advantage of them, joining the natives in laughing at their hopelessness in Siberia, and it felt wrong.

I dumped my bag, pressed the switch for my computer and walked straight back downstairs to the coffee room. Aleks, returned to his old desk, eyeballed me from his position of power.

Isobel, a news reporter, was in there stirring a tea bag.

'Hello stranger; you been away again?'

I told her about the recording trip. 'Feels like I've been on another planet, actually. But nothing changes when you come back.'

'Oh, I don't know about that. Not with Willie Grierson's death.'

'Death?'

Grigory walked in. 'Hello,' he said to me. My mind paralysed with the shock of what I heard, the biggest critic of Russian policy dead as we approached the next election, I just looked at him. We hadn't been in touch since I'd left. 'We thought you'd disappeared into the wilds of Siberia,' he said with a smile.

'Grierson's dead?'

'Yes,' he said, his eyes following Isobel as she walked out with her tea, 'heart attack. We think. Are you alright? Did you enjoy yourself?'

'Who says it was a heart attack?'

'A doctor. He's having an autopsy.'

'Well, that's convenient.'

He cocked his head to the side and narrowed his eyes, trying to penetrate my frosty facade. 'No.'

I brushed past him, all longing to see him evaporated, and walked back up to my desk. Outside a crowd had gathered to watch as three police cars with several officers now remonstrated with the Russians at the jeep. They were still laughing at them.

Boris tapped at the glass.

We made up, of course, after I calmed down and took stock. Maybe it was true. Maybe it was a natural death. I had to believe him, even if the country didn't. Despite the arrival of spring the mood was frosty. The Siberian cold had seeped into our spirit. The country was bracing itself against the inevitable Russian onslaught. People hurried past me, racing home when before they would have taken it easy, chatting to friends on the phone. Late night shops that I passed after another lengthy day were empty, few people stayed on for a drink after work. They released last minute tickets for the Six Nations rugby after French fans didn't want to travel to Edinburgh. I sang Oh Flower of Scotland with tears in my eyes, my country being able to defend their try line but not their land. There were Russians in the stands, drunk, leery and inappropriate. France scored and they celebrated, falling out on the stairs, tumbling down and causing a woman to fall in the people avalanche. Finally, someone, portly, aged, bearded and Barboured, stood up and roared for them to leave. There was posturing, the remaining Russians not on their arses standing on the upper steps and leaning over to try to grab and abuse, then a swelling in the crowd. Scots, French and security, without any coordination but with one mind, manhandled and carried them out, arms and legs held aloft.

The original protester, not having moved from his original position where he'd stoically eye balled the Russians as they'd jeered and yelled at him, looked around at the stand, taking a measure of us.

'I don't know about you!' he cried, his voice sounding like it might have addressed the haggis to large halls, 'but I've had enough of their shite!' There were cheers and then a rush of applause.

He looked like he was about to say more, then he realised there was a match going on. He steadied himself, and turned to watch the scrum amid a swelling of agreement in the crowd.

I realised then that we'd finally reached a tipping point. The squatters had to be evicted, and I wasn't the only one resenting their presence. We were still occupied, really, but that small show of solidarity gave me reassurance that there was still the old Scottish pride there. I looked back and to my right, Grigory standing watching the scene impassively, the tickets a present from him, intentionally apart. He caught my eye and studied my expression. I wanted to see if he understood the mood, then I wanted to check he wasn't taking note of who was there. He just seemed to be watching. He gave me a wink. I switched my attention back to the match. We won.

...

'Even if the SDP only win six seats or so, it will be enough for the Tories to form a government,' I said. It was election day. Everything was up for grabs. Like a giant dinosaur, the SNP infrastructure couldn't lumber about carrying all that weight. Fissures had driven the party into factions. The formation of the SDP had caused a bleed of its core support.

'The Tories would never form a coalition with terrorists.' He shovelled salad in his mouth, his eyes flicking from me toward the rolling news. The ballots were about to close.

'The SDP aren't terrorists.'

'The IRA aren't terrorists.'

'Don't be a prick,' I said, 'it's hardly the same. Anyway, you said yourself that they aren't a terrorist group.'

'Willie Grierson wasn't a terrorist. I think he was even a romantic.' He nodded. 'Which is why we would never have assassinated him. Better the devil you know, as you like to say.'

'Anyway, you're in the shit, no matter what the final numbers are. SNP are out.'

'You should be careful what you wish for.'

'If the only way for this to end is to finally fight it, then we have to get it over and done with. Face the fire and burst through it. Don't wait around to be burned alive.'

'The SDP are not the answer. You shouldn't vote for them.'

'How do you know I voted for them?'

'You just admitted it.' He tilted his wine glass at me.

'No, I didn't.'

He pulled a face. The ticker line stated that the ballots were shut.

'Are you staying up?' he asked.

'No. Are you?' He nodded. 'What's the point? Better put your alarm on for 3am or some time and watch it then when the votes are counted.'

'No, I might stay up. Just keep an eye on things.'

I picked up my plate and loaded it into the dishwasher in the kitchen I now knew so well. I didn't know if we were fools, believing no one saw me slipping into Grigory's stairwell or him letting himself in my door and hadn't connected that we were together. After the last Russian trip Grigory had turned up at my door when it was dark, ringing the bell after I'd just been on the phone with my parents. I opened it and he came in, closing the door behind him and pressing his hand against my cheek which I slumped against, pulling me to his chest and holding me.

'Are you alright?'

I didn't say anything, just leant against him, breathing in his smell of cologne, cleanliness and stale smoke. 'I'm so tired of this.' He kissed my head and we'd pulled apart. I looked at him, anticipating more from him. 'I hate seeing you at work. I find it difficult.'

He nodded. 'We didn't kill Willie Grierson.'

'Maybe nobody told you.'

'Maybe.'

And we'd sat down and I'd told him about the trip and he told me any news that I'd missed. And it was again, like we were commentators hired by opposite sides, watching this drama unfold, pretending we weren't part of it too.

He nudged me awake, leaning in and saying gently. 'SDP twenty seats.' I opened my eyes, saw him propped up on the bed, kneeling on the floor, looking tired. 6am.

'Have you stayed up?'

'Mostly. I slept on the sofa here and there.'

'So what's that mean?' He looked confused. Too tired for mental connections. 'Coalition?'

He smiled at his admission. 'Tories fifty two.'

'Have they agreed?'

He looked like he'd been beaten into submission. He was

exhausted. 'I think so, I don't know. It looks like they had pre-election talks that we didn't know about.'

'Ah ha!' I sat up. I prodded him in the chest. 'I was right! You were wrong! I voted Tory so you were wrong twice!'

He grabbed my finger, stopping my prodding, pushing it back against the bed while he stood and rolled over me, ending up beside me. 'I am so tired. I should have set my alarm for the early morning. I wish someone had told me to do that.'

'Oh dear. You'd better have some coffee. Get ready to pack your bags, dude. You guys are outta here!'

He pressed his hands against his face 'Oh Anna. If it's cheered you up, I'm happy.'

'Shall we have a 'cheerio to Moscow' party in the office?'

He looked at me. 'Do you want me to go?'

'No, but you should. Then you could come back. On a visa. Work in something valuable. Like renewables. Sell Scottish renewable technology to the Russians. That would challenge you.' I leant over and plopped my head on his chest. He wrapped his arm around me. My head rose as he took a deep breath, and then sunk back down again. I lifted myself off, studying his face. 'Are you worried?'

He paused before answering. 'A little. We've stayed too long. You're right. I wanted to withdraw everyone from outside the bases. We're too conspicuous.'

I rolled to rest chest-to-chest with him. 'But some people wanted to stay to dominate the country?'

He didn't quite nod, but I knew him well enough that it was an admission nonetheless. He stroked my head. 'Maybe with a little more forceful resistance my colleagues might realise we've done enough.'

I didn't think that was likely. I don't think Grigory did either.

I passed through reception a day later.

'They've been given three weeks to get out.' Sam said, staring at the lit TV screen that dominated the wall all day every day.

'Who?' I said, pausing by the stairwell.

'The red squirrel. Who do you think?' He jerked his chin towards the ceiling, then hissed, 'the Russians!'

I walked in and stared at the screen. Our new First Minister, Margaret McClaren, stood at a podium giving her terms. The Orkney and Rosyth bases were contracts the government were willing to renegotiate, but all other Russian military and non-military personnel off base were instructed to leave the country within 21 days. Beyond that time the Scottish Government were no longer engaging with the Russians on any matters outwith the bases: the Scottish Army would be ordered to assist in their removal, and we would be reaching out to all international offers of assistance to return Scotland to a fully autonomous state.

Sam gave a curt snort of agreement. 'About time.'

I felt a tingling through my body as I realised the tipping point had been reached. About time, indeed.

CHAPTER 26

The Russians didn't show any signs of going. Grigory worked late. I'd hear his key in the lock and the thud of his shoes being kicked off. He'd appear in the sitting room, the kitchen or the bedroom; wherever I'd settled down, and give me a tired smile and a kiss. Sometimes he'd hold me and ask me why I didn't want to move to Moscow with him, although he knew the answers by heart. Sometimes he'd not want to talk, would instead eat the warmed-up dinner I'd made in silence in front of the TV. Sometimes he'd just crawl into bed beside me and, without a word, fall asleep.

We were sliding into war. Jennifer told me to move back downstairs. I did. Boris stood by my desk demanding I move back up. I left, walking past sandbags piled up by the Balmoral Hotel and queues of men outside the council offices offering to conscript. Grigory called me, telling me I should go back into the office.

'I don't know who I'm working for any more,' I replied. 'Can't I stay away until they sort it out?'

'You need to go back.'

'Will anyone even notice if I'm not there?'

'How do I know about it?'

I made my way back in, stopping to let a car packed full of shopping bags turn in the road. I paused, and texted Grigory. Should I be going food shopping?

No need.

Then.

Actually, yes. Do that.

I returned home, jumped in the car, and carried out a haphazard shop of tinned food, dried pasta, yeast, flours...

And then threw a case of wine in the trolley. I bought frozen croissants, sun dried tomatoes... I googled what was rationed in the war, and then decided just to buy items I liked. Surely the government would take care of the rest? I queued behind five other trolleys stacked high and queued to get out the car park, which was filling rapidly. By that night some shops were bare. Petrol stations were empty once again. I was in work, watching Jennifer argue with the patience of a saint with Boris and Aleks about the new relationship they were to have with SBC producers. There was no official collaboration now. Marc had been given unpaid leave on medical grounds. Jennifer was in charge.

With Margaret McClaren holding no punches in Holyrood and Jennifer showing the first SBC balls I'd seen since the Rockall occupation, I wondered if women had been in charge from the off whether we'd be in this mess at all.

'Stay there,' spat Aleks at me as he marched after Jennifer.

'No Anna, of course you can go home now,' said my official editor.

'Just wait,' ordered Boris as he followed.

'I actually don't have any work to do,' I called after them, then threw myself back in my swivel chair and spun it around. Julian scratched his head. We sat beside each other now, him in Andrew's old seat.

'Are you going to leave?'

I pivoted on my foot, rocking the chair back and forward. 'It's probably best not to.'

He stretched out, his neck clicking.

'Want to order pizza?'

So the Russians didn't leave and we didn't fight, and I thought this phoney war would last forever. Then one morning in June, I woke to incredible news. As the sun rose early, a new border was drawn. Grigory hadn't returned that night, so I sat alone with my toast and saw the line sketched out – rising up through Melrose, cutting across Motherwell, curving around Glasgow, up and around Loch Lomond and across to the Atlantic. A free Scotland. Disputed were patches of the Highlands, Stirling and Perth, where the authorities couldn't guarantee a Russian-free zone. I was officially in occupied territory. The army had seized areas they knew they could control. The front line had been mapped out.

I went to text Grigory but the mobile network was down. I decided to call from my landline, but it was busy. Then it rang of its own accord – it was Viktor. I was to come to work.

'Is Jennifer there?'

'Yes,' he replied, 'everyone is here.

We stood in the news room, on and around the sofa which would feature on TV interviews, and at the desks which were usually hidden from view. Boris, and his superior, the bird-loving Mikhail, addressed us.

'You will have seen or heard that elements in your country have declared war on us. This has forced our hand. Of course until now we have indulged the accusations of improper behaviour on our part. We have tolerated the Scottish Government's refusal to comply with agreements freely made. We have been very kind.

'Now we are in charge and you work for us. You do not trade information with those in the rebel areas of the country. I hope that is clear. Now, I want to meet with the news team. The rest of you go back to your desks and await instruction.'

He swivelled on his heels and pointed at some people and another group was formed. I slid off the sofa and followed the line through to my office.

Boris reallocated our desks. The empty seats were to be taken up – Russian media workers were to fill them. I was back upstairs, with the rest of my feature radio buddies and some online, given my old desk. I lugged up a few books which I piled high to remind me to keep ignoring them and turned to face Andrew.

'Hello!' His was an unexpected face.

'Hello. I'm joining you here.'

'Weren't you in...' Australia? I paused because I wasn't sure who knew what or whether they should. I was so pleased to see him.

'Sydney. Visa ran out, so they turfed me out too. Thought it best to come in rather than be caught not being in. Rather peeved, to be honest. Give it another ten days with this stramash and I could have claimed political asylum.'

'In Australia?'

He sighed. 'I know. Should have gone to Canada. Much more accommodating. Oh well, lifelong hacks like me thrive on being where the action is!' He grimaced, releasing his fake enthusiasm, and sprawled onto his seat, which I was pleased to see was in Viktor's old place in front of me. A pile of books, papers, tea bags and folders were dumped in the walkway beside him.

Viktor appeared, looking uncomfortable in his role of bossing people about, giving a lengthy glance to his old desk, and Andrew turned to study the action out of the window.

'Hey, is this yours?' He asked. Andrew rotated his seat. 'Yes, afraid so.'

'Are you planning on putting it on your desk?'

Andrew seemed to ponder the question, frowning with his choices. 'Not right now, no.' He gestured between his desk surface and the mess on the floor. 'If I put it up here I won't have any space to work in.'

'Hey Viktor,' I said. We'd been ordered not to leave the office. 'I'll be your best friend if you get me a latte.'

'I thought we were already best friends,' he said, a hint of a smile, back on steady ground.

'But we're not,' interjected Andrew, swivelling round. 'Be a good chap: two lattes. And a cake if they've got any decent ones on display.' He made a show of patting around his pockets. I had my wallet to hand.

'Get one for yourself, dude,' as I handed over a note. Viktor studied it then trotted off. I looked at Andrew, scratching something off the desk with a ruler. 'Are you going to clear that up?'

He paused and sat up, rotating a little to face me. 'Anna, let me advise you on a little secret that someone like me, whose been around for a while, can tell you. In the BBC if you want to leave your crap somewhere, the trick is just to leave it long enough that people stop noticing and give up asking you to clear it up. It then becomes an extension of your space.'

'Andrew, this isn't the BBC any more. This isn't even the SBC. This is Russianburgh now.'

He drew a little symbolic square around us with his finger. 'This bit can be the BBC can't it? Be just like old times.'

I laughed. I admired him for trying.

Viktor returned, with carrot cake that we all poked at with the tiny disposable forks, and sat on a pile of books while we gossiped in hushed voices. We didn't have any work to do. The news teams were frantic – gathering, reporting, censoring – but I don't think Boris quite knew what to do with us yet. Beverley came over at one point and attempted to ask Andrew a question about a programme but he brushed her away saying he'd yet to negotiate his role here.

'I think it will be the same,' insisted Viktor, missing the point.

Andrew waved his arm at him, 'Not how I understand it, Viktor. Beverley, we can chat when I have confirmation.'

He rolled his eyes as she walked away. 'Even military occupation doesn't get me a break in here. So Viktor, how long is this going to be the status quo?'

'This, eh, how we are today? Well...'

'Doesn't it depend on whether Mikhail and his cronies get the go-ahead for the war they want?' I asked.

Viktor looked surprised. 'Did Grigory tell you that?'

I flushed. 'No! Why would he tell me that?'

'He likes you. He tells you things. I know that.'

Andrew's eyes were swivelling from me to Viktor,

detecting discomfort. 'Which one's Grigory?'

'The other guy we went to St Petersburg with. Remember, we went on a bit of an adventure together?' Hopefully that would do.

'Yeah,' Viktor laughed now. Our travails there now all rosy glowed and joked about. 'I got us a little lost, but Anna found some berries so it was okay.'

'But Grigory doesn't work in here?' Andrew still wasn't quite satisfied.

'No,' I said, 'remember in the very beginning he was one of the ones who negotiated the whole arrangement of the collaborations with the Russians. He's a spokesperson too for them.' He was a lot more than that, I knew, but I wanted to move off from Grigory. Andrew was starting to remember who he was.

'Anna was a wildcard, but Grigory and I tamed her. Yes?' Viktor was relishing this.

'No,' I said.

'Anna wanted to do the Stupid Americans programme.'

Now we were moving away from Grigory and onto worse territory.

'What programme? Anna, have you turned on me?'

'No.' I shifted in my seat. I'd regretted the commune programme ever since the first edit when I realised quite how much of it played into Russian hands. 'There were a couple of slightly zany middle Americans who were finding themselves and religion in Siberia that I recorded with. It was good stuff. But, with hindsight...'

'Have you become a Russian propaganda machine?'

'Yeah!' laughed Viktor. I kicked him. He looked hurt, suddenly mournful.

'Sorry, Viktor. I do like you, but don't ever call me that.'

Andrew sat up a little and started rotating his chair away. 'Watch yourselves,' he said, 'Boris about.'

'You having a picnic?!' Boris's voice smacking us back into reality.

'No, I was almost working, actually.'

'Working? Everyone, Anna is actually working!'

'Well, I'm not now,' I said.

Boris didn't laugh. 'Come here, both of you, I have work for you.'

CHAPTER 27

On the surface not much changed with my day-to-day. I was sent recordings – Boris decided I was more useful assembling the programmes in the manner he liked than being the person who went out in Russia incommunicado gathering material, so I spent my days piecing together audio and churning out tiny programmes that were to subtly show how vibrant and cultured the mother nation was. I was busy.

There were chips on the surface though. Sanctions were escalated against Russia, so Moscow pillaged Scottish supplies, robbing us of little luxuries such as cheese, wines... gaps in the shelves that were never filled. There were splinters too. Stories of people being pulled out of work and home to be interviewed about their politics and whereabouts. An undercurrent that made you wary of your footing. Who you joked to. Whether you joked at all. Just keep your thoughts to yourself.

And the veneer had been completely stripped off. Roads blocked off to civilians to ensure rapid military coverage through town if needed. Sandbags around strategic buildings. Checkpoints everywhere, bridges a favourite. Dean Bridge, George IV bridge... I walked to work passing three elevated scaffold towers with machine guns on top. We were all being watched.

Usually the roads were open, the only inconvenience was a slight narrowing which caused congestion when it was busy. Sometimes there were scuffles, and the road would be immediately shut. One evening I got hemmed in at the end of Dean Bridge, where the New Town ended and the city suburbs began, all elevated thirty metres over the Water of Leith on a proud structure devised by Telford.

Some man, or group, I don't know, started it. All I could hear was muffled shouting, broken sentences and rough Russian. All I could see were shoulders and upturned collars. We were being compressed as a group and shoved back. Kettled.

'Oh, come on!' I shouted. I was almost home, and this was just posturing. With no guns fired in the city, tempers would flare. I started yelling at one of the soldiers in his own language, imploring as best I could. His eyes flicked towards me, then away.

Someone fell. A woman, who shrieked with discomfort and fright. People tried to create space around her. To help. But there was shoving at the front again. People shoving back in annoyance. People shouting. We became a mass of bodies all shoving and complaining, then a sizzle of fear trembled through us, a new terror of being trapped in a crowd after the recent spate of New Caledonia bomb attacks around checkpoints and gatherings of Russian soldiers. One woman near me started screaming that she needed out, her voice breaking into a screech and juddering my ear drum.

Suddenly an arm grabbed mine and hoisted me out, people knocked aside as I was yanked past. Vladimir's solid frame lifted me out.

'Come,' he said, and pulled me onto the pavement beyond a barrier. I bumbled into his uniform then snatched my hands back, not sure whether I felt more awkward touching him in any way, particularly in his uniform, or uncomfortable being seen to know him. He gave me a shove in the back. 'Go home.' I stumbled a step then turned back to him, about to thank him, but –

'You know; no one needs to be shoved about in there. It's ridiculous.'

'How's she got out?!' a man yelled, understandably.

'You want back in?' is all Vladimir said, his eyes cold, a

few people nearby staring.

'No.' I avoided looking at the masses and walked on, only glancing at the man pinned on the ground being handcuffed. The cause of the backlog.

I told Grigory about it that night, lying in bed after we'd been intimate. He lay on top of me, sweeping hair off my face, then rolled onto the side.

'You shouldn't question things like that.'

'You can't just walk on by.'

'Yes you can.'

I sat up. 'I very much doubt if our roles were reversed, you'd be keeping your mouth shut.'

'Yes I would.'

'No you wouldn't. You wouldn't.'

'Yes I would. Because I would know it would bring nothing but trouble.'

'So when's the bombing raid on Glasgow going to start?'

Grigory sighed and pulled on my arm to bring me closer. I lay on his stomach.

'No plans to bomb Glasgow. The independent state is more a problem for your government than for ours. When the renegade state agrees terms with Holyrood then we will back off.' He stroked my hair.

'That's not true. If it was true then things wouldn't have got this far.'

He didn't say anything. Something bothered me. I popped my head up and turned to see his face.

'Why did you say I shouldn't question things. I didn't tell you I'd questioned it.' I examined his features. Was it a fluke? No. 'Did Vladimir tell you?'

His hand lifted off my head and rubbed his own. 'He texted me.'

'Why did he text you? Does he know about us? Did you tell him?'

'No!' He gave me a tired, incredulous look. 'I know how to keep a secret, Anna. He probably texted me because he thought you were being stupid and felt I was better to tell you so. We are in a war-like situation, Anna. You don't go shouting at soldiers. He said you shouted at one of them in Russian. You need to contain yourself. Anna,' he sighed, 'you know if you are ever asked about us you mustn't lie.'

'Why would I be asked about you?'

'You might not be. But don't be in a situation where somebody needs the truth from you and you start spouting rubbish. You are a terrible liar and it would only get you into trouble.'

'Who says I'm a terrible liar? When have you ever seen me lie? Or, when do you think you have?' I found myself smiling at this. I couldn't recall ever lying to him. Apart from maybe reassuring him that I was biting my tongue in the office. I was still leaning on his torso. He ran a finger up my throat, over my jaw line and up to my cheekbones.

'Miss Aitken, I don't want to give you a complex, but you should be aware that you have the highest propensity to blush of any person I know. People who blush, can't lie.' I felt the heat rush after the trail of his finger, bursting red out onto my skin. Bastard.

It may well have been a problem for the Scottish Government, but the Russians sure took their protection of the rest of the country seriously. They were suspicious of all of us. Any one of us a potential informant, any one of us a car bomber. We had our usual bit of banter in the office, but it was generally in hushed tones, Andrew leaning back for a stretch, poking his head past my screen and making a pithy aside or a short anecdote that we would laugh about. Then Viktor's head would shoot up, he'd pivot at confirmation of a chat, and give us his anxious face. Sometimes we'd hear the rap of Boris's knuckles on the glass if the conversation got too joyful. It was all very serious. I edited programmes on the great state of our freshwater lochs, demonstrated by a diver who would pick and cook; a hillwalking series headed by a comedienne who hated walking; and a bizarre one following a group of soldiers who took it upon themselves to rid an estate of the grey squirrel in a weekend of shooting, in order to save the red. It was the classic case of feeding feel-good to the masses while news distorted the truth. The self-proclaimed 'free' Scotland was a hotbed of disorder, where mini fiefdoms were springing up and food shortages were occurring. This wasn't true, I was told, but the rest of Scotland had to be reassured they were in safe hands. Better Russian hands than the chaos of the terrorists.

Still, no bombs fell, and the only shots were across the new border, reminding each other they were still awake.

I found myself longing to be with Grigory, to be consoled that it was all smoke and mirrors, that the real action was happening in conversation around tables and not along the sight of rifles. He'd come home, usually I'd be first, cooking dinner in the kitchen, bottle of wine already open, and I'd ask him how his day was, and he'd tell me it was a tough one at the office and make some joke about Doris in marketing sending out a dodgy press release, and we'd kiss and I'd murmur about him having to get a promotion out of sales. I think we joked about it because the reality of the situation was so incredible it could be overwhelming. The implications of what could happen. How close we were to civil war. Whether it already was civil war.

Julian wasn't in the office one morning. Like the poor sods who were on business when the Berlin Wall went up, he'd been working in Aberdeen when the divide happened here, and had been 'persuaded' in some way to stay with us. I think they rented a place for him on the south of the city, and I think he was still living with his Mum in Govan, so maybe that was the deal. But he wasn't in that morning. Unusual. Julian was very disciplined and could sometimes work extraordinary hours.

Then he did come in, about 11am, looking ashen faced and exhausted. I went over to check he was okay, and to tell him to go home and sleep it off.

'I'm alright,' he said to his desk, reaching for his headphones.

'You don't look alright. Are you hung over?'

He smiled, almost to himself, as he watched the login screen appear. He typed in his password and finally looked up at me, then, embarrassed, looked away. 'I was questioned this morning. Early this morning.' Emphasis on 'early'.

'By who, the police? For what?'

'No.' He was almost whispering. 'By the FSB. Like they think I've been up to something for the other side.'

I scrunched my face up, thinking of what I wanted to say, then Boris ordered me into his office to talk radio.

I think some others were pulled in for questioning. Or some people started getting warnings about their behaviour. Whatever it was, our bizarre mash of Russian and SBC colleagues all started having an air of mistrust. Although we'd been vaguely careful about what we said around in and around our soundproofed rooms for a while, now we avoided saying anything at all. Sometimes conversations would just drop off mid-sentence by mutual agreement. People would nod at each other by the kettle. People started dropping names, as if by saying 'hi' instead of 'hi Isobel' I might be able to deny knowledge of something if any tapped audio came to be questioned.

Then they came for me.

CHAPTER 28

I'm not the best in the morning. Well, to be more accurate, I'm not the best if someone wakes me up from a glorious deep sleep and it's not someone I'm pleased to see. 5.30am and the doorbell goes. In my blurry state I thought maybe it was a fire, or maybe a drug addict offering to clean the stairs, but I heard the accent in the intercom and my heart started pounding.

I almost didn't let them in. I'd asked Julian why he'd opened the door to them, and he said that he didn't want to make a scene. And it's true. I didn't get the sense they were going to go away. I asked them what they wanted, and they said that it was important that I come in for questioning. The police wanted to speak to me. I asked them if they were the police. They said they were helping them. Then they said they would break down the door if I didn't open it. So I did.

They waited in the hallway while I threw on a layer of clothes. I walked out the house in a curious mixture of sleepy daze punctuated with acute fear. This wasn't serious, I kept telling myself. This isn't 1930s Berlin. This is just mild intimidation. I've done nothing wrong. They're just keeping me in check.

We sat at a small table in a stuffy room where the heating was too high. Two of them. Both with coffees, me without. Still tired. I'd been out there and made to wait, in this tiny storeroom-like place with no windows, for half an hour after the car journey, then they'd sauntered in, smelling of cigarettes and coffee. I watched them take their time to get settled. No recording device. Not that I could see.

'We know you are a member of New Caledonia.'

'I'm not.'

He raised a finger, holding me back. 'I haven't asked you a question. Please wait.' He looked at me. I looked back. I'd done nothing wrong. 'We know you are a member. We know, in fact, that you hate the Russian fraternity here and would do anything to undermine the collaboration we have with the Scottish Government. You have tried repeatedly to harm our efforts here. I want to know what you are planning on doing next.'

I waited. Still no question. I'd done nothing wrong.

'Who do you meet in New Caledonia?'

'No one. Not that I know of.' They both reacted to the caveat. I didn't want to be caught in a trap.

'You consort with Peter Gallagher.' Someone in my tri club. I barely knew him. He delivered some of those edits for me. Surely they wouldn't know that?

'I barely know that man. We might meet in a big bike gathering every so often. I don't know what he's involved in. I doubt he's involved in anything. I haven't spoken to him for months.'

'But you know him.'

I nodded. It wasn't a question. They both stared at me. I tried looking back in their pale blue eyes but my gaze gave way.

'You like to meet with people whose aim is to destroy your country. You meet with people who want to hurt your fellow countryman. That is treason. It's very serious.'

'No I don't.'

'From the moment we arrived here you have set about trying to undermine the diplomatic efforts our country and yours have been performing to reach an amicable agreement.'

'No I haven't.'

'You intentionally broadcast material which was insulting to the diplomatic relationship. You broadcast it against the wishes of your superiors.'

I swithered about disagreeing, but didn't.

'You regularly meet with New Caledonia members, whose intention is to hurt, maim and kill your fellow countrymen. That is true.'

'That's not true.'

'You pretend to attend training but instead you plot against your country. That is treason.'

'That's farcical.'

The spokesman's gaze hardened at my criticism. He looked pretty pissed off. He leant back and pulled a cigarette out of his pocket, lit it and inhaled then exhaled directly across the table into my face. Both of them stared at me. I tried not to flinch as the smoke stung my eyes.

'Who else do you know from New Caledonia?'

'I don't know anyone from New Caledonia. Or I don't know anyone who has told me they are in it.'

Was this ever going to end? I don't know where they were going with this.

'You go to your swimming on a Tuesday night and you consort with these terrorists, then what do you do? What do you do with that information?'

'After training I go home and have a shower. I don't like the showers there. Sometimes I do that. Most times. Then usually I watch telly. Then I go to bed. At home.' Mostly true. I saw Grigory most nights now. I went straight to his on Tuesdays.

'So this Tuesday just past you went home after you met with your New Caledonia friends and you had a shower and went to bed? Yes?'

'I went to training then went home, yeah. Eh, yeah.'

They saw the hesitation. I can't believe they asked about this Tuesday. Did someone see me not return home? I felt the flush rise again.

'Yes? Are you sure? You tell me what you did. You went and consorted with your New Caledonia friends and then you went straight home, that's what you say.'

I felt my stomach sinking towards the floor, my head whirring as I tried to avoid it. I'd just take it slowly. Hope they picked up another scent.

'I went to training, then afterwards I showered and went to bed. I didn't consort with my New Caledonia buddies, as you say.'

'But you know them?'

'No. Who? The people I train with?'

'The people you swim with. The people you work with.' He cocked his head sideways, his sidekick watching me through narrowed eyes, assessing my reaction. 'All your New Caledonia buddies as you say. What do you talk to them about?'

Before I could answer, the quiet one jumped in. 'Where did you go after training on Tuesday?'

Bugger. My mouth went dry. 'I went and had a shower.'

'Where?'

I searched the ceiling and the corners of a room for an answer and found none. 'I went to a friend's house.'

'You went to a friend's house?' The original interrogator pounced on this. 'But you said you always go home. You lied to me. I am very hurt. I thought you might not be a liar. But you lied. You went to a friend's house. Why did you go to your friend's house?'

'I just went to see them. I had a shower. I didn't lie.'

'You said you had a shower and then you went to bed. You had a shower at your friend's house and then you drove home and went to bed? Who is your friend? Did you talk about killing more of your Scottish friends with them?'

'No! I went to bed. There.'

'You went to bed at your friend's house? On your own?'

'No.' A headache emerged. This was happening. 'I went to bed with someone else. Why does this matter? It's none of your business.'

'It is our business if you are fucking someone who wants to blow my brains out. You travel over the country with

218

your work meeting people who we know have links to New Caledonia. You pretend to go and train with people who we know have links with New Caledonia. And now you are lying about what you do after these training sessions. What are you doing at this friend's house? Are you passing him, or her, information that could lead to another atrocity aimed at undermining the democratic process of this country, or are you fucking them for information?'

'No. Fuck off. I go round to someone's house and I stay there and it has nothing to do with New bloody Caledonia.'

'Whose house do you go to?'

It had finally come. I slumped a little in my seat. The smoke and the headache making me feel nauseous. 'It's Grigory Rancovic's house,' I muttered.

He had his pen out. 'Who? What is the name?'

I looked directly at him, savouring what I could out of my unexpected answer. 'Grigory Rancovic. He's in the diplomatic team for your little takeover here.'

He dropped his pen. Stared at me. 'And what are you doing going to Grigory Rancovic's house on a Tuesday night?'

'He's my boyfriend.' I shrugged. 'I'm sleeping with him. Have been for some time.'

The admission made me feel cheap, but it worked. They exchanged glances then the quiet man disappeared from the room, the door clicking shut.

No. 1 questioner leant his podgy frame back in the chair and took a final drag on his cigarette before stubbing it out on the table. 'And does your boyfriend Grigory know that you like to consort with New Caledonia members?'

I'd had enough. 'Will you shut up about New Caledonia? I know nothing about them, I have no interest in meeting them, I do not do what you are saying I do.'

There was a moment of silence. I felt the air clear as the smoke clung to the ceiling. The door opened and the quiet man returned. He nodded at No. 1. He got up and left me, sitting there, on my own.

...

Grigory arrived within half an hour. I heard the door open from my position slumped over in my arms on the table, semi asleep, my hair sticking to the side of my face when I looked up. He gave a little sideways nod of the head towards the corridor and I got up.

He placed his hand on the small of my back as he guided me along the long corridor, upstairs and into a dull reception area manned by bored soldiers. It was a sunny day, my tired eyes squinting against the light.

We got in the car and he paused before he turned on the ignition. 'Are you alright?'

I slowly turned to look at him. I was so tired. 'I'm tired.'

'But they just asked you questions, right? Nothing...?' He tapered off, too hesitant to suggest his colleagues could hurt me.

'They just asked me questions. Really stupid, tenuous questions. And they blew smoke in my face.'

He smiled at this and patted my leg. 'We can wash your clothes.'

He set off, and I realised we were out in the industrial estate near the airport. 'You know,' I said, too tired to form my words but aware I should say something, 'I'm not using you for anything. Like information.'

'Don't worry about it, Anna. They're just trying to put a little fear in anyone they think might chance it with the opposition. They don't think you're doing anything. Not now.'

He drove us back into town. I appreciated the trees, and the blue sky, my small taste of Russian incarceration giving a shiny sheen to the outside world. Not now ran through my mind a little, but I let it float away. It wasn't until we reached the outskirts of my area that my attention focused on something else.

'You don't think they'll tell anyone about us, would they?

Like, Boris doesn't need to know. Or Aleks. Or Viktor. Of any of my lot?'

'It's done, Anna. Too late.' He pulled into my road and stopped outside and turned to me. 'It doesn't matter. Really it doesn't.'

'It does matter. Oh God.' I put my head in my hands, mostly due to exhaustion more than anything else, but the realisation I was going to deal with this was too much at 6.30am after limited sleep. I felt him stroke my head.

'It really doesn't matter. What matters is that you're okay, and now I can protect you.'

I looked up, creasing my face in scorn. 'Protect me how?'

'Well, if Aleks gives you any trouble, I'll deal with him.' He gave me a smile, and I couldn't but give him a tired smile, despite the queasiness in my stomach.

I showered, dressed and grabbed a big coffee on my way to work. I resolved in the shower that if I couldn't control the Russians releasing this information I could at least try to moderate its impact.

I called Andrew as soon as I thought it was reasonable and asked him to meet me early in Princes Street Gardens, on the bridge above the train lines. I refused to tell him what about. Grigory once told me to assume everything was tapped.

He looked anxious, his graduate scarf wrapped up to his jowls in an attempt to seem incognito, but not looking remotely like the stream of commuters pressing on to Waverley Station. 'If you are about to say anything about New Caledonia I'm sewing my ears shut. I am an impartial observer, my role in history to document what is passing just now in Scotland.'

'Shut up, Andrew. For a while now I've been seeing Grigory Rancovic. You know, the diplomatic dude who goes on the telly? I went to Moscow with him on that trip. This has not remotely impacted my editorial judgement on any of the programmes I've worked on. He hasn't interfered with any recordings. I haven't told him anything personal about anybody. Well, nobody I liked. So I just wanted to reassure you that my role hasn't been compromised at all.'

'Grigory Rancovic?'

'Yes. We kept it quiet because I was worried that people would think my role would be untenable...'

'With the dark hair and the glasses?'

'Yes. The Moscow programmes, and the Russian ones were entirely exec'd by Boris, it had nothing to do with him. Like, I've been really vigilant in continuously asking myself whether I was editing and recording in compliance with SBC values, and I'm confident and clear in my conscience that I have been.'

'You've been shagging a Ruski?'

I sighed. His mouth was hanging open. 'Yes, Andrew, but that's not really important now. What's important is that you know that this hasn't compromised me work wise and secondly, I really want Jennifer to know before the Russians get the pleasure of telling her. She has to know before then, and I'm happy for her to tell them, if she must, that she's known for months. And I can't tell her. I don't have access to her now. You know her.'

'You want me to tell Jennifer?' A bizarre euphoric look was spreading across his face. 'Absolutely!' He brushed past me in his haste. 'I can grab her off the Fife train!' And off he rushed, desperate to fulfil his duty of being the bearer of top gossip to someone who mattered.

I stood in the Gardens, frozen in indecision, in case, perhaps, Jennifer would be brought to me and I would have to explain myself. Then I came to my senses and forged on towards the office. I told myself that it was so early no one could possibly know. I'd rather be in the office and for Boris to find out, if he would at all, than have to do some walk of shame with all eyes on me.

It was still early, so the office was pretty empty and I took my seat without any emotional explosions. Boris was nowhere to be seen, and I guessed Viktor wasn't in yet.

'Anna!' I was wrong. Viktor crossed the office. I hunched over my keyboard in anticipation for the verbal blow. 'You know you've got a song about suicide in your diving programme?'

I stared at him blankly. 'What?'

He sniggered and told me the title. It was about drowning. I snorted. 'Very apt. Thanks pal, I'll sort it.'

He gave his goofy smile, as he always did when his honest delight in helping someone was appreciated, and retreated to his desk.

This was fine, I could get on with things and the world would still tick along whether I had a relationship with Grigory or not. Jolly good.

I had a meeting booked with Boris to go over some future content. With the disturbed night I was pretty exhausted but I battled through. At the end Boris told me to read an article he'd fished out, and see if it would enhance anything I'd written. He stood up, me too, hoping the day would move a little faster now.

'If you've any problems reading the article let me know, it's in quite academic terms,' he said, and I realised with horror it was in Russian. He held the door open for me. Sometimes he acted in a vaguely chivalrous manner like this. 'Of course,' he said, leaning into me as I passed, 'if you have any problems you could also ask your boyfriend.' He smiled, in the know, and I rolled my eyes and returned to my desk.

I crossed the office and saw Viktor raise his head from his monitor and look at me. He pointed at the monitor and dropped his mouth open in a show of shock. Then he gave his head a little shake of surprise. I walked on. I felt people were talking about me. A few heads together, a few eyeballs following my movements.

I hovered by my desk, then picked up my cup. I wanted out the room. Down in the tea room the kettle boiled and I stared at the steam, my mind slumping.

'Hello!' It was Isobel from the Newsroom.

'Hiya.' Monotonal.

'You all right?'

'Yeah,' I turned sideways against the counter and looked at her as the kettle clicked and steamed. 'I had the pleasure of a tête-a-tête with good cop bad cop in the early hours this morning.'

'Oh,' she said, eyes wide, suddenly understanding. 'So is that when it all came out then? You and Grigory.'

I hadn't expected that it would be round the Newsroom too. That was quick. She saw my surprised expression, and gave me a nudge.

'Don't worry. I'd choose him too. Definitely the pick of the crop.' She gave me a wink and fished a Tupperware out the fridge before swooping back out the room. I always did like Isobel.

The day dragged on as my tiredness held back the clock. I'd been aware of Beverley's raised comments on 'suspecting just as much' and a few extra glances from various seats, but nothing too upsetting. It wasn't until the end of the day I felt the atmosphere quieten as I saved my project. A pausing of the typing and a softening of voices. Then I looked up and Grigory was a metre away, coat draped over his arm, briefcase in hand. He gave me a smile.

'You want to grab some food?'

I looked at him, stupefied for a second, fighting the instinct to crawl under my desk or shriek at him a question about why he'd done that so brazenly in the office. Then I smiled back. 'Sure,' I said, and, ignoring the flush I could feel flowering on my cheeks, I shut down my computer and walked out, head high, alongside my enemy boyfriend.

CHAPTER 29

I was so emotionally and physically tired after the day I'd had that we ate a quick pizza and headed home. But the next night we lingered over dinner, enjoying the luxury. I decided to tell a couple of close friends about Grigory, who were delighted for me, well, to my face. So much so I invited him to gatecrash a drinks after-work session, which he did with aplomb, and strangely, since it was revealed under great duress, I finally let myself enjoy my relationship in a conventional way.

At some deep level I felt connected to this man, ties that felt secure but which were pummelled by political gales. Now the secrecy was lifted I think some part of me had expected total alignment with him. Plain sailing. I'm not saying we didn't draw closer as the shields around us dropped. We did. We spent that summer's weekends strolling around town. We went up to Fife and ate and walked along the coast. We played nine holes, very badly, and drowned our golfing sorrows in ice cream that melted over our fingers and mixed with sand. We couldn't go to the Kyles of Bute – the standoff between the regimes meant Grigory couldn't pass through the checkpoints without provoking trouble – so instead he took me away for weekends. He insisted on treating me because he hadn't done so thus far, so we ended up enjoying an amazing summer of boutique hotels and great spa weekends – the upheaval meaning lots of foreign visitors stayed away, so in essence we had the pick of the best places.

I loved this man. I knew it. I loved his intelligence, his wit, his arms, even his touch of arrogance. I loved the way I might pass his office and look in, and his eyes would lift, catch mine, and the smile would sneak in around the corner of his lips as he talked on the phone. I loved the way he held me, pushing hair off my face and holding my gaze with confident eyes and saying nothing until I became bashful and squirmed away. I loved the silences he held. I admit it – I loved his power. The official command of power he held, but also his aura of power that men recognised when he spoke or gazed.

Some men use a smoothness to disguise. Confident chat to cover gaps of substance. Grigory wasn't like that. Any smoothness in his delivery was based on a true belief. A logic. And the strength of his argument was laid upon foundations that I discovered were immovable. Those scars. Suffered while serving his country. This branded medal of honour was worn with devotion.

He was as unshakable in his nationalistic devotion as his religion. It too was a solid foundation, not that you'd notice it from any action or word – we were living in sin in any case – but he did attend mass and he did view his orthodoxy as the One True Faith. This consolidated his belief in Russia too. In most ways I'd admired him for that. In some ways I feared him for it.

...

'You alright?'

We'd just eaten some pasta which Grigory had stabbed with a vengeance and eaten out of duty. He hadn't said anything, just glowered at his plate. I expected a non-committal answer about work.

'My sister.'

'Your younger sister?'

'Yes. I only have one.' He looked up, a little twinkle reappearing. 'One is enough.' He swirled his wine, resting his hand on the table, holding the base of his wine glass.

'Is she alright? She's not...?' He didn't talk about his family that much. I knew she was a bit of a free spirit, but maybe that was just relative to the ambitious Grigory.

'I don't know how she is.' He released his glass and crossed his arms, still leaning on the table. 'She's doing whatever she wants wherever she wants, but the latest is that she's in Paris, supposedly doing a fashion course, but Anatoly is pretty sure she's just hanging around taking drugs.' He leant back on the chair and cupped the back of his head in his hands, looking for support. 'He wants me to go and find her. Sort her out.'

'Why you?'

It was the question he wanted. He jerked his hand out, stabbing at the frustration of it. 'Because my father can't go because my mother will want to know why he's going to Paris and he can't tell her it's because his daughter is hanging around with drug addicts and spending too much money or she will get very upset. My brother can't go because his fiancée wants him there to await the birth, so it falls to me.' He slapped his arms onto the table. 'It's always me.'

'Going to Paris isn't a bad thing. I wish I could go to Paris. But I can't. Count yourself lucky.'

He stared at me and blinked. 'You want to come to Paris? Come with me to Paris.' A grin spread across his face.

'I can't come with you. I can't leave the country.'

But he wasn't listening, the cogs turning.

'I can get you a pass.' Then he pointed a finger at me and laid down the law. 'But you must come back. You mustn't run off to Switzerland, or London or wherever. I wouldn't like that.'

'I wouldn't run off.' This was too good an opportunity to miss. I didn't realise I had cabin fever from travel envy until he'd suggested it.

'Promise?'

'Promise.'

'You must go to Paris and come back with me?'

'Yes!'

'Okay. Good.'

...

So we went to Paris. We held hands as we walked with no feeling of self-consciousness along the Seine. I felt the city of love was living up to his name.

We ate out and well on the Friday night and made good use of our hotel room until mid morning before we wandered around the city – Notre Dame, Montmartre and the Louvre. We sat out for café crème and ate steak haché in a busy bistro. Then as the day grew older Grigory started getting frustrated.

'She said she'd call me. She knows I'm here. She's not replying.' Each statement a declaration of provocation.

We were drinking red wine, watching the world go by, flapping at pigeons, and he was aware the clock meant more than just the romantic weekend going by. He had his task. He shifted in his seat, jabbed at his phone. 'She said something about a party. Anatoly knows a brother of a friend who is her friend and she said Dina was going to a party. She's hanging around with some German aristo with too much money.' He leant back, patting on his armrest with nervous energy. 'She's annoying me. She always does this. She thinks the whole world revolves around her. I hate women like that.' He glanced at me, then smiled. There was a further backstory there that I hadn't cracked into, I was sure.

We ate a lavish dinner, then Grigory got his confirmation. 'She's told her friend she's going to this party. So let's go.'

'Now?' I was rather enjoying myself.

'Now.' He stood up, took a swig of wine, and turned to get the bill off the waiter. The atmosphere had changed: he was building himself up for a confrontation.

The taxi took us past the Eiffel Tower as we entered the stately Faubourg Saint-Germain area of Paris. We stopped outside a solid-looking door, sitting below ornate stonework and impressive window ironwork latticing. Music was pumping.

'What are you going to do? Just talk to her?'

'Well I need to see if she's here first. The first task is to get in.'

The buzzer let us in without question, but the next door was a little trickier. A tall skinny man, with a thick tuft of dark hair flopping over his chiseled face answered, and he slumped against the doorway, barricading our way in, as he studied us. He gave me a slow drunken smile and opened the door a few more inches, nodding me in and I entered under his arm, having to brush against his body to squeeze through. Grigory remained. I glanced back as the gap shut, and saw him assessing his diplomatic approach as he tried to gain entry.

His sister still hadn't answered the phone. I had entered a wide hallway with a curving staircase winding around in front of me up to another level and a balcony going full circle. People, young people, loitered in small groups, not saying much, or stood individually on phones, or sat on each other, slumped over chairs. I had to watch where I stood over abandoned glasses, and blink against the fug of smoke. The beat was reverberating strongest in a room off to the right, where lights alternated red, green, blue and to my left a smoke machine density of weed fumes were billowing out into the hallway.

I tried to act as if I belonged, which I doubted I pulled off, as I climbed the staircase in the manner of a seasoned guest. There were lots of women here with long blonde hair and willowy figures, looking like the small picture I'd seen on Grigory's phone. I heard snatches of French, twangy euro-trashy international school English, then Russian. I turned as two women sandwiching a short man went down the stairs. I followed round the balcony, peeking into rooms, then stood leaning against the rail, waiting for Grigory or some sign of what to do.

'Hey!' A seriously stoned smiley man leant against the railing beside me. 'You having a good time?'

'Yeah, absolutely.' I tried to slow my speech down. I didn't want my abrupt tones to give me away. Despite my own drinking with dinner I was relatively sober. 'Great party.'

'Great, yeah. Oh wow!'

At that moment there was a yell and another tall blonde woman stomped out the fug of smoke room and stormed towards the door, shouting. Dina entering stage left, I assumed. Another man was with her, tugging at her sleeve half-heartedly as she wrenched the doorman aside and faced Grigory. The speech was fast and blotted with swear words so I couldn't entirely follow, but it was accusations of being treated like a child; of 'why can't you leave me alone'; she just wanted to live her life; she was an adult... Grigory tried to step in, but doorman blocked him. Dina was shrieking at him to fuck off. She told him to run back to Dad, but also not to dare tell anyone about her. The door was slammed shut.

'Wow!' declared my companion. 'Not good. Some people need to chill out.'

'Hmm,' I said, 'Oh well.'

'Yeah!'

Dina stood in the hallway, pouting and raging about her treatment. She stabbed into her phone and jerked away the kisses and fumblings her adoring partner was trying to soothe her with. I started wondering about my getaway.

Then there was a crash. And another. The door was being smashed in.

'Wow!' my companion laughed at the drama. 'Someone is angry. Anger management!' I looked at him and saw the dopey wide eyes bright with excitement, his perfect teeth showing a grin.

Finally, two more blows and the door burst open. The doorman couldn't hold the fuming dervish that was Grigory. He shoved him aside, throwing the man into an ornamental table, gilded photographs and a vase smashing onto the floor, his teeth gritted and his eyes burning in a way that shocked me. He yelled at Dina, shouting at her to grow up, to talk to her parents, to stop acting like a child. Dina started screaming, there was a tussle with her partner and then others burst out of the marijuana room with surprising speed and lunged at Grigory, trying to pin him down, but Grigory was fuelled with rage now, and they couldn't control him as he kept bawling and tussling with him.

'He's angry,' my neighbouring commentator analysed. The balcony was full now with too-cool Europeans, gazing down with disdain on the scene like Roman amphitheatre spectators.

'Yeah,' I said, realising he wouldn't be able to translate having decided he was likely German, 'I think they're related. I think it might be her brother.'

'Cool. Good intel. Fair. Family issues are important.' He nodded sagely, approving.

Finally, they managed to control Grigory, three of them squashing him flat on the floor, then gaining grip on his arms and literally carrying and throwing him out. I hoped he wasn't too hurt.

There was a silence, and the sound of glass being stood on. Downstairs the immaculate hallway looked like the aftermath of a bomb blast. Even the portrait now rested at an angle on the wall.

'Oh jeez, what a mess,' I said.

'Yeah!' laughed the man. People started filtering back into the upper rooms with their superior air of boredom.

'Whose place is this? What a nightmare.'

My companion laughed. 'It's my parents'. So funny.'

I looked at him in horror, but saw no sign of worry in his face. I wondered if that would change in the morning, or whether he was so rich someone would come and sort this out for him, as maybe they had before.

There was now a group by the door and neighbours had arrived. I guessed they were neighbours – they were middle aged, sober and seriously annoyed. I heard talk of the police being called.

'Do you happen to have a back door here?'

'You wanna smoke? You can do that inside, I don't care. It's a friendly place.'

'Eh, yeah, but I'd just like to take in the stars for a moment first.'

'Cool. Nice idea. Out there and then the gate's open.'

'Great, thanks. Great party.'

'Yeah, thank you.' I left him at the balcony looking down at the scene with stoned delight.

Indeed, it was easy to get out and back on the road. Grigory wasn't out the front. I tried calling him but he didn't answer. It was worrying. I'd never seen him like that.

I called a taxi and retreated to the hotel. There I found him. He sat on the bed watching something on the TV, his eyes boring into the screen. He barely lifted them when I entered.

I stood by the bed and waited. Finally he looked at me.

'You all right?' I asked.

He shrugged and looked back at the screen. His knuckles on his right hand were bleeding and I thought I could see puffiness around his face where it might be swelling.

I walked round to his side to see what he was watching. Die Hard in French. 'Can you understand this?' I said. Anything to change the subject.

'No. But I think this John McClane is going to do alright.' He smiled and reached out his hand to me, holding mine with his fingers, his flesh all scuffed. 'It's okay.'

I just looked at him, feeling sorry for him, then I realised I felt sorry for him that his legendary cool was lost and he felt sorry for himself.

'Anna,' he was staring at me. 'Promise me something?'

'Hmm, all right.' I wasn't happy with blind promises.

'Promise me you'll never become one of those stupid women. I can't stand hysterical women.'

I laughed softly and leant forward to give him a kiss on the head. His face looked sore. 'I'll promise that if you promise not to smash down my door if I decide I don't want to chat with you.'

He sniffed and looked back at the screen, the reflection flitting over his eyeballs. Then he switched it off.

He leant back and took both my hands in his and guided me to sit on the bed. I could tell he still carried adrenaline. His breathing was controlled and his movements consciously slow.

He looked at me for a while before he spoke.

'I don't like to lose my temper,' he finally said.

'Well, I think it was understandable...'

'I didn't lose my temper today. I used it.' His eyes bore into me. 'I had to use it to get in that building.' He shrugged. 'I didn't get my sister out but I think she knows where she stands now in my mind.'

He let go of my hands and shifted on the bed, wincing as he did so. I went to move and he stopped me with a hand on my shoulder.

'I have...' he stopped. I could see he was brooding whether to reveal something. I froze in anticipation. 'I was once to be married. To a nice woman. I had known her a long time. But she betrayed me. She changed into a different person. She wanted a different life, with those sorts of people, those sorts of men,' he flicked a finger towards an imaginary social aristocracy, 'and she betrayed me,' he repeated.

I didn't say anything. I waited for the conclusion.

'You mustn't betray me, Anna. I wouldn't... like it.'

I nodded. I had no intention of betraying him. He stroked my cheek and smiled. I smiled back but felt a shimmer of something – fear? – as I realised I was now in deep with this man.

The next day we returned to Scotland, just in time for the beginning of the end.

CHAPTER 30

We'd passed Dunblane and were coming down by Stirling, William Wallace glaring at us on our left, the Trossachs stretching out the right.

'Hey!' yelled Grigory, grabbing the wheel. I switched my attention to the road, then glanced back and forth to the road to the right.

'Are they tanks?! Like, loads of tanks.'

'Yes, it might be,' he said, cool as a cucumber.

'Is that for the rebels?'

He laughed. 'A present, you mean? Maybe.' He realised I was shocked and added, 'We have to ensure the rebel Scots know we mean business. The government are behind us.'

'The Scottish Government approved Russian tanks roaming Scottish roads?'

'The Scottish Government are terrified of civil war. There are republicans crossing the Irish Sea ready for a fight. There are funds from the American diaspora who are bringing in weapons through Dublin. The pro-union government at Westminster has battalions on standby 100 miles from here. It's not just an argument about a rock anymore.'

'Holyrood are prepared to be occupied rather than face their own people?'

'Holyrood doesn't want blood filling the Clyde.'

Like so much of what had happened, it rendered me speechless. We drove home in virtual silence, passing army vehicles and checkpoints that no longer seemed incongruous.

I pulled in outside my flat and rested my head on the steering wheel. 'I don't think I can do this anymore,' I whispered. I lifted my heavy head up but kept my gaze looking ahead. 'How can it end? It can only end in unhappiness.'

The car ticked over as it cooled down. A woman with a pram walked past. Grigory cleared his throat. 'I was thinking you were the woman I would marry.'

I felt the tears stirring. 'I don't know, Grigory. What a world to be thinking about the future in.'

'Time goes on. We must live through it.'

'But you're creating it.'

'Anna,' he grasped my shoulder, 'please don't let this overcome you. This is politics, you're above this.'

I opened my door. 'I don't think so, Grigory. It's all you, sometimes you're all I see.'

He followed me to the door but didn't try to push his way in. He looked so sad. I couldn't speak.

'Call me tomorrow, Anna.'

I nodded and closed the door.

I stayed up for hours, imagining being with him then trying to imagine being without him. It hurt too much to be without him. I texted him at 2am. It's okay.

Good. He wrote back within seconds. See you tomorrow.

I'd finally handed myself to him.

I saw him after work. He gave me a strained smile.

'I'm sorry,' I said, giving him a kiss on the lips and a stroke of the cheek. He looked tired. Rugged.

'It's not about us,' he replied.

He switched his gaze to watch who was coming out after me, then he looked at me again. 'It's not about us,' he repeated.

We walked back up the Royal Mile, across the bridge and along George Street. Summer had decided to throw in the kitchen sink, giving us a burst of heat as we approached October. It was Thursday so the shops still had their doors open and people reclined outside the restaurants smoking, drinking and soaking in the precious rays. We hovered outside a fashion boutique, Grigory with his arm draped over my shoulder, as we window-shopped and strolled. On days like this it all felt very normal.

I clasped his hand which dangled over my shoulder. He kissed my head and we walked back along towards the edge of the New Town with its Barbours and Range Rovers, Labradors and chinos, kids playing in the private gardens, cars rolling along the cobbles.

We passed the checkpoint at the end of Dean Bridge. Grigory nodded through, I had my driving licence checked.

'Is it just me or are they getting more jittery?' I asked. He was staring at his phone which had just pinged.

'I have to go to Orkney tonight.' The breeze whipped my hair across my face and we progressed onto the shelter street off the bridge road. 'I think it will be just a night. I don't know.'

'All right. Hope the weather holds for you.'

We turned to face each other. 'It's always cold in Orkney.'

'I don't think that's necessarily true,' I countered.

'It's always cold when I go.'

'I think you're turning soft, Mr Moscow.'

He gave me a kiss with smiling lips, cupping my face in his hands and giving me an extra kiss on the nose, then we said goodbye, him filtering off to his flat and me continuing on down the road. I'd make a shepherds pie for Saturday. It would keep if he was late.

CHAPTER 31

The buzzer jolted me out of my sleep, although there'd been a buzzer in my dream, an oven door that wouldn't open, a concoction about to explode. Then hammering at the front door. It must be the men upstairs, or they would be at the outer security door. Maybe it's a fire. I ran through, swaying groggily, and opened the door.

Strangers, in uniform. Russian uniform. Three of them.

'You must pack a bag and be ready in ten minutes.'

I stared at them, mounting horror raising within me. 'Ready for what?' My voice squeaked.

'Ready for a trip. Bring a coat. Where is your phone?' He looked over my shoulder where my phone rested on the kitchen surface, and pushed past me to pick it up and slipped it into his breast pocket.

'Hey!' I lunged to take it off him, but he grabbed my wrist, twisting it slightly and led me towards my room.

'You should pack a bag immediately or you will have to go without anything, and you will not like that. You will be cold.' I was shunted into my room, where I hesitated for a fraction, and then rushed to grab some clothes – jumper, jeans, underwear, a book, some toiletries, another top, another pair of trousers... all thrown into a bag in disarray without a clue of where I was going.

'Can I get changed?'

He nodded, stepping back slightly. I pushed the door towards him, but he held it ajar. 'Not shut.' He said.

I threw on some clothes, was allowed to go to the loo, and then was manhandled out the door.

'Should I lock it? Where are we going? I don't understand.

237

You can't do this.'

The soldier took the key from my fingers with another twist and locked the door. His colleague, holding my arm in his hand, steered me out of the security door and down the steps to the pavement. 'You can't take that.' I stated to the soldier, who ignored me and slid the keys into his pocket to join my phone. I felt my head being pushed down as I was shoved into the back of a large car with a sliding door that, following the soldier sitting down in the row of seats in front of me and my suitcase being thrown in, clanged shut.

The street lamps pinged past as I witnessed my beloved city sit back and watch me being taken against my will, through the suburbs, out towards the airport. The industrial estate? No, the airport itself. We joined a queue of cars going through the roundabouts, trailing towards the departure drop off. Panic was rising. 'Where am I going?'

'You can see where you are going,' came the reply from the front with a touch of sarcasm.

'No, where am I going after that? This is ridiculous. Illegal. Not what has been agreed with our governments.' Silence. 'Give me my phone.' No movement. 'Give me my phone. If you are arresting me I have a right to make a phone call. I have a right to have representation.'

The car stopped and the soldier opened the door, then pulled the seat in front of me forward, giving me access. Having not wanted to get in the car, I was now terrified of getting out. I wasn't the only one who had found my voice. Now I could see there were others: bewildered men, crying women, angry figures, confused faces; all being pushed and ushered into the building with soldiers, everywhere, with guns and more soldiers grouping with soft bags on the ground and guns slung from their arms, outside the terminal, looking like fresh arrivals.

I was led by the shoulder into the terminal, passing a man being dragged and yelling, who I recognised too late as Graeme. I tried to turn, to engage with him in some way, but another hand grasped me around my upper arm and propelled me into the building.

Crying, dragging, bewilderment... the horror of those hours are meshed together in a patchwork of witnessed emotions and snapshots of scenes. The man physically forced into the plane seat; the soldiers laughing at the front of the aisle; the small bottle of water and cheese sandwich we were all handed; having to put my hand up to go to the loo; the buses with my bag on my lap; the grey tower blocks; the snow; the guns; the dogs; the bunks; the nailed windows; the door being shut and the silence of me with my roommate as we stared at each other.

We weren't going to jail; we were told that. This was an internment camp. We were a threat to the safety of the Scottish people. We had all carried out activities which were a threat to the aims of the Scottish Government, in alliance, with the Russian Government. We were now at war; did they not already mention that?

Images of gas chambers, the Great Escape, starvation and death marches haunted my day thoughts, dreams of being buried alive and trapped in sunken submarines plagued my nights. But in reality it wasn't like that. Stripping away the fears and restrictions and despite the basic nature of the facilities, we weren't treated badly. Locked in at night, two to a room, but free to mingle in the communal rooms and allowed out in a yard space for three hours a day, either side of a lunch. Lots of potatoes, toast and tea.

My roommate was a political activist called Nadia. She was furious and despairing, as she had been for the previous year. Now, too, she was justified, although it didn't bring her happiness. The others were a mixture of bloggers, writers, activists, political researchers, journalists.... and they'd all swapped battle stories, recounting where they earned their stripes and booked their own seat on the internment flight. I'd given my own version – my recording of Mikhail, the variations on the programmes, my run-ins with Aleks cobbled together, and it made sense that I was thrown on this plane. But. The niggle grew to a torrent. The insecurity gnawed at me. It was him. The whole time it was him. The reassurances, how he'd taken me under his wing, controlled me, twisted me into seeing his point of view. How I'd toed the line. The American programme, my guts flinched when I thought of that programme, laughing at the naive as they attempted to exist in Siberia. The joke was on me. I almost rejected him. I insulted him. I betrayed him in his mind? He left and I was taken. How convenient. He didn't say goodbye. I was used then sent away. Would they be laughing at me now?

CHAPTER 32

Nadia sat picking the last of her purple nail polish off as we heard the first of the doors being unlocked. I dropped the curtain edge, letting it obscure my view again. I stared out at that gate and the road for hours a day.

'Coming for a wander?' I asked.

'No, ta. I'm going to sit here and continue with this exciting task, thank you, Anna.'

I waited for our own clanging lock then left her and walked to the far end of the corridor. Glancing left and right I'd see socked feet propped up on the beds, women standing up and stretching, magazines being reread. Most people seemed to have resigned themselves to the rhythm of the day now. They'd set their internal clocks to hibernation mode, slowed down to fill the hours. I was still desperate to move, to get out.

I turned at the stairs. Women weren't allowed upstairs to the male dormitories. I retreated back past our room and passed the remaining rooms until I reached the communal areas.

Graeme stood receiving a mug of coffee. He still twitched about. Luckily they gave us cigarettes so he could pace from room to doorway. There were a handful of them who smoked and a few others had taken it up to pass the time. I said my hellos and took a tea.

I started my turn of the rectangular yard as soon as the door was opened at eleven. Graeme was there, in his usual spot, coffee in one hand, fag in another. He raised his eyebrows in greeting then looked away. We'd nothing to say to each other.

I walked along the frozen mud studded with stones, round the corner and the little perimeter where it became a stunted L and passed the soldiers' mess hall, along the row of jeeps in the car park that we would be shouted away from, back into the main yard. I couldn't stand the fences and walls outside either, but I could look up. Looking up inside just showed me chipped plaster and damp.

Generally, the guards didn't speak to us. I don't think they spoke English anyway. They just stared and smoked. Sometimes they drank, mostly when they were off duty, but they might join a friend in the watchtower or in their common room, laughter bellowing out into the long corridor. The place used to be a hospital, I think. The men were in bigger rooms with rows of camp beds, but we women were fewer, twelve in total, and we got the smaller rooms.

We sat at long trestle tables eating soup for lunch. I would stay longer but I knew they'd close the door again at two and it was a long twenty-one hours until my next fresh air hit.

Nadia had emerged and was drinking tea with her soup, which in my mind was a waste of two potentially segregated activities. The conversation was stunted and subdued. It looked like snow.

I supped and got out again. I performed lunges across part of the yard and sumo squatted along one fence. I jogged another part. My body yearned to release itself, to stretch out my legs and stride the earth, swing my arms, sweat and leap. I could feel myself folding up like a collapsing deckchair.

As I jogged I imagined myself setting off from my flat. The light, the hill, the sound of the birds and the traffic. Princes Street, the Meadows, the climb up and around Arthur's Seat. The ripples on Duddingston Loch. The morning shadows on the golf course. The shimmer on the Firth of Forth. The swans on the loch. The protesters camped outside Holyrood. The climb back up to Princes Street, then... I'd stumble. Which road first? Which traffic lights? Where did I switch pavements? The routes were becoming distant.

'Anna!' I had to go in. Closing time. I saw Graeme stub his cigarette out and return inside. I followed him.

'If this is a full war, can you imagine how long we will be here?' Nadia sat on the edge of her bed as I lay facing the damp in the ceiling, trying to avoid my nightmares. She liked to talk about it. I didn't. Thinking about it was hardly bearable. She'd ruminate for hours, tapping her nails against the metal bed, tugging at the curtains as if she might see something exciting. But it was just space and sky out there. Cold space and sky, and nowhere we could go. 'We'll be old. Our eggs frazzled. Any chance of a family gone. Do you think we can ever go back to a normal life?'

'It's been twenty-three days, Nadia. Come on.' I kicked my leg against the bed, the bounce rippled up the springs, my memory of the shared secrets. It's just politics. The intimacies. The promises of our future together that I'd brush off. All lies.

'Yeah, it's nothing. Can you imagine that this is only the beginning? It could be the best part.'

I didn't want to think of it. I pressed my hands against my eyelids, squeezing the darkness into a display of light and swirls, trying to see something that wasn't walls. This couldn't be the beginning, could it? Please let it be the middle, the end.

There'd been a snow dump overnight and throughout the morning. Winter was coming and the chill permeated my jeans, bit at my lips. I kept walking, though. It helped. I started mentally drifting away, used to the rhythm of the circuit and the points that didn't change – the rough blob of cement poking out a gap in the wall, the broken gutter, the chipped paving slab. Most people were inside. Two smokers outside the main door, but they stamped their feet and flicked their cigarettes away as soon as they could. It was going to get much colder, so they'd have to get used to it. I was wearing some base layers and a jumper under my coat, thick socks and I'd had the presence of mind to pack my winter boots that were serving me well. I flicked my eyes up towards the watch tower. Beyond the snowflakes the soldiers smoked and stared out into the distance. I tried to pretend they weren't there. I'd mastered the timing to maximise the free view, avoiding all military vehicles parked, barbed wire and watchtowers. My breath appeared in front of me, mixing with the snow, shunted out by the icy air that filled my throat and my lungs, then I breathed that out too, having heated it and walked through it.

'Morning,' another journalist greeted me. He wrote for the Sunday Herald and had been a little too truthful in his political column a few too many times. He wore hiking boots to stomp through the snow.

'Hello,' I replied, forcing a smile.

'They say it's going to snow more today,' he said, bashing his hands together. His nose was veined and red and his regular appearances outside and tendency to erupt inside made me wonder if this confinement was a forced abstinence programme.

'Who said?'

'The chaps. One of them who serves the tea.'

'Oh right,' it didn't matter. Of course it would snow. It was Russia.

We studied the sky, indeed looking heavy and impenetrable, and agreed more snow was likely.

'Do you remember the winter of bad snow at home?' This was inevitable. Every remark on our current situation being pivoted around and redirected into a reflection of home. I didn't know quite which year he was referring to, so we scrolled through them discarding the stormy years and the mild Hogmanays, then finding it. The Year the Buses Stopped. A bad year for snow.

Again, as always, we withdrew from our memories and

brought our immediate environment back into focus. We knew nothing of snowy winters, we with our trifling bus stoppages.

I walked on, my companion took refuge inside. Two more laps then lunch.

The snow started falling thicker. It stuck to my eyelashes and I blinked it away. It helped shield my view of the fences. I could imagine being anywhere. A lorry, having dumped its load of food to the storehouse, revved its way back then paused as it waited for another van to move, waiting in turn for the opening of the main gate. I'd seen them come and go from my room. Gates were only opened when we were confined to indoors. It had a white and blue tarpaulin stretched around it. A lorry in the yard. The snow swirling. Men chatting. A lorry in the yard right now. It's never in the yard when I'm out. Must have been late because of the snow and the roads. A lorry in the yard. Metres away, about to disappear. Snow. Everyone in. My heart started pounding. The engine switched gear as the gate swung open. Everyone's inside. It's snowing. The Scots think this is as bad as it's going to get. They're soft. Just open the gate. No head count. A rev.

Behind the canvas of the lorry's frame, beyond the sight of the watchtower but in full view of the mess room if they happened to be watching through the snow, I ran. The lorry shifted. I sprinted, jumping, grabbing at the canvas, desperate to feel a flap or a curve on the taut material. All smooth and hard.

I lunged up the vehicle, grabbing, trying to find a loose piece and some way in. I was almost at the cab, with every tick of the clock I could feel my exposure increase. It would just take one soldier to peer through the snow of their window. One extra glance in the rear view window of the driver. A rev. A shout. Another shout back, not at me. Last chance; a pause. I crouched and grabbed, fumbling for a handle, finding a space in front of the wheel. I swung under, picked myself up, held my legs taut, tensed my whole body. The lorry rolled forward. The cab swung round and straightened up. I hooked my legs over some tubes and shifted, grunting and praying, shunting my back against a hard surface. The ground started whirring inches beneath my bum. A lurch over a pot hole, but I held fast. And there I stayed.

Now I listened. We bumped and roared along the road and I visualised us disappearing into the birch, Nadia at the window dreaming of the road home. The muscles in my armpit started to ache. My neck felt stiff. I shifted. The lorry lurched and I shrieked and grasped, nudged into the reality that one slip and I'd be crushed to death. I listened again. No sirens, but would there be sirens? No change in speed. I held on, and hoped.

I knew they'd do a headcount at two, when they'd close the doors and check the yard. They were used to calling me in. Maybe they'd glance around outside and think I was in and just close the door, and not check until we had to go to our rooms after dinner. I had to assume it would be an hour before they'd notice, and then they'd realise the gate had been open. Then they'd think of the van or the lorry. I had to get away.

How long – twenty minutes? Forty miles an hour; fifty; sixty? Fifteen miles maybe. I tried to calculate odds. Think how they would search. What they would use. Roads. Dogs. Radius. Terrain. Transport. I couldn't get off while it was moving, but at some point the strain in my arms would turn to shudders. At some point I'd let go. I had to be in control of my limbs when I let go.

I held on for another fifteen minutes, then we stopped. Seize the moment, I thought. You can only grasp a chance and if you've failed: you've failed. I prised my legs out of where they were moulded into place against cables and metal and dropped down. My heart pounding and my body jangling I scrambled in front of the wheel. The engine revved and my heart skipped a beat before I dashed for it, stumbling and falling into the snowy verge as the wheels turned and the body of the lorry drove on, pulling out onto the road, thankfully turning right as I dived left. I forced myself up and groped and scrambled further, into the birch and snow drifts. Adrenaline pumped life into my muscles as I swept my arms at the snow, fumbling into the wood. There I slipped and ran and groped my way deeper and deeper, further away from the road. Of course they'll know you got in here. I condemned myself, I thought, plunging out exactly where they would expect it. Of course I would leave when the lorry stopped. My tracks will be all over that junction. I swore at myself, and ploughed on. Through the slush and soggy ground where the snow didn't lie properly. Just heading on. Heading away. Hoping I wasn't looping back.

At one point I stopped. Legs shaking, and tried to get my bearings. Where's the sun? Behind the clouds. Maybe straight ahead? I looked at the trees. The lichen. I'd read lichen grew mostly on the southern side. Yes, there it was. I traced my hands over the white scales on a tree, then flinched. No scent. Who was I kidding? My scent must be dripping all over this place. But if the snow was slush here, maybe it would be different.

My room faced south west. The road out west. I'd go west, and hope I was going directly away from where I started. I started jogging again. I was heading into a forest that could be greater than any in my own country, and a winter that had devoured armies.

The light began to drop. They'd be on to me now. They must be. With tiredness my spirits fell. The elation that had accompanied my initial dash for freedom had been sucked away into the frosty mud. I began to despair. What idiot dives into the Russian wilderness in a bid for freedom? I mustered courage thinking of the stories I'd read. The survivors. The treks. And then I stopped, pausing on a fallen trunk, the cold permeating my feet and slowly gnawing its way to my core. I sat, looking for deviations in the cloudy sky where a moon could be seen, then telling myself a clear sky would be colder. A twitch in the silence reminded me that it was unlikely I was alone. What could punctuate my misery – an elk? A bear?

Then I heard another sound, that initially I thought was a road. A reverberation. Then a metallic judder. A railway line.

I trudged, then jogged towards the sound, aware it might disappear and I'd have lost all hope of finding it. It was dark now, my feet stumbling over tree roots and slipping on hidden bumps. The ground gradually came a little brighter to my eyes, then I entered a clearing and was standing by the line. I stepped back, looked both ways and strained my eyes to see a train. There was nothing. Which way was west now? I could follow the easier terrain on the track. I looked up to the sky, but it was blanketed in clouds and I couldn't read the stars anyway. I looked back at the trees, and started to backtrack down the siding to study the lichen, when I heard it again. The train.

I slipped trying to twist my body on the slushy hill, so saw it as I lay on my stomach. A freight train, trundling along. Going west? Going east? Going to safety or into the lion's den? I couldn't tell but I didn't have time to piss around in the dark forest to find out. It was moving and I was stagnant. I scrambled up, and stood, watching the dark units charging past me. I wanted on. I ordered my cold stiff legs to move and started jogging, then running, as controlled as I could, slipping and swearing as the cars swept past me, then I saw a handle on one, and steps, and I lunged and missed, then the next one which I saw too late, then the next. I grabbed, and swung, and shrieked as my hand twisted the wrong way pulling my elbow forwards, but I carried through my body, swinging onto the train, kicking with my feet, trying to scrabble up, grasping with my other hand as the car rocked and tried to dislodge me. Then I was on. Standing on a step, panting, snot and sweat and hair over my face, the cold air battering my body, my arms and legs shaking with adrenaline.

I was on, and moving. Please let me be moving away.

I clung on to the side for a few minutes, calming myself, speaking out loud as I told myself I was doing fine. I hauled myself up to see what I was on. It was a long flat container. I'd wondered about trying to get in between the cars to be shielded from the wind, but when I got to the top there was no roof. The box was filed with coal.

I lifted my aching legs over the side and crunched down onto the surface. Holding on to the edge I carefully made my way to the front, the coal shifting under my feet. When I reached the front corner I sank down onto my knees, sheltering from the wind. Now, crouching against the side, my arms tucked in between my thighs and stomach, I sat, totally hidden from view.

...

A jolt woke me. I sat up, a stab of pain through my neck as I looked over the edge. There were lights now in the distance, and the sound of traffic on wet roads. I panicked for a moment, wanting to stay away from anyone, but then rationalised that maybe being in the thick of things could offer me more protection. I was cold; so cold. There wasn't snow on the ground here, but the air was bitter. I unfurled my legs and crouched poised over the edge as I waited and watched. If this train stopped here, I didn't want to be around when there might be guards and railway men watching and noting. The debris by the track was becoming more frequent, the number of tracks parallel increasing in the reflected orange glow from the roads.

I eased my frozen legs over the edge and grasped the ladder, slowly making my way down. The train was trundling now, meandering through tunnels, under bridges and switching tracks in its slow clumsy movements. During one of these I was partially jolted off the ladder, my feet dislodged, swinging wildly over the rolling wheels. I clung on, but during the next slow down, as the cars shunted together slightly, I took advantage and jumped off, the ground hammering through my cold bones.

I paused, crouched, frightened that I gave too loud a gasp as I landed, terrified that my invisible trackers might be about to pounce. Nothing. I got up and jogged over the tracks, four sets, and along the sidings until I came to a point I could scramble up and away from the tracks. I passed row after rows of containers, rotund and block-like chunky machinery. It looked like a railway graveyard. Finally, I came to a fence and beyond it a road. High with barbed wire. I tracked along it, cursing my luck, until I came to a gate. High, with barbed wire. If I couldn't go round it, I'd have to go over it. I'd passed a piece of material. I returned and found the matting, lugging it to a site in the fence where I thought the climb possible. I threw it over my shoulder and climbed my way up the post, finding footholds in the bending wire that made me think I wasn't the first to do this. I grunted as I dragged the wet matting off my shoulder and slugged it over the wire before dragging myself over the top. My body flipped over, and before I could grab hold of anything, I plummeted to the ground with a thump. It happened so fast I lay in shock, then gradually picked myself up.

It was now past two in the morning. I was hungry and cold. I started walking towards what I thought was the centre. This was no hick town; this was a city. Cars still flowed on the multi-laned roads, lights were on, streets busy. I realised it was Friday night. At the camp every day was the same.

Groups loitered outside clubs and eateries, men and women stood out smoking, chatting, laughing and lunging precariously at each other with the confidence of drunks. I weaved through people oblivious to me. Grubby, small and determined to avoid eye contact. I looked purposeful but lacked direction. I didn't know where to go. The dark streets and looming apartment blocks intimidated me. The exposed streets that were still awake threatened me. Despair enveloped me again. I needed warmth, but the obvious places, train stations, subways, they all seemed to dangerous. Then I realised I was at the edge of a graveyard. The spires of a church disappeared up into the night. I stared at it, wanting its sanctity to envelop me, aware that it would be long shut or else it would be a Mecca for the entire city's homeless. I leant against the wall and tried to think.

'Hello, dear.'

I turned. An elderly lady had addressed me, her eyes concerned, her face hardened. I hadn't heard her approaching. I couldn't think how long I'd been standing there. She was wearing a coat but didn't look like she'd been out for long. She looked warm. 'I saw you,' she said, her voice thick and slow. 'You look lost. You need some soup. Everyone should eat more soup. Yes.' She nodded at me, continuously, for about a minute. I became aware that I hadn't said anything, acknowledged her statement. The thought of soup made me want to cry.

'I am lost,' I said, 'and I'm tired.'

'Yes, yes, poor child.' She beckoned me to follow her and when I hesitated she put her arm around my shoulder and guided me along. I found myself leaning into her and her musty, warm smell.

CHAPTER 33

Her name was Lena and we were in Nizhny Novgorod. I looked out at the lights of the big city, stretching out further than I'd anticipated when I walked through what must have been a suburb. She'd brought me to what looked like a decaying high rise, the lift creaking up floor after floor, but her flat was warm and welcoming. Soup brewed in the small kitchen. Ornate rugs hung on the walls. Family photos decorated the surfaces. She liked porcelain flowers which peppered the places not occupied by frames. Her TV gave me a flashback to my childhood with pull out buttons.

'You just sit, and take off that jacket. Your legs, you must be cold.'

'Thank you. Are you not tired?' I couldn't believe she was up.

'Tired, child? I worked nights as a nurse for years and years. The hour doesn't affect me now. I sleep when I choose.'

She fluttered around me, hanging up my clothes, ushering me to a seat to drink her hot borscht, which seeped into me like golden nectar. Lena was saying something to me again, but in my tired state I'd filtered out the Russian. Plus, I'd told her my name was Natasha.

I had a bath, nearly falling asleep. Then I did fall asleep, on the sofa covered in layers of rugs and blankets, so comfortable it could have been the Ritz.

When I woke it was mid-morning. I sat up and saw Lena in the kitchen with her apron and slippers on. It became apparent that last night she had taken me for some lost soul. A desperate woman yearning for sanctity of the church to shield her. Her nursing instinct had identified a victim from her elevated perch, so she had come to save her. I couldn't complain as part of it was true.

'Ah, good morning! You must have some food, and then we will discuss what you will do today.'

I let her usher me around. I wondered whether she missed taking care of her children and her patients. She was a natural carer.

I had tea, still appreciating the warmth. Last night I'd asked for a map, an idea forming in my mind, and I knew where I wanted to go.

'Thank you, Lena. Today I think I must travel on, but you have helped me so much.' She took the compliment with a nod of agreement.

'Yes, yes. I have worked with many women. Many women who have needed help and I know the problems.' She leant forward, increasing the privacy in her private apartment. 'You know if you need help I can help you find it, God help me, sometimes women just need help.' She crossed herself, suggesting a sin her religion would despair of.

'I just need to go on. I thought I might get the train, but...'

'You don't have money?' My hesitation told her the answer. The last thing I wanted was to take money from an old lady in a dilapidated Soviet-era one-bedroomed flat. 'I can show you how to get on the trains.' I looked confused. She laughed and tapped my arm. 'Oh! My brother used to travel, all over Russia he travelled. I know all the rules. We just go down to the tracks and I will get you on a train. No problem! They will be good to you. But...' she held her finger up, 'you must take care of yourself. The world, my God, can eat women up. You must not go back to what you know is not good for you.'

I digested this, not wanting to lie or draw attention to

myself. 'I want to go to Vladimir.'

She nodded. 'Yes, yes. And you know someone there?' I almost nodded. 'You are from the east, are you not?' I sort of nodded again, her returning the gesture. 'I could tell, from your accent.' She held her hands up. 'I won't ask. Oh! The women whose stories I could tell you. We all have our crosses, oh we do! But I must give you something.'

She bustled away into her bedroom, coming back with a burgundy jacket and fur hat. 'You must have these. They belong to my daughter, a long time ago, so she has no need for them now. You must have them.'

I accepted them with thanks and soon we were on the way out.

Lena drove me in a very loud, very small, very clean car. In the light I didn't recognise any of the sights, and we could have been driving to the other side of the city but when we passed a high fence with some material draped over the top I realised we were returning towards the area I'd disembarked from the previous evening.

This time, however, we drove into a yard which was more alive with activity. Lena got out to speak to what seemed like a security man. After a few minutes of chatting and gesturing towards me and the trains, she returned to the car.

'I was right. I know about these trains and the people. My brother, oh, he travelled all over Russia on the trains. Come with me.'

She walked me to a small office and told me to wait, while men in overalls and railway uniforms came and went. Then she returned, telling me it was sorted. She fumbled in her purse.

'No, no no,' I objected.

She dismissed my protests and pressed 1,500 rubles into my hands, then pulled me into a hug, patting my back. 'May God be with you and show you the way home.'

I thanked her, and also for the bread, cheese and water she'd wrapped for me. She had been my guardian angel.

254

A man showed me to a line of cars in a freight train. Inside another man was already sitting. They exchanged words, the railway man instructing him to not go near me. The man looked bemused and agreed. So in I jumped.

It was a long journey. Darkness fell while I sat on that cold floor. I was glad for the snacks Lena had given me. I was glad for the extra clothing. I was really glad when my companion got off at the first stop allowing me to take a moment to hop off and relieve myself. Then I had the carriage to myself, and his discarded newspaper.

I leant over with shaking hands and opened it up. Front page, tanks in somewhere – Falkirk? I felt anger stirring. But what about me? Nothing. No picture of me, no picture of the detention camp, nothing I could interpret as sending out a nationwide search party. Maybe if I lay low I could get away with it... but how could I last?

It was cold, but sheltered. The hours passed, and with every hour I told myself I was an hour closer to freedom. I managed to nap, curled up in a ball, lying on the newspaper and a blanket of paper on top of me, but my nerves kept waking me. Little money, no food supply, just a tenuous hope I might be able to find the one place I'd seen on a map that could offer shelter.

I arrived as I had done on my previous journey – in the dark. Stiff, cold but keen to get out, I nodded my thanks to anyone I thought might be looking in my direction and stepped out into Yaroslavl, a town sitting north of my destination. I wasn't going to Vladimir. Sergey, the impressive man of Siberian self-sufficiency, had pointed out the town of Rostov, I'd remembered the name from my slog through War and Peace, which sat at the top of Lake Nero, which in turn sat due south from Yaroslavl. It was on Lake Nero that Sergey's family had their dacha. Maybe he'd be there. Maybe he'd help me. It was my only idea, my only hope.

I didn't want to spend the precious money Lena had given me, so I rallied myself and stepped out, working my way through the roads towards the motorway, and headed in the direction stated as being towards Yaroslavl. Usually there was pavement, separated from the road by barriers, as I passed by residences and parks. Despite it approaching midnight there was a decent level of traffic, some of it spraying surface water towards me, some of it narrowly missing me as I dodged across junctions. I needed to take it easy, I told it myself, this was going to be a long trip.

I was glad again for my coat and hat, swallowing me up, giving me armour against the exposure. I told myself I was a nurse walking home, a relative finished babysitting... I kept walking, and soon the pavements disappeared and I was walking on a rough hard shoulder of the roads, alongside the cars and lorries which were now thinning out, sometimes stepping out into the muddy grass verge when I felt it became dangerous. Tonight it was clear. The moon showed me the way when the tail lights vanished, illuminating the edge of the road, the water on the grass glinting, my breath forming clouds ahead and the vanishing into the air.

I walked. I walked more. I made myself walk for three hours, then I gave myself a break and let myself eat a little bread and cheese and drink some of the water. I sat on a rock, dipped down from the road, and watched the white headlights arrive then the red lights disappear away.

I walked, kept on going, ignoring the blisters forming as my boot interiors submitted to the damp, ignoring the denim chafing on my thighs and around my waist. I kept walking, towards the orange haze in the distance, pas neat houses with dark windows then on again in darkness, until I saw the sunrise brewing in the east.

In a line of trees I took shelter, slumping by a trunk and closing my eyes. I woke to the sound of a lorry thumping by and bright sunlight. Once again I stretched out aching legs and forced myself to push on, but I lifted my waistband away from my stomach and saw the welts forming as the denim chafed. I had to move on, regardless.

Traffic had picked up again, the cars queued, but kept flowing slowly on the road. I kept my hat low and my gaze on the ground as much as I could, staying as far as I could from the traffic, not wanting to draw any attention to myself.

I drank some more water, trying to ration it sensibly, and I walked into the town. I became just another commuter with somewhere to go. The road forked and I took the road that looked straightest, instinctively. I knew the town sat on the north west point of the lake, and I knew I had to travel further on round the lake. Since I'd galvanised myself to get to the town, my legs suddenly gained weights when I tried to move forward. I forced myself on, travelling along what seemed like an endless suburban road, but my body had had enough.

I sat on a bench beside some religious buildings. I knew it would be hard, but this was tougher than I was prepared for. I finished the bread and cheese, my mouth feeling dry but I needed to ration my water. I let myself rest for a moment, feeling my head slump onto my chest, the air cooling around my neck, but then I forced myself to press on.

Mile after mile I walked, and I started to despair that I'd taken the wrong road when the houses stretched out in front and no town centre appeared, then they petered out and I was through it. Finally. Again I sat down, this time straight onto the frosty grass. I didn't know how long it would be until I found my location, I knew it was unlikely I might even recognise it. As always, I'd underestimated the scale of this place, but I was closer, I must be.

Once again the road stretched out. My head was aching from dehydration. It wasn't incurable – I would eventually find water in a place so prone to snow. I kept walking, stumbling every so often. There was a woman in the distance that I was slowly gaining on, standing at a table. I finally got there – apples, she was selling piles of apples. They looked so red, juicy and delicious. My mouth started salivating. I stopped and stared at them for a while before I was aware that I was staring without having acknowledged the presence of the seller. I snapped out of it and decided it was worth it. I asked for an apple, carefully pulling out my money and she counted out my change. I thanked her and bit into the apple. Divine. I shuffled off, but she stopped me. I turned, panic rising that she might be about to snare me, but she stuffed another apple into my hand and told me just to take it.

'Thank you,' I said, truly grateful, and I continued on my way.

Two hours passed. The sun was thinking about heading in for the night. I thought, finally, I might be approaching my destination, hoping that I hadn't grossly underestimated the scale of my search, swinging my gaze from left to right as I studied the layout of each house as they thinned out on the landscape. I knew it would be relatively small yet some of these were proper family houses. Some looked like sheds. This could be a needle in a haystack. I started looking for places to lay down for the night as it would be pointless looking when I couldn't see. Then I saw it, the blue house, the red shed at the end of the drive where Sergey had posed with his parents. I felt my body deflate at the prospect of rest, then a rising apprehension that he might not be there.

I crossed the road and walked up a dirt driveway lined by a wooden fence. I couldn't see any lights and weeds were scattered on the ground. I walked round to the back of the house. A frost was forming on the empty vegetable beds, plant pots were stacked in a crooked tower by the door. No signs of life.

I slowly turned around, verifying it was the house I'd seen in the picture, aware a wrong decision could lead to an arrest. Yes, he'd stood there with his parents. I was sure of it. I peeked in the darkened windows, seeing the neat kitchen.

No fresh fruit on display. I poked at the letter box and felt mail. I decided to risk it.

I knocked on the door. Nothing. I tried the handle. Didn't budge. I decided to see if the Gods were going to favour me and rooted around beneath the plant pots and around any crevices I could see. No keys. It was starting to snow. I assessed my options and couldn't find more than one. I picked up a plant pot, upturning it in my hand, and held it against the small glass window of the door, eyeing up my target, then pulled it back ready to hit. I felt movement and something slithered over my hand. I shrieked and dropped the pot, it shattering over the ground, my shaking hand flicking away whatever it was. I swore at myself and my pathetic nature. I bent to pick up one of the bigger pieces to use by the corner of the plot and I saw a glint. A key. My heart skipped a beat as I picked it up and tried it in the lock. Stiff, but it turned, and the door opened.

A small wooden table and chairs sat alongside the side of the room reserved for cooking. Another small cupboard hosted an electric hob on the surface and below sat the plates shielded by a curtain. Shelves were stacked with tins and plates carrying pictures I recognised as food, but was too tired to identify. A dish towel hung, stained but clean. Further in there was a small sofa and two chairs in front of an old TV. Bookshelves contained battered novels and stacks of magazines. A family photo pairing with the one I'd seen at Sergey's Siberian residence was propped up on the shelf too. I was in the right dacha.

A wooden stairway which looked homemade led upstairs, and I held on to the polished bannister as I climbed it, passing whimsical paintings of countryside scenes. Boats, picnics, trees. Two bedrooms under the eaves, one with a double bed, neatly covered with a spread that looked richly embroidered, but now faded, draped across the metal frame. A small chest of drawers and two bed side tables. The other, across the small landing, contained two metal framed beds, each with pretty bedspreads across them, separated by a small chest. I was so tired. I peeled my jeans away from my raw legs and hung them with my overcoat and hat on a chair by the wardrobe and got into bed, still wearing my own jacket, and fell soundly asleep.

CHAPTER 34

The next morning was so quiet. A morning in the sanctity of a hidden building, I thought. Then I looked at the window. The world was blanketed in snow. I stood, misting the single pane glass, watching it fall, covering the vegetable plots and erasing any tracks I might have made. My own prison, entered voluntarily. But I didn't know how long I could last here.

My jeans were stiff and my skin hurt as I tried to pull them on, so I left them, wrapping myself in my coat, just wearing my socks on my legs I returned downstairs. I could hear the road in the distance, but inside the cottage was silent. And cold.

Beans, peas, pulses, fish and some sort of meat were canned on the shelves. There was enough food, if I rationed with discipline, for a couple of weeks. There wasn't running water. There wasn't a tap. My head throbbed with dehydration.

The floor was cold in my socks. I shuffled through to the living room and saw the logs stacked that I hadn't noticed the night before. I contemplated the risk of lighting a fire, and decided it was lower than the risk of becoming ill if I didn't heat the place at all. At this point I'd made up my mind that this Goldilocks role I was playing would be okay with Sergey. He was a reasonable man from what I'd sensed. Deep down I believed that I could trust him.

I spent a while lighting the fire, hunched over in my pants and jacket, trying not to waste matches as I blew at the paper and urged the kindling to light. Then I sat in front of the small flames and ate sweetcorn, straight from a tin, with a fork, before drinking the juice. I'd need all the nutrition I could get. Finally, I eased back on my jeans and boot and ventured outside. A tap jutted out a few metres from the back, and only, door, wrapped in insulation. I turned it, held my breath, and out came water. Further away an outhouse looking neither insulated or appealing, turned out to be the toilet. It was clean, and cold. I returned inside to fetch a few containers and brought in water to use.

I gave myself a wash with a cloth, in front of the fire, from a bowl heated with kettle water, then I had a cup of tea with a teabag I found in a tin. I found a radio, and listened to cheery pop music. The electricity worked fine, but I didn't plan on drawing attention to myself too much with lights.

That's how I spent the rest of that day, and the next, and the next, holed up in my tiny dacha. I created a little comfort zone around my fire, the sofa pulled up close, a chair beside as a table. I read parts of books, until I arrived at sections where the lack of a dictionary rendered the plot indecipherable.

I poked around in every cupboard and every cranny. I found a rifle and a carton of bullets in the wardrobe in the double bedroom. I lifted it out, slowly looking at the mechanism, clicking the safety and managing to open the chamber. It was loaded. I carefully put it back.

I carried firewood in from the shed and assessed my fairly distant neighbours which consisted, from what I could see, of two empty houses and one which I could avoid being in the line of sight if I kept away from the far right corner of the garden. I mixed together cans and cooked them on the hob, making fairly thin soups and dreaming about bread. I performed a dance around the little kitchen table when I found a sealed packet of biscuits, smelling them and taking one, then climbing up on a chair to place them out of my reach. I was bored, and stiff from sitting around, but I gradually started to feel quite safe in there, if I ignored the growing pile of tins by the door. I would have to deal with that soon.

The temperature had plunged further. The snow remained, fluffy where I hadn't touched it. The dirt driveway a smooth cloud of undisturbed snow. I stuck to the loo seat one day and panicked, imagining leaving part of my buttocks on the plastic, but a bit of wriggling rendered the lift off painless.

The dacha had old maps, and I retraced my pilgrimage with my finger, then tried to determine where I might have been in the camp, but Russia was too wide and my directions too unreliable. It looked like anything further south was more remote. First thing day four I decided to walk back towards the nearest shop and see what I could afford and whether there was a pay phone I could use. I needed money. I would need a permit, an ID, for any respectable work. I wasn't prepared to do anything else. Yet.

I set out, plunging into the snow by the fence and onto the road, hoping to keep my tracks as discrete as possible. Two hours later and I found a small shop. A cheerful plump lady stood behind the till, giving me a smile, watching me as I toured around, calculating prices. I bought bread and potatoes, enough to last me a week, and enough to give me a little money left over. I needed to find a phone.

'Is there a phone for the public somewhere near here?' I asked before I left.

Yes, there was, but in town. I thanked her, sighing inwardly, and made the long journey back to the cottage. I'd try another day when I could muster the energy.

The next day I decided to examine the contents of the shed a little more thoroughly. I hoped wood had been stored there, as well as the pile stacked along the outside, but it was just antiquated gardening tools and outdoor furniture.

'Hello!'

I jumped at the sound from behind me, and spun around to see someone approaching the far corner, from the direction of the inhabited house.

'Hello!' I replied, feigning confidence.

'Who are you?' A thick set man with a beard and shaggy eyebrows. A sort to share a bottle of vodka with Sergey, I'd wager.

'I'm a friend of, I'm a cousin, well not close, of Sergey's' I babbled, hoping he'd mistake my contorted Russian for shyness. The surprise threw out my concentration.

He lifted his chin in consideration and took a measure of me. Slender, young, female, and pottering about in a summer cottage in the snow.

'Is Sergey coming to visit?'

I looked at the dacha as if that might give me the answer then replied 'I hope so. I don't think he has plans to though.'

'Ah.' He stroked his beard. 'I haven't seen Sergey in a long time. I'd like to see him.' He considered this. 'Are you comfortable in there?'

'Yes,' I frowned, 'yes. I needed to get away from the city for a while. I needed some peace and Sergey said I could stay here.'

'Do you have enough wood?'

I didn't, and he could see it my face as I weighed up the answer.

'I will bring you some wood later.' I held a hand up to my protestation. 'Of course I will. A friend of Sergey's...' and he smiled and said goodbye before trudging off through the snow.

I watched his back, and then stepped forward to see if anyone else was watching him from his dacha. I couldn't see anyone, but I couldn't see anything behind the reflections in the windows.

I didn't hear him return, but wood was piled up outside the door the next morning. I was so grateful, but annoyed as I'd managed to concoct a story about a lost phone which might enable me to ask to use his own to call my mum, offering him money. It was risky, but I had to risk it now. There was a greater chance he might have a number for Sergey and decide to check out my story first. The prospect filled me with worry for that day, then I pushed it out of my head. I was heading towards the Russian winter with barely any money and no transport. Speaking to Sergey would be a good thing, as long as he didn't call the police.

I spent the next three days eating my small portions of bread and tinned goods, reading and carrying out my elaborate circuit of exercises I'd devised using the small space and furniture available. I was slowly going nuts.

I perfected my story and tried to walk round to the neighbour's house to say thank you for the wood, but he wasn't in. I clomped back across the snow, looking out towards the road, and remembered how I looked out towards the road that projected from the camp, and had that same feeling of being trapped as those cars fled to freedom.

My fear of being caught subsided and I started to rage at my predicament. At my own arrogant resistance that printed my name on the flight list. At my government's weakness. At Grigory's betrayal. I'd poke at the fire and imagine stabbing him in the face, again and again. Not so tough without an army behind you, eh, Grigory? Then I'd find myself welling up at how I was so deceived into thinking he loved me. And letting me love him in return.

CHAPTER 35

I was sitting there listening to the cracking of the fire and reading through an old travel magazine when I heard an engine and the soft tread of tyres on snow. My heart missed a beat and I froze, then slowly lifted my head to strain to hear more. The engine stopped.

I ran upstairs as quietly as I could, the adrenaline pumping, and peered out the corner of the window in the roof of the main bedroom. It was a jeep, sitting in the middle of the drive about ten feet from the edge of the house. I could feel myself shaking as the door opened.

A foot sunk into the snow and the jeep rocked as the weight transferred out. I ducked as I saw my breath cast a mist on the window then tried to hide myself as I looked. Grigory was standing by the car. He swung the door shut. A red mist descended on me.

I threw open the wardrobe and grabbed the rifle and went downstairs. I ducked as I passed the small side window in the living area and slid into my boots. I slipped out the door and stepped into the garden, holding the rifle with both hands in a firing position before striding out into the drive. Grigory stopped mid-step and froze.

'Hello,' I said, looking down the barrel of the gun at him.

He held his hands out, as if he was contemplating holding them above his head, but he wasn't sure. 'Anna.'

I gave a curt nod. 'How did you find me?'

'I, are you alright?'

'How did you find me?' Maybe it didn't matter, but I wanted to be the one asking questions while I still had the upper hand. Maybe I could shoot him and steal his car.

Maybe I could get him to take me somewhere better. Maybe I could get money off him and kill him. No idea.

'Viktor guessed. This isn't the first place I've looked. God, Anna, how did you get here?'

'I was put on a plane, Grigory. You know that.'

'I know. Anna. You weren't on that list. I saw the list. You weren't on it. You weren't supposed to be on it. Aleks put you on it.'

'Yeah, I'm sure that's true. You didn't know.'

He dropped his hands, and put one to his chest. 'I didn't know. I swear I didn't know. God, Anna.' He stared at me, and conflicting emotions floated over his face. Concern, anger, arrogance. 'You think I would hurt you? You think I would betray you? I would die for you. I've risked my career, and my liberty to find you. I've been driving for days and looking in every fucking cave and wood for you. I've lied to my superiors to find you.'

He implored me with his eyes to believe him. My feelings of love and betrayal and hate collided within me.

'I really want to shoot someone.' I could feel my arms sagging under the weight of the rifle, my body trembling with the cold instead of the adrenaline. I wanted to believe him.

'Well, I should be bottom of that list.' He dropped his arms and took a step towards me. I lowered the rifle. 'I brought you food. Do you have food?' He reached towards his jacket. I jerked the rifle up again.

'Don't!'

He jumped at the gesture. 'Anna! I'm not going to hurt you. Fuck, Anna. My car keys.'

'Take your phone out.' He looked incredulous. 'Take your phone out. They took mine away from me, you can at least take yours out.'

He slowly reached into his trouser pocket and pulled out his phone.

'Chuck it on the ground.'

'Anna, the ground is wet.'

'Oh fuck off. Put it on the car bonnet then.' I jerked the end of my rifle towards the jeep. Grigory did as he was told. 'What else have you got on you? If you've got a gun you'd better bloody well put that on the car bonnet too.'

He made a show of opening his pockets. His wallet. A receipt. His car keys. I ordered them to all go on the car bonnet. 'Step aside.' I gestured again with the rifle towards the edge of the snowy track. He did so, stumbling a little. I walked forward and took his phone and car keys.

'You aren't holding that gun properly.'

'I could still club you with it though, you fucking prick.'

He nodded in acknowledgement, then smiled gently. 'I brought you KitKats.'

I lowered the rifle again, and sniffed back tears. 'Well hurry up and get them out, for God's sake, or I will shoot you. But Grigory,' I said, as I went around the back of the jeep as I beeped it open, 'I could quite happily kill you now.'

He lifted a box out. I could see packets, cartons and tins. He shut the boot and followed me in.

I put the rifle on the table, then changed my mind and propped it up on the floor. Grigory placed the box on the table.

'You look thin,' he said, appraising me. He held his arms out in expectation, a sad look on his face. I let him hug me, my hands held to my front, then I softened and wrapped them around him, smelling his mixture of cigarettes and cologne. He kissed me on the forehead, tried to stroke my hair, but I pulled away. I couldn't trust him, just yet, although I yearned to just release myself to him.

'I bet I stink,' I said.

He shrugged. 'You smell fine. How long have you been here?' he asked, looking around the room.

'Over a week.'

'What were you going to do?'

I didn't answer as I poured some water from a jug into the kettle and turned on the hob. I looked at him properly then. He did look tired, his eyes shadowed under his glasses, the grey in his hair picked out by white light.

'Did you really bring KitKats?'

He smiled and leant over the box. 'Of course I did. All the way from Edinburgh.' At the sound of my city my emotions erupted, and I started crying. He dropped the packet and grabbed me, drawing me close and squeezing me, kissing my head, telling me he was sorry, sorry, sorry.

We stood like that until the kettle screamed. I pulled myself away and made the tea. We took the biscuits and the drinks around to the dwindling fire. Grigory stocked it with fuel and I moved the sofa further back and the chairs in closer. I sat on a chair. Grigory noticed my decision and sat on the opposite chair. He looked at the staircase.

'You sleep down here?'

'No. In a bed upstairs.'

'Is it not cold?'

'Yes, but I'm not...' I wanted to say, a squatter, uncivilised, but words escaped me. He held up his hand to stop me struggling. He took a sip of tea. 'How did you find me?' I couldn't believe he was here.

He nodded. 'I thought you'd go to the border. Mongolia. Perhaps start where you'd visited at Irkutsk. Viktor was sure you'd go to Moscow and find one of your contributors there. So I called round, and one didn't answer repeatedly, which made me suspicious. I flew to Moscow – I said I was visiting my new nephew and niece so it was easy to get leave for a few days...'

'Oh, did he have....'

'Yes, all fine,' he dismissed it with his hand. 'I still haven't seen them. But, I went to the appropriate apartment for that woman Kat, saw her husband. Well, he's an asshole, and he wouldn't say if she was in. So I watched. I didn't think she was there, so I tried to persuade him to tell me where she was. And he wouldn't. So I became convinced she was somewhere helping you. He must have thought I was a stalker or something. He threatened to call the police.' He rubbed his hands in front of the fire and sniffed. 'So then two days later she returned, or maybe she was there longer but I didn't know. But I tried the apartment again and she was there. She denied all knowledge of seeing you. So then,' he waggled his finger at the fire and smiled his wry smile, 'so then I was convinced she was hiding you, and I staked her out on her shopping trips and her wanderings.' He looked at me and laughed. 'Fortunately Viktor called me around that time so I didn't have to go full Paris on her. He'd mentioned Sergey and had managed to get hold of him, but Sergey hadn't seen you, of course. But Sergey called him back and said his neighbour at Lake Nero had called him to say some pretty little woman was staying in his dacha.'

'What did Sergey say? Was he angry? I was going to pay him back.'

'He told him to make sure you had wood, and anything else you needed.'

I smiled then. So that was another person who had helped me. I felt the tears come, but I sniffed then back. I sighed. 'Could I have gone through the border?'

He shook his head. 'I doubt it. Unless you had money, but I still thought you might go there.' He shrugged. 'I didn't know. No idea. It doesn't matter, you're okay now. Are you okay?'

'Do you want one?' I asked, not ready to answer the question, gesturing towards the chocolate.

'You have them.'

I crunched away and finally felt ready to ask, 'What can I do?'

He put his mug on the floor, leant forward to address me and started playing with his nails.

'I told you, you weren't on that list. You believe me, right?

I didn't know.'

I gave a slight nod. I had to believe him to give me a choice. He continued.

'You weren't on the official list. We had a list. We're at war now, and it's standard to detain people who pose a threat. We're looking after them.' His voice softened, he looked concerned. 'We were looking after you, there, weren't we?'

I sighed again. 'Yeah, I suppose as unlawful imprisonment goes.'

'It's not... okay, okay. So you weren't on the list. Boris called me, actually, in the morning, to check I knew. He knew something was wrong. I flew out, the next plane, back to Edinburgh. It was too late. Mikhail pretty much laughed in my face. You know him and Aleks are friends? Well, Aleks is his little stooge.' He stared at the fire. 'He hates me. He wanted to do anything to upset me. You know I wasn't needed in Orkney, really.'

'I made you shepherds pie, for after Orkney.'

He nodded, not really listening. 'They just wanted me out the way. He's stupid. He's just made me angry.' It was silent for a while, then Grigory shook his head a fraction to shift away from his thoughts and looked back at me. 'So. I went above him, to Moscow. You know they've wanted me back in Moscow for a while? I've resisted.' He smiled. 'I like Scotland. I have reasons to stay, you being number one, but I went back, above him, and spoke to General Orlov. Boris backed me up. Viktor backed me up. You shouldn't have been on that list. It wasn't approved. You aren't a threat. I've promised, I've guaranteed it.'

'I can go back?'

He pressed his lips together. 'No.' He saw me frown, and leant forward to take my hand. 'Moscow believes you aren't a threat. But Mikhail Burkov is in charge of the situation in Scotland now. He'll arrest you if you go back.'

I stared at the rug. So I was still a prisoner. 'So I'm in limbo. I have to move...?'

'I've guaranteed you aren't a threat. I've, it's been difficult, Anna. We don't like admitting mistakes. We don't make mistakes. Orlov is happy for you to be free if I found you first, if I could guarantee you'd toe the line. You can't go telling people you were wrongfully arrested. You shouldn't mention the camp. You can't tell your parents that.'

'What?'

'We're at war, Anna. Russia doesn't make mistakes. Officers don't have feuds and send other officers' girlfriends to internment camps just to piss them off.'

'So what do I do?'

He looked at me intently and took my hand. 'You can marry me. I can guarantee your safety if you're my wife. General Orlov will believe your intentions if you marry me and stay with me in Moscow.'

'Married?' I pulled my hand away.

'Yes. General Orlov doesn't believe that you won't go running away to France and shout about your treatment, he doesn't think you'll stick with me. He didn't believe that I could vouch for you. Unless we were married.'

'So you can control me?'

'So it's proof you love me. And you'll stick with me instead of running off to London.'

That's exactly what I would do, given my freedom. 'What if he doesn't? What if I show up and it's handcuffs.'

'He will. He's promised.'

I rubbed my head. I hated this man until half an hour ago, now he was my only salvation. But marriage: did I love him forever?

'When would we have to get married?'

'We'd get married when we got back to Moscow. As soon as we can. I'm sorry, it won't be a lavish wedding.' He smiled at me, hoping for a reaction. I shook my head in despair.

'You'd, like, own me.'

'No I wouldn't.'

'Isn't that what marriage is? Belonging to someone?'

'Belonging to each other.'

'But I can't leave your side.'

It was his turn to sigh. He leant back in his chair. 'What do you want me to do? Can you think of something else? You're a wanted woman. It was everything I could do that they didn't concoct some evil shit about you and launch a national man hunt. How did you get out?'

'I'm not telling you.' He smirked in disbelief. 'Right fine,' I said, 'let's get married. I'm sorry.'

He nodded and picked up the tea cups and walked through to the kitchen.

'Get your things.'

That didn't take long.

CHAPTER 36

It was snowing as we drove towards Moscow. I sat in the passenger seat in a state of composed anxiety. We were driving to the Ministry of Defence. To the bear pit.

Grigory was switching to strategy in Moscow while the fighting took place in Scotland. A front of sorts had formed through the north and east of Glasgow. He said it wouldn't take long. They were being patient. They would starve us – them – out, letting any civilians who wanted out, out.

He spoke like it was a war game. Not my people being shot at. 'There are so many mercenaries, Anna. Anyone who wants to have a go with a gun has flown in.' I resisted passing comment. I'd read the news when I got to his home. Our home, I guess.

We hit the rush hour and crawled into central Moscow, the snow pelting the car's windscreen.

'You're lucky you weren't out in this,' Grigory remarked.

I stayed silent. The nerves had encompassed my whole body, making it difficult to swallow and I had to concentrate on my breathing. I jumped when he put his hand on me. 'It's okay,' he asserted.

He drew up to a car park and showed ID to a security man in military uniform. We were let in and walked in the snow towards the building. It loomed over me. Grigory cupped his hand under my elbow, to check any fall or to keep me close, I wasn't sure. Another showing of passes and conversation which I didn't quite follow before we were let through and entered a lift. As the door shut I felt the incarceration. Grigory placed his arm around my back, cupping my waist. He gave me a little squeeze. The door opened to a vision of stately marble and windows. I froze, unable to propel myself forward, but Grigory pulled me gently and we walked out into the corridor, me flinching as the doors shut behind us. 'Come on,' is all he said. I could feel the tension in his body, a stiffening of his torso and a tenseness in his speech. Maybe it was being around the military again.

A secretary took a look at me before listening to Grigory. She made a phone call and we were ushered in, to General Orlov.

He looked in his late fifties, and if he wasn't wearing his mass of stars, honours and badges, I would have guessed him to be a middle manager. Until he looked at me, and then I felt his power.

'So this is the cause of all the worry,' he said once Grigory had introduced me 'I suppose you should take a seat.'

He studied me some more then addressed Grigory. 'You found her quite quickly, for someone who had no idea where she was.'

'I got a lead.'

'That was very fortunate.' He stared at Grigory, who acknowledged the remark, then he gave me another appraisal. 'Well, I'm glad you are safe. We were very worried about you. Little girls shouldn't go running away into Russia without preparation. You wouldn't be the first to suffer from it.' He tapped his fingers on his desk. 'So now you must tell me how you escaped from your lodgings.'

I paused, not wanting to close any potential chance for anyone else, but beneath the civility he looked like a man of low tolerance. I sensed Grigory about to encourage me. He shifted in his seat.

'I escaped under a lorry,' I said, almost a whisper. I took a sideways glance at Grigory. His mouth had dropped open.

'A delivery lorry?'

'Yes. It was just leaving. Then I got off and managed to climb on a train.'

General Orlov digested this with a curt nod, glanced

at Grigory and moved on. 'I understand you are in a relationship with this man.' He jerked his head towards Grigory and a smile curved around the edges of his mouth. I gave a faint nod. 'So it's true,' he said. 'I suppose I should say congratulations.' He studied me a little longer. 'I'm afraid I must ask for some privacy with Grigory. If you would please wait.'

The door opened and a man appeared. He nodded at General Orlov's instructions to accompany me and gestured towards me to stand up. I looked at Grigory for reassurance, but he just nodded. I stood up and walked out into the corridor, looking back for a sign as the office door was shut.

'Come,' he instructed me and we moved to a small meeting room. He stood by the door and I sat at the table. I accepted his offer of water, which he called in, not leaving me for a moment.

We sat in silence for twenty minutes. A clock ticked away the time on the wall. I heard people walking past. I wondered if it was Grigory amongst them. The panic stirred itself and rose into my chest.

His phone rang. I jumped. He answered and agreed with a curt 'Yes, sir.'

'You must come with me.'

'Is Grigory coming?'

'I don't know of Grigory.'

We were met in the corridor by another man in an officer's uniform. They escorted me along the corridor. I looked into offices, sideways, then behind me, to see him, but Grigory was gone.

'This way,' the man said. We walked out the building and down the steps to a waiting car. My breath shortened in panic and I looked at up the steps at the imposing building. The windows stared down at me. Was he watching me from up there?

'In, please.' The man applied some weight onto my shoulders and gently pushed me in. The uniformed man sat in front. We left my companion watching us as we drew away from the steps, then he made his way back towards the building.

We sat in silence. 'Where are we going?' I asked.

The soldier turned his head and laughed. 'You don't know? Maybe it's a surprise.'

That made my heart pound. I started sweating. We drove through junctions, weaved through traffic and then finally stopped. I leant to open my door but the handle just gave way. A man opened it, appearing from nowhere, and greeted my companion as he stepped out.

They walked me into another official looking building. A police station, I thought. I jerked my head around for one last look of Grigory. No sign.

We walked on, in past a high reception desk, through a doorway down a corridor, then into a bigger room. There were rows of chairs and two people at the front.

He turned around. Grigory. He gave me a smile and I shuddered with relief and made myself fight back tears. I saw his frown, then understanding. He put his hand around my waist.

'Where were you?' I whispered.

'We had to talk. Sorry.'

'Now' said the other man, 'Are we all ready?'

Grigory looked at me. 'You okay?'

'Now?!'

'Yes.' He gave a short laugh.

'Don't you have banns or anything?'

'Not this time. General Orlov made special arrangements.'

I looked back at my previous companions, now making themselves comfortable, suddenly just witnesses and not jailers.

'Did you not think to tell her?' Grigory asked.

The officer shrugged. 'I thought it was a surprise.' He laughed too.

We turned to the registrar who gave us a nod and began.

'We are gathered here today...'

I felt Grigory squeeze my hand. I squeezed back.

Afterwards Grigory kept hold of my hand in between shaking others. I received congratulations from the pair, who, it turned out, were a friend and the famous brother. The friend joked that perhaps Grigory should take a little more care of his wife's appearance. Tall, broad, Anatoly just looked mildly disapproving. He gave me a stiff kiss, his bristles brushing my cheek, then he ignored me. We drove back to the Ministry of Defence.

'So will you be working here now?' I asked as we approached.

He nodded, a smile across his face. 'Yes.'

'Are you pleased with how this has worked out?'

He took my hand and rubbed it. 'I'm pleased you are safe. I'm delighted you are with me. I know you will not be happy at being here, but please do give it a chance. And yes, this will be very good for me. This is where the strategy is. I can have influence here, away from the small petty world in Edinburgh.'

We pulled up and got out.

'We'll pick up my car and go and buy you some clean clothes.' Grigory looked proprietorially at me. 'We'll need to get you dressed up Moscow-style: you are my wife now.'

'Grigory, don't say stuff like that. Or, repeatedly say I'm your wife, please. Or, wait. Say it rarely at first.' The magnitude of the day's events was leaving me dizzy.

Grigory grasped my shoulders. 'Are you alright? We'll get some food.'

I was looking up at the front of the building. The blue, white and red draped down the multitude of floors, the gold gilding giving it an ironic sense of glamour.

'Is he in there? Could he be in there right now?'

'Mikhail?' Grigory asked, reading my thoughts. I

imagined Mikhail standing at a window, looking down at us and sneering. 'I don't think so,' Grigory said, 'If he is, I hope he's angry.'

He gave me a little squeeze. 'The future isn't relevant now for the people in there,' he nodded up to the window. 'The future is for us.' He could see I was unsure. Our fates were intertwined, I knew it. 'We're on the same side now Anna. Whatever happens you're on my side now.'

'What about my side?'

'It's the same side.'

My eyes shifted away, towards the threatening bulk of Moscow, weighed down by the snow. I felt a finger lift my chin. Grigory was waiting for an answer.

'We fight our corner together.'

'What if you come from a different corner?'

'It will be your corner.'

I lifted his hand from my face. A chill wind made me tremble. It was cold. Grigory made a move to the car.

'Grigory,' I said, holding his hand back. 'It can't just be your future now and I tag along.'

'Anna. If I wanted that I wouldn't be with you. I wouldn't have gone for the girl who defied not only Russia but her own boss to stand for her principles. Come on,' he tried to lead me away. I resisted. He leant into me.

'Anna. What do you want me to do?'

I knew the answer immediately. 'I want you to take down Mikhail Burkov, and I want you to get me, us, back to Scotland one day.'

He kissed me on the forehead and leant in towards my ear. 'Of course. With you by my side.'

He leaned back to see my reaction.

I smiled and nodded. He wrapped his arm around me and we went to begin our next chapter, together.

...

279

Note and Acknowledgements

In 2014 I wandered along to an open meeting discussing the merits of independence. The large school auditorium soon buzzed with enthusiasm, and Nicola Sturgeon, alongside her Green and business independence allies, extolled the reliable price of oil that would prop up the Scottish economy and the ease of staying with the pound. These were the only opposition quibbles, they implied. The audience appeared to agree.

I felt very alone as I sat, watching this optimistic spectacle and the few differing views shouted down by the crowd, too intimidated to ask the question that had dominated my mind over the previous few days. What would we do if we were invaded? Realistically, if Russia were to lay siege to an oil rig or an island before we were stably ensconced in NATO or the EU, could we withstand them?

The thought grew and developed, and became *Russian Doll.*

The world is changing unpredictably and at a fantastic rate. There was no President Trump when I completed my first draft, with a USA withdrawing from global issues. There was no Brexit. However Anna and Grigory's adventures continue, I imagine no fiction will be able to reflect the reality of a Russia determined to undermine Western stability, and dissatisfied populations voting for change.

From that time until now I need to acknowledge the support I've enjoyed in getting this far with the novel. My husband James has supported my efforts throughout. Thanks to Richard Happer for editing the original manuscript, and Valerie and James Lloyd for additional sweeps for errors. Gordon Lawrie at Comely Bank Publishing was instrumental in encouraging me to progress to this print edition and was heavily involved in the production process. I hope his faith in the story was worth the effort.

Lucy Lloyd, November 2017